FALL FOR THEIR LIES

CRAIG BEZANT

HENRY HERBERT SERIES

Bury Our Secrets

Pay For Your Mistakes

Fall For Their Lies

Crime writer Craig Bezant hails from Perth,
Western Australia. He is the author of the Henry
Herbert crime series, and the children's adventure novel,
The Flats. His short fiction has also appeared in numerous
magazines and online publications.

Craig created the award-nominated Eclecticism
E-zine before co-founding Dark Prints Press (2010-14),
editing and publishing the work of over 100
of the world's best crime and horror authors.
He won the 2012 Australian Shadows Award
for Best Edited Publication (Surviving the End).

'FALL FOR THEIR LIES'

International print edition - Australian English

Copyright © Craig Bezant 2024

www.craigbezant.com

ISBN Print edition   978-0-6456895-4-9

ISBN eBook edition 978-0-6456895-5-6

Cover image by JTART / Evannovostro /Shutterstock.com

Cover design by Craig Bezant

Typeset in Palatino and League Gothic

To the amazing teachers out there. My old colleagues. Those who taught and inspired me.

Many of the locations within this novel are real.

The story itself is fictional, which means creative flair has been given

to locations and characters – descriptions and actions are purely for

plot and entertainment and are not intended as critiques

of existing entities, people, or places.

Enjoy, and come visit Western Australia soon.

CHAPTER ZERO
DISMISSING MY EXISTENCE

I gaze at the ocean as a light breeze ruffles my hair, try to find the beauty in the unfolding sunset. It's something I don't do often enough—watch the sun disappear, the sky fill with hues of orange, pink and purple. I never stare up at the stars, either. In the northern suburbs of Perth, where I live, the light pollution makes me forget they're up there, all around us. I should do these things more often. There are only so many times in your life you get to appreciate wonders we don't even have to pay for.

I pull back from a stretch of wooden railing, turn to take in the sprawling suburb behind me. I've visited Yanchep more in the last two weeks than the rest of my life. When I was a kid, we'd come this way for one of two things: Atlantis, Perth's version of Sea World, which didn't last long, an enormous statue of Neptune rotting away somewhere; and the national park, always busy with picnics, boat hire on the lake, and cave tours. If I didn't have to go into another cave in my lifetime, I'd be happy.

I start heading for my car, parked near a café. The place is closed now but I've already been there three times today, ordered my triple-shot coffees, scanned the rooms for faces. Searching for one in particular. Never having any luck finding her.

I get in my car, take the winding road back to civilisation. When I was young, Yanchep used to feel hours away, even though it wasn't. Now, the coastal area is growing, Perth suburbs sprawling northward to meet it. A couple of years ago, there was something in the news about it hitting over ten thousand residents.

Again, I'm just looking for one.

I find a familiar pocket of housing. The road is improved, the bitumen dark, which doesn't match the houses. Most are leftovers from the seventies, resisting the area's redevelopment. Those that gave up are now empty lots of white sand. There are only a few eyesores as fresh as the road.

I reach a roundabout, pass one of the new, two-storey monstrosities, pull into the vacant land beside it. Idle the engine, wait for someone to emerge, ask what I'm doing. Ask why I've parked here several times a day.

When I'm sure that nobody gives a shit that I'm here—just another investor trying to visualise the matching monstrosity they'll develop—I cut the engine, get out my car. Stretch. Listen to the faint sound of crashing waves from the coast I'd just left. It's part of my self-taught immersion therapy. Take in the ocean's raw energy. Try not to imagine my cousin, Trent, falling to his death into its depths, shot cliffside by the sweet grandmother I'd never had, Leonie Haynes. It's not the ocean's fault its waves swept Trent's body away. Anger and despair fuelled Leonie, making her take Trent's life in retribution for Trent's parents killing her foster daughter, Tiffany. For burying her in a cave I never want to set foot in again.

I take a concrete path, walk by the monstrosity. Seagulls circle overhead, mewing for their next meal. Despite the time of day, we're well into summer now and the heat knows it. There's no cloud cover. White sand, paths and roofing have reflected sunshine all day. I glance at the two-storey house. Its front yard is all limestone walls and artificial lawn. It's worth a million, at least. I can't imagine having a million dollars in my lifetime. Right now, I'm jobless, although I'm about to shift into another career.

A lady appears on the opposite side of the road, her dog jerking her along on its lead. She glances at me, does a double-take, then succumbs to the dog's pull, heading away from me.

I'm jobless, but recognisable. I've been the subject of several news reports over the last month. My face has been on the front page of our local newspaper. Twice. Which makes it hard for moments like these, when I need to blend with the suburb's everyday happenings.

I pass the monstrosity, ease onto the lawn of its neighbour—a remnant from the seventies, one of the first houses to be built in the area. It has rose bushes running alongside its tan-bricked walls, the tops of palm trees visible out the back. I take a paved path towards its front door.

My high school friend, Sergeant Gary Winters, helped me find this house. Getting to the address was part puzzle-solving, part luck. A life-changing sequence of events that started with the death of my uncle, Graham; led to the discovery that my father had an affair before he died, which gave me a half-sister, Lillian. Who I'm hoping to meet now. Who's evaded me for the last two weeks.

I knock on the front door. Wait. There's no security screen, just a thick wooden door with a thin slat of frosted glass down half its length. I assume the inhabitants can see out, or see a shadow. So, if Lillian were inside, she would know someone was waiting for her. I don't think she's inside, though. Two weeks ago, I pieced together the landline number leading to this house. Called it. Heard Lilian's voice for the first time. Cried with relief, with the knowledge she was alive. Then she'd told me it wasn't the right time, that she would speak to me later. Dismissing my existence.

I could have left it there, respected her wishes. But my family killed her foster sister, has had Lillian on the run for the last three years. Her foster mother is in hospital, recovering from an awful stab wound, and when she's healthy enough, authorities will whisk her straight to prison, the aftermath of her anger-fuelled retribution. Lillian needs to be around for that. To help bury Tiffany. To see that I can help her, that I'm not like the rest of my murderous, illegally-spy-on-everyone-in-their-hometown family.

I remove a lock pick set from my pocket. It's stored in a tiny cloth case, a gift from my amazing wife of fifteen years, Lucy. I'm not sure if it's legal to own, but Amazon shipped it in one day and nobody questioned the purchase. I *should* remember the legalities. I trained in the police academy after leaving school. Was an officer for two years before receiving my own awful stab wound. After reconnecting with Sergeant Gary Winters, while preparing for Uncle Graham's funeral and exposing my father's family, he offered me a place in his department. So, Gary believes I remember more about the law than I do. After rejecting his offer, he's helped me prepare for a side-career as a Private Investigator, my licence arriving in the mail any day now. Watching this house has given me plenty of surveillance hours to add to my credibility.

I take two thin bars of metal, slide them into the lock.

My first act before I officially start my PI business is to break into the house I've been surveilling. I don't need to remember the legalities of what I'm doing, but I don't care. And this doesn't make me like the rest of my family. Desperation has brought me to this point. Two weeks of surveilling this house, praying I'd see any sign of life within. But nobody has come and gone. Nothing delivered to the mailbox or door. Common sense tells me I'm going to step into an empty building, but my eyes need to confirm this. I spoke to my half-sister on the landline that's attached to this address. So, she was here at one point. If there's a shred of evidence pointing to where she's gone, I have to risk everything to find it.

Three minutes of fumbling the picks and the door clicks open. I look around, check for more dog walkers and other people passing by. Nobody. I wonder what the police response time is around here, if anyone has called in the suspicious man hovering outside the rose bush house. I glance at the monstrosity next door, picture someone watching from a second-storey window. Nobody.

I turn the handle, open the door. Slip inside, clicking the door and its lock back into place. Stand still in the entryway, listen for any telltale signs of life within. Nobody. No television or radio, talking or snoring, creaking or clunking, water trickling or utensil scratching.

I'm alone.

I step into a lounge room. Curtains line the windows facing out to the street. I let my eyes adjust to the shadows, hesitant to flick on a light switch. It takes a few minutes for everything to take form around me. There's a two-seater couch covered with a throw rug; a wooden cabinet made to house a television. Empty. No other decorations, no paintings or framed photographs or other signs of a regular inhabitant.

I work my way through the room into a dining area, find a light switch on the wall. If someone was going to burst out of a hiding place, they'd have done it by now. I flick on the light. In the dining area, there's one chair at a tiny wooden table. No crumbs on any surface, no signs anyone's used it to eat; unless they fastidiously clean up after themselves. I enter the connecting kitchen, take a peek in the fridge. Empty, but still running. I open a few cupboards above a long bench. Several cans of nonperishable items. Not enough to make a meal. There's nothing in the sink, the drying rack empty. There's a potted plant on a ledge above it, more curtains robbing it of sunlight. I work my way back to a passageway, assume it leads to bedrooms and a bathroom. Maybe a laundry, since I'm yet to see one.

There's a squeak outside. I hurry to the lounge room curtains, pull one aside enough to peer out at the street. A tradie's ute, pulling into the driveway across the road.

I let go of the curtain with a sigh. Head for the passageway, to the first doorway down its dark length. If that was the police pulling up here, what would I have done? Hidden in the room? Run out the back? If I got myself arrested, what would Gary say? He's already suspended while they investigate officers within his department; an investigation my actions were responsible for. Adding this highlight to his list would hardly work wonders for our friendship.

I shake off the thought, peer through the threshold of the first room, reach out to flick on the light. My reflection stares back at me in a bathroom mirror. I look tired. Real tired, the bags under my eyes adding years to my actual forty-one on this planet. My brown hair, cut short before a recent television interview, is flat and greasy. When did I last wash it? I shake my head, flick off the light. I don't enjoy looking at my reflection at the best of times. Today's just a reminder of how much this has affected me. Of why I've resorted to breaking in to this house.

There's a laundry area next, white goods missing. I check two cupboards; both are empty besides a solitary towel. There are two bedrooms deeper within. Well, one of them would suit a bedroom, or study, but it's absent of any telling furniture. The last room has a queen bed inside, atop a wooden frame. It's fitted with sheets, but they are straight and crisp and have had no one lie atop them. There's nothing else in the room of any value.

So, an empty house leaving me empty-handed.

I work my way back to the dining area, take a seat. Scan the rooms surrounding me from a lower angle. When I was looking for her, Lillian had taped a business card inside a letterbox, left pre-recorded song samples on an answering service, wrote extra numbers on Uno cards—all to lead here. Maybe there's one more hidden clue? Something to make sense of her current absence.

I find myself looking into the kitchen, staring at the plant on the ledge. It's a pink orchid. Tall yet drooping towards the aluminium basin below. When was the last time someone watered it? How long did they expect it to survive, the only sign of life in the house?

I get up, walk to the plant. Lift its pot off the ledge. The only life in the house, so it feels out of place. I feel the pink petals. They're real. Check the moss it's planted in. It's dry. But just to the side of the pot, peaking out of the brown, fur-like texture, is the edge of a plastic Ziplock bag. I lower the pot to the sink, work the bag out of its hiding spot. Hold it to the light.

A small bag, drug-dealer's choice. Except this has a slip of paper wedged inside, instead of marijuana or cocaine.

I remove the paper. Unfold it. Stare at the handwritten message.

December 20, listen to my year of birth.

So, I'm not leaving empty-handed. I'm leaving with another bizarre clue. I would love nothing more than to scream, attention be damned, but I should look on the bright side. Lillian isn't here, but she expected me to enter at some point. To find this clue. She would have hoped I'd taken less than two weeks to break in. Because December 20 is only eight days away.

CHAPTER ONE
CHILLI'S GOT A KICK

Summer sunlight in Perth stops you from sleeping in. It laughs at heavy drapes, finding its way through the tiniest crack or pinprick, seeking your eyes. Burning you. Telling you, *Wake up, there's so much to do today*.

I grab a pillow, pull it over my head. Just for once, I'd like to pretend there's nothing I need to do. I reach an arm across the mattress, search for Lucy. She's already gone to work, though. Of course, it's not the weekend yet. It's Friday. The last teaching Friday of the year, since her school finishes next Thursday, the nineteenth. She will be brighter than the sun when she gets home.

I can hear lots of thumps, the padding of footsteps. They thump closer, reaching the bedroom's threshold.

'Uncle Henry?' two voices chorus.

They don't even wait for a response. They can sense I'm awake. Seconds later, two heavy bodies land on my back, the pillow ripped from my grasp.

'Uncle Henry!'

'No, it's not.' I slide my arms out, get ready to push. 'It's the tickle monster, and you made it angry!'

The children giggle as I lift my body, turning to topple them on the mattress. Through sleep-encrusted eyes, I look down at Katie and Thomas. Eight and almost-five. If they didn't wake me up like this every damn morning, they'd be cute. I roar, then form claws with my fingers and tickle their tummies, arms, feet, resisting the bucking of their limbs.

'Kids, stop annoying your uncle.'

Sarah appears at the door. My wife's sister. The sunlight catches the red dye in her hair, glowing fire on her scalp. She folds her arms in a mock angry-parent pose, then breaks down with a smile.

'You're lucky your mum's rescuing you,' I call out as the kids scurry off the bed.

'Sure, rescuing them.' Sarah hugs her children, nods to me. 'Mum made Nasi Lemak for breakfast. I made coffee.'

'Give me a few minutes.'

They disappear. I concede defeat to the sun, rise from bed and make sure my hair isn't stuck to one side. It feels less greasy now, after the long shower I had upon my return. After everything that's happened, I could stay here in my room, enjoy this moment to myself a bit longer. I don't want too long with my own thoughts, though. Don't want to think about how I will fill the next eight days before trying to contact Lillian again.

I leave my room, work my way through my house, find everyone in the kitchen-slash-dining area. Sarah, her kids, and her parents. My in-laws have been on a *brief* visit from Singapore that has now turned into an extended stay. We've given my sister-in-law and her kids a room while she avoids her husband, Desmond, who's hidden a gambling addiction since the start of their marriage. They're working things out, but it's a long road to recovery.

'Henry.' My mother-in-law, Win, rises to greet me. Despite her slight frame, she pulls out the neighbouring chair as if it's weightless. 'I made you Nasi Lemak. Eat, eat.'

'Smells amazing.'

Some people wouldn't find the competitive smells of coconut rice, egg, sambal and fried fish amazing in the morning. I've had years of this food, though, embracing Lucy's heritage, and it's so much better than the toast and Vegemite my Aussie parents raised me on. Well, *parent*, since dad died when I was a teenager.

'Take some peanuts,' my father-in-law, Aqil, says, holding out a bowl. He winks at me. His way of saying hello.

'And don't forget cucumber,' Win adds. 'Chilli's got a kick.'

Sarah sits beside me, hands me a mug. 'Maybe drink the coffee before you lose your sense of taste?'

'Is this the coffee you got me from Melbourne?' I ask.

'You've got about a kilo left.'

We laugh, drink, eat, talk. The kids have found a box of crayons and are colouring printouts of SpongeBob SquarePants.

If someone were to visit now, they'd think they'd stumbled upon a perfect family.

'You not in the paper today,' Win says, smiling.

Aqil ruffles the newspaper in his hands. 'Going to be forty degrees today. Few days of forty predicted.'

'Great.' Yesterday was thirty-nine degrees. What's one more degree? I'm already looking over at the air-conditioner. Forty-one years of summers and I'm still not used to the extreme temperatures.

The doorbell rings.

'I've got it,' I say. It's my house, after all.

I head to the front door. There's a young man waiting with an envelope. His van's in the driveway. I can make out the courier logo. The man asks for my name, then scans the package and hands it over. Months ago, I didn't get much mail. Even my bills appear online. Then I received a letter from Uncle Graham, asking me to do his eulogy, giving me a list that revealed how far my family had gone to protect their secrets. After that, I've been receiving letters far too often. Information from the legal system, including court dates, statements from lawyers. Random people telling me I either did the right or wrong thing 'dobbing' my family in. I was also receiving letters from Leonie Haynes, telling me what Lillian was like when she helped raise her.

Leonie won't talk to me now, though, so I doubt I'll get another letter from her. I have to get my updates from the hospital and The Bear, Senior Constable Leigh Collins, who's also suspended while they investigate Gary's department. The Bear and I got off to a rocky start, but he's softened up to me now. A big, bald-yet-hairy-everywhere-else man who's good to have on your side.

I rip the envelope open as I return to the dining table. It's nothing to do with my family. It's the paperwork confirming I've registered my Private Investigator business. A decision backed by my amazing wife, who's going to help me get off the ground once her school's out for the summer.

'That looks fancy,' Aqil says, examining the licence. 'You want me to be your first case?'

'What case do you have for me?' I ask, humouring him.

'What happened to the weather here? It's as humid as Singapore and twice as sunny.'

He smiles as he hands the licence back. We've been talking about going to Singapore for Christmas, spending time with Lucy's extended family. After that, when they remain in Singapore, I'll miss corny jokes like these. And the strange feeling of having a large, loving family in the house.

I head over to a small desk, my makeshift office, and take a photo of the licence, send it to Gary. He's the reason I got it so quickly, his recommendation getting me fast-tracked through the system.

My phone rings. Didn't take him long. Probably going to offer me my first job as a consultant. An actual job, not like the one Aqil offered.

'Don't forget to eat,' Win calls out as I grab my phone.

I don't recognise the number. Maybe Gary's calling from the hospital? I know he's been visiting Leonie, too.

I answer the call. It's not Gary. They identify themselves as a lawyer from a firm I've never heard of. Their voice flows between one of refined, feminine grace to a nasal-twanged, closet bogan.

'Listen,' I say, cutting off their introductory spiel, 'I have my own lawyer for all this kind of—'

'You're not in trouble, Mister Herbert. I represent a client who has named you as someone likely to help their case.'

I glance at the paperwork on the table. Business already?

'Who?'

'Joseph Pooles.'

The name is familiar, but I can't place it. 'Why has he named me?'

'He was your mentor.'

'From teaching?'

'Correct.'

After leaving the police force, I dabbled in a variety of jobs before retraining as a Primary School teacher; inspired by Lucy and a need to help young children. I almost managed ten years at my school before the extra-curricular demands outweighed the help I felt I could provide. Proving my wife's a far better, more resilient human than I'll ever be.

I cycle through the mentor teachers I had when I went through my university degree. There were six or seven of them, since Edith Cowan University liked to encourage as many practicums as possible. The memory is already stirring. The first eight-week practicum from my final year. Joseph Pooles. He'd been teaching for about five years. And given that I was a mature student, he'd revelled in the fact that I was a year older than him. Calling me grandpa instead of treating me as an equal. The most I'd learned from him were the bad habits you had to work hard to avoid.

'I barely know him,' I say, because it's the truth.

'He knows that. But he's seen you in the paper, where you mentioned you were starting a PI business, and…' I overhear a sigh '…Look, things aren't looking good for him. He needs any extra help he can get, so he mentioned you. If you could come to my office, we'll discuss the case and arrange a time to visit him.'

Things aren't looking good for him? My mind cycles through the list of things he could have done. Being a teacher's bad enough; being a male teacher means working through the stigma left behind from evil men staining the profession. Mental and physical abuse of students. Abuse of power. There's no way I can have anything to do with this case if that's what he's accused of.

'What have they got him for?'

'They've arrested him for murder.'

'A student?'

'No. A parent.'

CHAPTER TWO
CLUTCHING AT STRAWS

The lawyer's office is in Subiaco. Like Yanchep, I haven't been near this area for years. When I was a kid, it was a vibrant place. Two tourist-pulling markets, toy stores, chocolatiers, mouth-watering food. There was even a stadium and a kids' hospital. It's different now. Old haunts closed down, replaced, revitalised; but nostalgia isn't important at the moment.

I need to hear what my mentor teacher did. Well, a quick Google search has told me what he's accused of, but I need to *hear* it.

The office is inside an old heritage house. I introduce myself to the person at the front desk and I'm asked to wait. A few minutes later, a short blonde-haired woman greets me with the switching accent I caught on the phone. She can't be over thirty. Maybe the only one in her firm willing to take the case? I'll ask her that later.

She leads me down a passageway to her office. It's large enough for a desk with chairs on either side, two bookshelves full of leather-bound hardbacks, document holders, and not much else. The room smells of vanilla, a diffuser on the table to cover any lingering mustiness.

'Please, have a seat,' the lawyer offers.

She has a nameplate on the desk. *Jensen Healy.* Thank God, I couldn't remember her first name from her phone call, her news stunning my brain.

She sits opposite, opens a manilla folder and draws out a photograph. She slides the photo to me.

I look at it. 'Joseph grew a beard, I see.'

'You confirm this is the Joseph Pooles you know?'

'Yes, I confirm it.'

She tucks the photograph back into the folder, pulls out a lined piece of paper. A pen appears in her other hand. 'For notes,' she says, registering my gaze.

Jensen asks me a few questions about myself. Age, when and where I worked as a teacher, my qualifications as a Private Investigator, how much contact I've had with Joseph. She puts the pen down after my last answer.

'You haven't seen him at all?' she repeats.

'Not since my prac.'

'Not at teachers' conferences, nights out, that sort of thing?'

'Sorry.'

'No calls or emails to each other, wanting to know how each other's going in their career?'

'No mentor teacher I've had has ever done that,' I say. Should they have? Did I leave the kind of impression that makes people want to avoid contacting you? I can't have. I found employment fast, gained permanency after two years, worked for nine years at the same school. That would only have happened if I were a capable teacher, right? Then again, nobody's contacted me since I left the profession. Shit.

Jensen hands me some printouts of newspaper articles. Not the ones I read about the murder, but ones about me and my family. 'Joseph said he'd seen you in the papers. I had a look myself.'

I cringe at my photograph. 'I solved a couple of mysteries, by chance. I'm still yet to see the end of it.' Since trial dates have moved around, because Leonie Haynes silenced a lot of witnesses who'd been there when Tiffany was murdered. 'I've got the stain of murder around me, so if that's what Joseph's accused of, I don't know how I could help.'

Jensen leans back in her chair. 'Maybe hear the case first, okay? From our perspective.'

I nod. What the hell.

'Yesterday, Joseph… We'll just call him Joseph… He had a parent-teacher meeting at the end of the day.'

Ah, the old parent conference. 'What time?'

'It started at four.'

Of course. Everyone thinks teachers knock off at three, when the kids go home. Anyone who knows them would say they stay at work for as long as needed, then bring more home. Never turning off.

'Just the one parent?' I ask.

'Father. Year Five student. Meeting about his low grades and general shit behaviour.' Jensen looks horrified, realising how crassly she'd just surmised things.

'Don't worry, I'm used to shit behaviour.'

She smiles. 'Joseph said this guy would not leave. The meeting had been going about forty-five minutes. Things got heated. Joseph offered to go get coffees for the both of them. Thought it would be a good break, give the father some time to realise he'd worn out his welcome. Oh, did I mention Joseph's school has several storeys of classrooms?'

'No. He's not at Ocean Reef?'

'He took a position at a private school four years ago. They'd usually be finished for the year but they trialled a three-week midyear break, so they have one week remaining. Anyway, the building is important. Joseph's room is two storeys up, in the middle. He comes out of the staffroom with the coffees, and—'

'The father is on the ground?' In the news report, there was a crude image of a chalk outline on paving. Something whipped up using stock photography.

'Correct. He's fallen two storeys onto the brick courtyard.'

I squirm in my seat. 'Let me guess. No other witnesses?'

'There was a long staff meeting the day before. Report editing. Yesterday, everyone got out of the Junior School early.'

So much for teachers staying back.

'I find it hard to believe nobody else was around.'

'Okay, so not everyone. One teacher was there. Miss Silver. In her room, first floor. Diagonally to the right of Joseph's room. And the principal was in her office.'

'Did one of them at least hear anything? If things got heated, they could have heard, right?'

'We're going through that now. Covering all angles.'

'So, again, what do you need me to do?'

Jensen struggles to find the words.

'Interview the teachers?' I offer. 'The other parents?'

'In a way.'

'Wait. Was the kid there? At the interview?'

Jensen shakes her head. 'He has two brothers. An older one was taking part in a swim meet, part of events run by the Senior School. The place has its own pool, right near the Junior School. The three boys were all there, the two younger ones helping, watching. Dad was going to join them after the interview. Swim meet finished at five.'

'And mum?'

'Works for an airline. Separated but not officially divorced. She was due to see them on the weekend.'

I shake my head. I'm not a police officer anymore, nor a teacher. I'm not the person who Joseph Pooles needs helping him.

'Are the police feeding you enough information?'

'Joseph had a one-on-one meeting with the parent. There are no witnesses to the murder. They will do everything they can to build a case against Joseph, and only Joseph. They will maintain there was a disagreement, a struggle, and Joseph threw the father off the balcony.'

'What was the disagreement about? Bad grades?'

'They can make anything up. Nobody but Joseph will contradict it. Maybe he snapped, called the father a dickhead. Called the kid a dickhead. The father snapped back, a struggle ensued.'

'*Did* he call them dickheads?'

Jensen shrugs.

'What do you need from me, then? Don't you have your own team to look through everything?'

'I haven't told you everything yet,' Jensen says, dismissing my questions. 'But I think you should speak to Joseph. You need to hear it from him.'

'Before I say no, you mean?'

Jensen closes the manila folder. 'Before you say no.'

Do I want to help? If Joseph Pooles has reached out to an ex-prac student he only had in his life for a couple of months, he's clutching at straws. There may be no way to help him even if he's innocent, especially if the police are confident in convicting him.

It's my first case, though, without spending a cent on advertising. And if Joseph *is* innocent, and I help prove that, then my face will be on the news for something unrelated to my family, growing my business exponentially. Besides, it's the diversion I need while I deal with the fallout from Margaret River, while counting down the date to Lillian's next clue.

Do I discuss my fee now?

'When should I meet with Joseph?' I ask instead.

Jensen shifts her chair back, stands. 'I was thinking right now.'

CHAPTER THREE
ANGRY FROM THE START

Jensen drives us to Hakea Prison in Canning Vale, where they've remanded Joseph. It's one of four maximum security prisons in the state. I'm ashamed to say my relatives are in two of the four. Turning that into a percentage makes it sound even worse.

The parking lot is almost empty, everyone filling the earlier morning visiting hour; a quick hello before the day heats to apocalyptic proportions.

'Are any reporters bothering Joseph yet?' I ask as Jensen pulls into a space.

'They can't get to him here, and my boss is deferring any calls.'

'Leaving the public to make up their own opinion?'

We exit the car, head for the visitors' entrance.

'You know,' Jensen says, 'there are already people on social media siding with Joseph, branding the father the monster.'

Of course they are.

'*About time someone stood up to abusive parents*, stuff like that.'

'Which would only be true if Joseph murdered said parent,' I point out.

There was a slight smirk on Jensen's face. It has vanished, now.

We enter the building, go through the sign in procedure. Confirm an appointment Jensen made, complete a visitor identification form, place our phones in a deposit box. Then we're waved through with a handheld metal detector wand. Rather than following lines to the visitors' area, we're led to an isolated room. We take a seat with our backs to the door. Wait.

'There'll be a conflict of interest with this case,' I say. 'A past mentee finding information to save his mentor?'

'This is Perth,' Jensen says. 'Everybody knows somebody. Besides, you said you haven't talked to him in over a decade.'

'True.'

We sit in silence for the next few minutes. Then the door clicks open and I turn to see Joseph led inside. He's handcuffed to the table, seated on a chair opposite. It all reminds me of the video conference call I had with Aunty Janice. She'd been sitting in a similar room, her lawyer present. But she'd seemed far more relaxed, in control. Without saying a word, Joseph looks defeated in his starched prison clothes. He's got a huge purple ring around his left eye. His curly brown hair is smushed to one side and his beard looks dry and lifeless, jagged tufts of hair pointing everywhere.

Joseph watches one guard step into the corner of the room. Maybe he's waiting for Jensen to ask for some client confidentiality? When she doesn't, Joseph switches his gaze to me, finally registers my presence. 'Henry Herbert?' A flutter of a smile. 'You came.'

I point to the eye. 'In here, or at the—'

'He punched me. I told him his kid needs to actually read a book to improve his reading and he punched me.' Joseph glances at Jensen. 'Thank you for getting Henry to help.'

'Technically, he hasn't agreed to help, yet,' she replies. 'He needs to hear your side of events, first.'

'Didn't you tell him?'

I lean forward, try to catch his gaze, hold it. 'I need to hear it from you.'

Joseph shakes his head. 'I didn't kill him.'

'That's not enough. Tell me what happened.'

Joseph rocks on his chair, glances at the guard.

'Can you give us some privacy?' I ask the man.

The guard grunts, shuffles out of the room. He doesn't go far, though; I can see his shadow in a gap beneath the door.

'Go on,' I prompt Joseph.

'We met,' he says. 'Hooray! This parent's been avoiding me all year, waits until the second-last week to see me. You know the type? Does nothing then comes down hard on you for the low marks you've told them you're about to reveal in their kid's report.'

I know the type. The parent who'd rather blame everything but their own absence.

'Was he angry from the start?'

'Furious. I was supposed to meet him and the wife but they couldn't agree to a date. He scheduled last minute and I thought why not, I'll just get it done and out the way.'

'Why was he furious?'

'I emailed, telling them about the low marks their boy was about to receive.'

'Was this the first time they knew about his marks?'

'He's been a D student since he started. We've got tonnes of support in place for him. We have to report individual assessment marks to parents all year on the SEQTA platform, and we have interim reports and semester reports going through their overall marks and effort. You know all this, you would've done it yourself. And before you say anything, yes, I tried calling them; many times. They never picked up their phones. Plus, we have school-wide parent interview days at the start of each term and they never made a booking. It's why I resorted to email.'

Joseph tries to catch his breath, his face red. His frustration emerged without much provocation. Did it fuel his anger during the parent meeting? Enough to push the father over the railing?

I know that if the teacher is doing their job, poor grades are never a surprise for the parents. From memory, Joseph wasn't the type of teacher to take such communication seriously. He tried to avoid several parent meetings while he was mentoring me. So, did everything happen as he described? Have further years of experience improved his professionalism?

'What's the father's name?' I ask, because I'm yet to put a name to everyone involved.

'Heath Hallid. Another double-H, like you.'

'And the boy's name? The one you're teaching.'

'Blake.'

'What was Blake good at?'

Joseph flutters a smile. All teachers know marks aren't everything. 'Anything computers. Terrible at math but the kid could already code his own mobile app. His dad wasn't having that, though. The college has an unhealthy emphasis on sport, which plays right to people like Heath. He wanted his son to be doing all the sports he could no longer do. His older brother was in the swim squad. That's where the boys were at the time.'

'What year is the older brother in?

'Bailey? Year nine.'

'And the younger one?'

'Reilly. Year two.'

Two more teachers to talk to regarding Heath Hallid. Given he rarely made an appearance, though, I'm wondering if they'll have much to add.

'The swim meet Heath was supposed to go to afterwards, it was still going during your meeting?'

'It would have had a few heats left.'

'Could anyone have come over from it?'

'Well yes, but… to get there and back in such a brief space of time, and to leave and not be seen…'

I glance at Jensen. 'We're canvassing for witnesses. Police will be, too.'

'Okay,' I say. 'So, you tell Heath that his son needs to read, he hits you. What happens next?'

Maybe, if I go in a few tangents, I'll catch Joseph off-guard.

'I ask him to leave,' he says, not missing a beat. 'The guy looks shocked he hit me. Apologises. I ask him to leave again. The man looks like he's about to cry. He mentions his separation. I feel for him a bit. I offer to go get us a coffee from the staffroom, giving us a quick break. He says we can talk for about twenty more minutes, then he has to get his kids from the pool. I'm relieved there's an actual cutoff time to this travesty. I leave him in my room, go downstairs. Get the coffees but take my time doing it, eating away at those twenty minutes. I come back out and there's this lump of clothes in the courtyard. And then I realise it's a person, and I see what's left of the face, and, well…' Joseph gulps, closes his eyes and tries to shake the image away.

When he opens his eyes again, they're rimmed with tears.

This guy is one big emotional roller coaster.

'When you made the coffees,' I persist, 'did you talk to anyone else in the staffroom?'

'No.'

'Receptionist? Principal?'

'The staff building has two entrances. One side has an area for the receptionist, deputy, principal, and school psych. The other side has the teacher lounge. I went in the lounge way. There's a solid door blocking the view between both areas. There's a passageway joining them, toilets along that stretch.'

'And how much time did you eat away making the coffee?'

'At least five minutes.'

'Are you sure it was five minutes?'

Joseph seems puzzled.

'You didn't stop to put ice on your face? You said you were taking your time making the coffee, so maybe you did that, too?'

'To be honest, I didn't think to put ice on my face. Shock made me go through the motions with the coffee machine.'

'Nobody heard you? Walked past the building? Saw that you were distressed?'

'If they did, I wasn't paying attention. The rest of my brain was working through how I'd end the meeting with that man, whether I should report him.'

'And when you saw him in the courtyard?'

'I froze beside him. A coffee in each hand.'

'You called for help?'

'I don't know what I did. I thought I did, but I couldn't hear myself. I just… I kept looking at the body, and… But not much later, one of the other teachers appeared. Kristen. She's on the floor down from me. She screamed. Asked me what I'd done. Then the principal ran out, and from that point on it was more of a blur.'

Joseph leans back in his chair, looking more exhausted than when he entered. I glance at Jensen, who raises an eyebrow that seems to ask, *So, you interested?*

Am I interested? Will I be helping free an innocent man or a murderer? Have I heard the complete story, or is there something missing? Joseph seems innocent. He's deflated, hurt, worried. And I may have heard his complete story, or most of his story, but there are elements missing. A five-minute window when Heath Hallid was alone. A five-minute window for someone to hear or see Joseph in the staffroom. After which, a teacher just appeared in the courtyard, followed by the principal; Joseph immediately accused of killing the father.

'What did you do with the coffees?' I ask.

Joseph looks puzzled.

'The coffees you brought out into the courtyard?'

'I guess… Tali took them out of my hands, I think. She's the principal.'

I picture Joseph standing there, staring down at Heath's body, so locked in shock that he couldn't even drop the coffee cups. Then I picture the opposite scenario, a man so confident he held them firm, even took a sip, looking down at the broken body. Two ways it could have gone. Either way, I'm intrigued.

'Is there a wife, partner, someone we need to talk to, to tell them what's happening to you?'

If there was, this would have already been done. I just want to hear him say it.

'I'm alone.'

I thought so. I don't know how it impacts the case, I just feel it does.

'You hit forty and realise you've dedicated your whole life to a job that's now put you in prison. All the people I mentored over the years, never would have thought this could happen to any of them.'

I turn to Jensen. The media are going to portray a loner who cracked after years of teaching, a quiet monster waiting for his chance to strike. I need to know what his co-workers think of him, what his students thought. His experience with other parents. Whether he'd reserved his lack of communication for the Hallids or if it was a common trait. A lot to investigate, with only four days of school left.

'I'll do it,' I say to Jensen. Then to Joseph, 'I'll help. And I have an idea how.'

CHAPTER FOUR
FOSTERING SUPPORT AND HEALING

Almost sixteen years I've been married to Lucy, and I still get giddy when she comes home from work. Earlier in our relationship, it was the sight of her caramel skin, her long black hair and sparkling green eyes. And her smile, always putting one on my face. What's built far beyond the physical attraction is the knowledge that she's the perfect complement to me, making me better in every way.

So, I hate to see her down.

She enters our house a zombie, her smile long gone. Sarah's kids run up and say hello and she flashes a brief look of happiness, but when she gets to me it's gone. I was a teacher long enough to know there are numerous reasons for the drain of energy. Tough kid, difficult parent, awful lesson, unrealistic demands from management, no breaks, no coffee, uncovering something awful about a student's situation, and so much more. All the things that could have pushed Joseph over the edge.

Still, I ask Lucy what's wrong.

'Just pooped,' she says. 'Lots to get through before the end of the year. Kym wants me to meet with the new teacher and do a handover on Monday, as if I don't have enough on my plate.'

Lucy's school knew she had been considering a move to Margaret River and offered her a deputy principal role to keep her. She'll be co-teaching with the other deputy next year, two days a week in the classroom and three in her new role. It's a change she deserves, but it will be a lot of work.

I give her a big hug, lead her to the bedroom. Shut the door.

'Honey, I said I'm pooped,' she says.

I smile. 'Just wanted to tell you about my day, without everyone else hearing.'

I let her know about the phone call, my visit to the lawyer, my visit to Hakea. Lucy heard about the murder. All of the teaching community is talking about it, obviously. Plus, it's all over Facebook. Lucy has a friend who teaches at Joseph's school. It was closed today. They're debating whether to close early for the holidays or keep going. Which may put a dent in my plans if they're closed.

'You think I should take the case?'

'You've already said yes, haven't you?'

'I can always reconsider. Contracts aren't signed.'

'You think he's innocent?'

'I want to believe he is, but…'

'You need to know more?'

'Much more.'

'Have you spoken with the police?'

'I think I have to investigate on the sly.' If someone attaches my name to everything that happened in Margaret River, the local police with ring the alarm bells.

Lucy sighs. 'I've had so many bloody frustrating parents over the years, but I can't imagine murdering them. My revenge is to make their kids better than they are.'

Something I tried to do for nine years. I know how frustrating parents can be, too. Truth be told, they were the reason I left my teaching position, their demands outweighing the joy of helping their children. Lucy is far more resilient than me. She'll be in education forever. Still, I agree with her. I can't imagine murdering a parent no matter how awful they are.

But that doesn't mean Joseph Pooles was as forgiving.

The teaching profession has had its share of monsters. Time will tell if my mentor is one of them.

Aqil knocks on the door, opens it before we respond.

'Everything okay, dad?' Lucy asks.

'Should we go out for dinner?' Aqil asks, oblivious to what he's just disturbed.

Lucy looks at me. 'Henry's got a case to work on, so…'

'No,' I say, 'not until Monday. You said you have a friend who teaches at the same school; you think you can get them in touch with me?'

'So, dinner?' Aqil asks, tapping the doorframe.

'Let's go Hillarys Boat Harbour,' Win calls out, walking up to her husband, our privacy gone, the conversation's momentum lost. 'Get the ocean breeze. You see the news? Big fire further north. Yanchep and beyond.'

Since visiting Joseph in prison, I've spent most of the day inside our home, avoiding the forty-degree heatwave outside. Reading those Facebook posts Lucy mentioned. Looking up what I can on Joseph and his career, which is very little. It doesn't surprise me that a large stretch of forest succumbed to the scorching temperature. Part of me prays Lillian's house has escaped the fire; the other part knows she's not there, anyway.

'Hillarys sounds great,' I say, trying to refocus.

Maybe I should drive up to Yanchep, just to check?

No. I should try to have a normal weekend with Lucy and her family, before I have to investigate a potential murderer; before I lose all focus to the message awaiting me from Lillian.

We swelter through two more forty-plus days, summer reminding us Christmas in Perth isn't all snow, sweaters and hot cocoa. The fires continue further north. I keep clicking on the Emergency Services map, tracking the spread, but it doesn't reach the area where Lillian's house is. We spend Saturday joining half the other suburb-dwelling residents at the shops, sticking to the cool air-con. The quest for Sunday lunch takes us to Cambridge International Food Court, the closest we can get to the Singaporean experience in northern suburbs Perth, since Lucy's parents are a little homesick for hawker-style food. Normal stuff, the weekend passing like it does for plenty of people.

Then my phone rings. It's the lawyer, Jensen.

We'd almost finished lunch, working through an Ice Kachang dessert. Lucy gives me a look that says, *Don't answer that.*

I have made little progress on Joseph's case, because I'm yet to visit his school, yet to talk to anyone else involved in the incident.

Everything I've read is rumours and speculation. I'm aware that means it's several days more that Joseph's sitting in prison, but his team of lawyers can also help him during this time.

I mouth an apology to Lucy, excuse myself, exit through the food court to the car park. My wife has already set things in motion for me tomorrow, she just wants me to spend the last hours of today pretending I'm not about to enter another world of secrets and murder.

There are many times in our relationship that I've been too slow to listen to her. Today will mark another of those moments.

'Everything alright?' I ask as I answer the call.

'My superiors liked your plan,' Jensen says. 'We've been in contact with your wife's teaching friend to confirm things.'

'The school's definitely open, then?'

'They want to finish the year fostering support and healing for their community.'

While trying to keep parents from withdrawing their children, I think.

'How's Joseph holding up?'

'Well, social media's painting him how we thought, people who don't even know him saying awful things about his character. We're going to have to work hard to sway a jury if this goes to trial.'

'You expected that, though.'

'We did. Hopefully, we can find people with nice things to say.'

'Or just find the murderer, if it's not him.'

There's a pause over the line, then, 'Yes. Proving his innocence is our priority.'

'How's Joseph actually going, though?' I repeat.

Another pause, then, 'I am visiting him Monday morning.'

In other words, he's fending for himself over the weekend. 'He definitely doesn't have any family?'

'There's a sister in Denmark. She's arranging a flight over.'

I picture Leonie Haynes waiting for her husband and son to arrange a flight from Singapore. Taking far longer than they should to arrive and provide mental support. Leading her anger to bubble over, for her to take matters into her own hands.

'Maybe have him watched,' I say.

'He'll be okay.' There's a rustle over the line. 'Ah. Now, I called because I wanted to make you aware we may have a problem.'

There's laughter behind me. I turn to give way to a family exiting, bags of takeaway in hand.

'Go on,' I prompt Jensen.

'Well, the police are handling it, but I think it affects every-thing.'

'What happened?'

'Heath Hallid's oldest son, Bailey, has gone missing.'

'Missing?'

'His mother said he's wandering. Said he's in shock about his dad. She's adamant he just needs some time and he'll come home, but she called the police all the same.'

'When did he leave home?'

'A few hours after his father's death.'

His father's death was Thursday. It's now Sunday.

'We're into the fourth day. Are the police taking it seriously?'

'The kid's fifteen. He can look after himself.'

'But…?'

'Seems coincidental, doesn't it? Father dies, kid goes missing. He could have had something to do with it, or he could know who did.'

'Hmmm.' I don't know how I feel about the concept of coincidence any more. 'But the police are handling it?'

'It's nothing we need you to investigate. It's awful to say, but a missing teen will draw the media attention away from Joseph.'

'Keep me updated,' I say, understanding what Jensen means no matter how horrible it sounds. 'Oh, did we discuss my fee on Friday?'

Jensen hangs up before answering. Leaving me with more questions than when I started the case. And the feeling that something is definitely not normal with the case itself.

My phone rings again. I almost answer, thinking Jensen's about to add another detail to the disappearance, then I see the number. It's my mother.

I let the call ring out.

Letting some parts of today remain normal.

CHAPTER FIVE
EASIER TO BLAME

Joseph Pooles mentored me at a small government school in the northern suburbs of Perth. Its focus was on connecting its local community, providing a safe space for its children to learn, with four main buildings and a tiny car park bordering a main road. The school he ended up at seems far different. It's in the southern suburbs, a boys-only school, and has two sections, a Junior School and Senior School. A one-stop Kindergarten to Year Twelve experience. Its grounds encompass the equivalent of the entire suburb Joseph's last school served. They're fenced off, keeping the local community out. There's a large sign near the gated entrance, with an embossed logo telling me I've reached Isidore College, in case I didn't know.

I drive my vehicle through the gated entrance. Past two stationary vans, their television station logos plastered on every surface. I ignore the reporters as they watch my car pass, take in the grand entrance. Bushland surrounds this first stretch, hiding it from outsider view. Then nature disperses and I reach a roundabout with a statue of someone important. The aforementioned Isidore? Ahead is another gate, but it's closed, blocking further access. I take the roundabout, head back towards the entrance, and find a turn to a carpark in a pocket of sunken land. I park, get out, follow a mother and son along a brick-paved path. Already, the sheer size of the looming buildings tells me a great deal more funding went into the infrastructure than any school I've taught at.

There's a huge castle-like building in the distance, part of the Senior School, but the Junior School is before that, separated by long stretches of grass and a smaller building that looks like a church. Given it's a Catholic College, it makes sense *if* it's a church. I follow signage to Administration, check in, wait for the deputy to come and grab me.

It's just gone eight. School starts at eight-thirty.

I sit on a leather sofa, wait five minutes. Ten. Check my phone, look for missed messages. Maybe this isn't going to work after all. My plan's pretty simple. I'm no longer teaching, but I still hold an accreditation to teach. I can act as a substitute. Get to know the school from the frontlines. Lucy's friend in the Senior School recommended me to relieve Joseph's class, her word golden to get me chosen ahead of the school's regulars. Assuming anyone would volunteer to teach here after Thursday's incident.

'Henry?'

I look up from my phone to see a man in his early fifties staring down at me. Almost my height, a touch over six feet tall; curly greying hair and wide-rimmed glasses; black suit a size too big, hanging off his tall yet thin frame.

He holds out a meaty hand that betrays the rest of his body. 'I'm Trevor, the deputy. Thanks for coming at such short notice.'

I rise from the couch, shake his hand. 'Thanks for considering me.'

There's a look on his face that tells me he had little choice. So, the regulars were unavailable. I don't know if that's a good or bad thing.

'Reporters didn't bother you, did they?'

'I only saw them in their vans.'

'Good. They're hovering by the gates, even though they shouldn't be on the grounds. If they bother you, please refer them to me.'

'What are they here for?' I ask, playing dumb.

Trevor adjusts his glasses. 'We have little time, so I'll walk you to the staffroom, then bring you up to class.' He points to the backpack in my hand. 'Any lunch you need to put in the fridge?'

I smile. He'll talk about the murder soon enough. 'Some leftovers, yeah.'

We leave the first building, walk into a courtyard. Tan brick paving framed by buildings on three sides, each structure two or three storeys high. I almost ask where Heath Hallid landed, stop myself. If I'm playing dumb, Trevor has to think I've avoided all news and social media.

'You any good with iPads?' he asks.

I've sold a mountain during a stint in retail electronics, but I don't tell him that, either. 'I'll manage.'

'We have one for each teacher. Your relief notes will be on there. You have a temporary email address, *ReliefTeach1*, and you'll have access to the class list for the role. We take the role first thing in the morning and first thing after lunch.'

'No problem.'

We reach the two-storey building and Trevor opens a glass door for me, waving me inside. The stretch of glass wall is tinted, hiding whatever lurks inside; which is a staffroom. A long table runs down the middle, a bench and fridge to the left, sink and coffee machine to the right. There's a couch further into the room. Someone's sitting on it, chatting away on a landline phone, the rest of the staffroom empty.

'I'll make some introductions at recess,' Trevor says. Then he clicks his fingers, like an idea has just sparked. 'Actually, you have duty at recess. Lunch then, I guess.'

I glance behind us at the glass wall. There's a darkened view of the courtyard outside. A staircase blocks some of it, but there's plenty of space to see a few kids running around, heading to their classrooms. I glance at the coffee machine. Wonder, if Joseph had just turned his head, what would he have seen?

After I put my lunch in the fridge, Trevor opens a door and leads me down a passageway. He points to another door for the staff toilets, then directs me straight to his tiny room. He picks up an iPad, some pieces of paper and a name badge, handing it all over. 'Name badge just says *Relief Teacher*. It's magnetic, easy to put on. I've got some notes about school conduct, duty expectations, etcetera, all printed out for you. You'll have some time to read all that before the bell goes.' He looks at his watch. 'If we hurry.'

He leads me past a reception desk, where he introduces me to a grey-haired woman who has the most appropriate smile for a warm welcome to school. Beyond her desk is a door leading to the principal's office. The door is closed, a nameplate telling me her name is Talitha Hills. I missed the grey-haired lady's name, turn to ask her but see Trevor's already exiting through another glass door. I excuse myself and hurry after him. We cover the width of the courtyard beneath a bridge connecting the two-storey building to a three storey one. A few kids hurry up the stairs ahead of us. We climb one flight, then another, to the upper storey. We walk along a concrete balcony a metre and a half in width, waist-height metal poles and panelling providing the only security to keep me falling. We pass one classroom, kids yelling inside. Trevor looks embarrassed, shrugs, keep moving. We reach the second door. A small group of kids are waiting outside it. They cheer when they see Trevor with a fob key. Cheering to get in class? Where the hell am I?

Trevor swipes the fob and the door clicks open. He asks the kids to wait outside a moment. They groan. He ushers me inside.

'Is that everyone?' I ask. There were six kids.

Trevor sighs. 'We don't know how many children we'll get today. It's already the last week. Families escape for an early holiday no matter how much we say their schooling is important. Also, there's the other unfortunate incident to consider.'

I don't respond, continuing to pretend I have no idea what he's talking about.

'A parent died here last Thursday,' Trevor explains, reluctance in his voice.

A parent *died*, no mention of *murder*.

'That's awful,' I say, trying to carry the appropriate level of surprise in my voice.

'Truly. The student was from this class. The teacher is on leave. So, if all things go as we expect, we will need relief for the rest of the week.' Trevor swipes an arm outward in dramatic fashion, drawing my attention to the classroom's layout. 'The boys will help you. If they don't, you have a teacher either side of this classroom. Now…' He pauses a moment, considers his question. 'We teach in the Catholic tradition. Are you Catholic?'

'No. But my wife's family is.'

'Then you're familiar with our many traditions?'

I nod.

'Just follow the notes,' Trevor says. 'Jesus was good, everyone do as he did. That sort of stuff.' Trevor looks at his watch again. 'I have to go now. Good luck.'

He doesn't wait to see if I have any questions. Nor does he continue deceiving me about the murdered parent and the teacher *on leave*. He opens the door and steps outside, inviting the kids in. I don't even make it to the teacher's desk—at the back of the classroom, far left—before I'm hit with an avalanche of questions.

'*What's your name?*'

'Mister Herbert.'

'*Do you know Mister Pooles?*'

'He helped me become a teacher.'

'*Are you a killer like him?*'

'Nobody's a killer.'

'*Blake's dad died. Did you know him?*'

'No.'

'*Why are you so tall?*'

I let the questions become static in my head, a vital skill learned over the years, and find a seat behind the teacher's desk. As I look up at the classroom, I feel a weird sense of unease and déjà vu at the same time. Last time I'd stepped foot onto school grounds, I was at Lucy's Primary School, telling her about the death of Tiffany and the possibility that Lillian was alive. Now, I'm pretending I'm just a regular substitute so I can investigate the potential murder of a parent.

I shake off the spectre of death and unlock the iPad Trevor gave me, using a code on the printout, then follow the instructions and access my notes. Someone's left me a pretty simple day. I'm not sure who prepared the notes, since Joseph's detained, but they've assigned a whole lot of time-filler activities. Apparently, the kids have a Christmas booklet to work through; they've been making their own board games and need to finalise those; there are a lot of Kahoot quizzes to run; plus, I need to finish the class novel. There's an Art lesson after recess and I'm going to relieve the Year Two class during that time. Blake Bailey's younger brother is in this year. If it's his classroom, someone is looking out for me.

The bell rings and I take attendance. There was a boy who arrived seconds before the bell, so we have seven in the class. I write my name on the board in case someone forgets, taking forever to find a whiteboard marker—end-of-year stationery blues. I wonder if the low student numbers are the same in the other classrooms or if it's because parents don't want to send their child to an accused murderer's classroom. If it's the latter, what does that say about the parents who sent their child?

If there are only seven children, I'm not likely to get called back tomorrow. Trevor will siphon the boys to the other classrooms, money saved. This might be my only day at the school. Not what I'd hoped, so I'll have to make it count. How do I make it count?

I read the class novel for a while. After a few minutes, I ask a student to turn the air-conditioning unit on, the heat baking us. The student has to go borrow a controller from another room, though, theirs lost. When he returns, I continue. The novel's about a boy who's been sitting unnoticed at the back of the class, a refugee who's waiting to hear the fate of his family. I ask the kids a few questions to gauge what's been happening. One of them wonders aloud about the parents, asks if they've been murdered, too. I should dismiss this, fast. Instead, I ask why they keep mentioning murder.

'Blake's dad was killed,' the same boy as before tells me.

'Did anyone see him killed?'

They shake their heads.

'Then how do we know he was killed?'

'My dad says Mister Pooles killed him,' the tallest boy in the class calls out.

'Did your dad see Mister Pooles do that?'

The boy looks confused.

'Sometimes,' I explain, 'what people say happened and what actually happened are two different things. Think about Mister Pooles. Before the death, was he a good teacher?'

'Yeah,' a few voices echo.

'He was great,' another says.

'And did he ever get angry?'

'Yes,' one boy offers.

'Did he ever yell?'

'Yes,' they chorus.

'When he got angry and yelled, did you ever think he was going to hurt you in any way?'

The boys shake their heads.

'When he yelled, it's only cause someone was being naughty,' a young boy with close-cropped hair explains. 'And that was after like a hundred warnings. Most of the time, he spoke soft, so if he yelled you knew you'd pushed him too far.'

Pushed him too far. I wonder if Blake's father pushed Joseph too far. The smack to the face wouldn't have helped.

'So, he yelled sometimes,' I say, 'just like your parents might, right?'

There are some mutters of agreement.

'And other than that, no violent behaviour. Yet everyone is saying he's a murderer?'

More murmurs. I can't tell if they get my point.

'Let the police do what they do,' I say. 'They'll find the person responsible and keep you all safe. Meanwhile, let's end the year by focusing on the good things that got us here. There are lots of opportunities to finish your Christmas booklet, to make your board games and to play some quizzes. Okay?'

Everyone nods.

'Wise words,' a voice cuts in.

I turn to the doorway to see a woman standing rigid, arms folded. She looks to be in her late forties, early fifties. She's a couple of inches taller than me, her thin frame rivalling Trevor's. Does nobody eat in this school, or has stress had an impact? Makeup is working hard to conceal dark rings around the woman's eyes, so perhaps stress is also affecting sleep. She's pulled her brown hair into a tight bun, stretched as tight and thin as the smile on her lips.

How long has she been standing there, listening?

'I'm Ms Hills,' she explains. 'The principal. Welcome.'

'Thank you,' I say, resting the class novel on my knee.

'Please come and see me by the end of the day.'

Before I can reply, she spins round and hurries off.

I turn to the boys. 'Sounds like I'm in trouble, right?'

They chuckle.

Off to the principal's office. This is why I left teaching: weird power-plays, office politics, parents demanding too much from teachers until they snap.

My time here is definitely limited. I'm on duty at recess, though. Wandering the school grounds, talking to the kids and some other teachers. If I have any kind of Private Investigator skills at all, that's when I'm going to use them the most.

I have to believe what I just told the boys, that we'll find the person who did this. If I don't, Joseph Pooles will spend the rest of his days in prison, because he's looking easier and easier to blame.

CHAPTER SIX
THERE WERE USUALLY SIGNS

Joseph Pooles was twenty-eight when he'd mentored me. I was almost turning thirty. He'd been a teacher for five years. The average teacher retention rate is five years. During our time together, it seemed like he would help affirm that statistic. He was disorganised, his desk a mess, his lessons poorly planned. He had over a hundred emails in his Inbox. But he didn't care. He had the relaxed attitude that fits so many Australians, at the detriment of professionalism.

His students always loved him, though. He cared more about the pastoral side of things than academics, focusing on his students' physical and emotional wellbeing. It's a great approach to take, but actual teaching has to take place, too. His co-workers would pull me aside during the practicum, tell me how they'd always have to work twice as hard with his students when they came into their class the following year. The kids were down in comprehension skills, writing, and basic computational abilities. The important areas. I had approached Joseph about this and his response was he didn't care. *It's only Primary School* was a favourite excuse, as if Primary School didn't contain the vital foundations for a lifetime of education. I'd thought that by the time I was into my own career, Joseph would have left or had someone ask him to leave the profession. I hadn't caught up with him, he'd never tracked me down and asked how I was progressing. Being called to help him with the murder was the first time we'd talked in over a decade.

Joseph had arrived at Isidore College four years ago, filling a vacant position. From the three duty teachers I'd talked to during recess, it seemed he was quiet his first year, adjusting to an unfamiliar environment. After that, he became a key member of staff. One of the few teachers to speak up against perceived injustices, questioning demands placed on staff. He clashed with the principal at times, but the others loved him for it.

Loved him. That's what my key Private Investigator skills got out of recess. The kids I spoke to loved him, said he was the best teacher they'd had. The staff here thought of him with fondness, too. That didn't mean he wasn't a killer, of course. Case histories of paedophilic teachers showed they built up trust with the people around them before revealing their true nature. People say the same of killers, but there were usually signs, weren't there?

After recess, I'd thought the Year Two class might give me further insight into Joseph or Heath Hallid. Blake's younger brother, Reilly, was absent of course. Everyone was eager to tell me his daddy went to heaven, but the Education Assistant hushed them. With her around, I wasn't able to do much but stick to the lesson plan, a Health session where I demonstrated the insane amount of sugar found in soft drinks. After that, we watched last week's end-of-year review episode of *Behind the News*, a kids show that'd been running for over fifty years. When I returned to the Year Five class, the lesson notes had me put on the same show. Leaving me sitting here, on Joseph's chair, staring at the same thing I just watched, feeling like I have very much wasted the one chance I will get.

Fuck it. The kids are sitting on the carpeting, staring up at the interactive whiteboard. Transfixed by the show. I have twenty minutes or so to do some snooping. I'm not going to get anything else out of the kids, unless there's a secret they might blurt, so I may as well try to find notes or photos or something of use to help me make sense of Joseph's relationship with the parents.

His desk is nothing like the one I remember him keeping. It's insanely clean. There's an *In* tray, a notepad, a tin with a few pencils and pens, a tissue box and a candle. That's it. Maybe the police swiped as much as they could for future evidence?

A small set of drawers sits under the desk. The top two drawers have more pens, sticky notes and other assorted stationery. There are also some medical supplies for cuts and sunburn. The bottom drawer is much deeper and has two metal bars on the sides. Perfect for hanging suspension folders. Except there are no suspension folders. The police have definitely taken those, which would have held notes on parents, along with Joseph's laptop and its accessories. I might have to find out who's working the case, see what they know, see what I can get access to. But I have very few connections in Perth and I'm not part of any police investigation. If they found out I was posing as a relief teacher to get answers, I might join Joseph.

I get up, wander the room. There's a wet area behind the wall housing the whiteboard, connected to the entry door. The kids have their own locker, two rows of them along the walls. Each one has a name on it. Some have posters with endless memes covering them, kids trying to express their identity through pop culture references. I read a few, chuckle, then get to a locker at the end, near a cupboard and sink. It's absent of a name and decorations, but it has a padlock on it. Interesting.

I look round the whiteboard wall, point to the nearest student, get them to come over.

'Whose locker is this?' I whisper, tapping the padlocked door.

'Mister Pooles,' he replies.

'Thanks.'

The boy returns to the carpeting as I stare at the locker. It's possible the police didn't search this because they assumed it belonged to a student. Joseph made use of spare storage, though. I hold the padlock. It's thick and heavy, something you'd put on a gate at home to keep people from intruding. I try to picture the contents of my backpack, try to remember if I packed the lock pick set Lucy bought me. No, I didn't think I'd be needing something like that at school. I should have, though. It's my first rookie error. So, if I don't have the tools, what alternative is there?

I can hear the episode ending, the show's theme tune starting. The boys will use the rest of their time before lunch to polish the board games they've been creating. Apparently, they're going to play them during the last two days. I go round the wall, give them their instructions. Stand there as they hustle off into small groups. Think more about that padlock. Lunch is coming up. Trevor was kind enough to give me the full forty minutes without a duty. If I can get that padlock off, I should have plenty of time to go through Joseph's things.

I return to the wet area. Blake's locker is there, with posters for video games like *Fortnite* and *Call of Duty*, popular games I recognise. Games he shouldn't be playing. With an older brother, that would have been hard to stop. There's a padlock on Blake's locker, too.

A boy enters the wet area, gets into his own locker, trying his best to ignore me.

'What happens if you forget your key?' I ask the boy before he leaves.

'Mister Pooles has spares in his desk, in a little pencil case,' he replies. Then a grin widens as he remembers something else. 'Or you get the cutters from the office.'

I thank him and hurry to the teacher's desk. There are no pencil cases in the drawers, perhaps seized, too.

I pick up the class phone, find the instructions on how to dial reception. Donna answers. Now I know her name. I make up a story about a boy who can't get his lunch after losing his locker key. She tells me to come and get the cutters when the bell goes; she'll leave them behind her desk.

I smile. In half an hour, I might discover some of Joseph's secrets. Maybe I haven't wasted my chance, after all?

CHAPTER SEVEN
THIS READS LIKE BLACKMAIL

The schools I taught at and attended never had lockers for their students, just benches outside the classrooms that everyone put their bags on. If students left their bag open, their lunch was free game to crows. It was a rite of school. Lockers seem so American, so Middle School. What has a Primary School student got to put in a locker, anyway?

I have to admit, though, using the bolt cutter on the padlock is fun. Wriggle the blades between a section of the shackle, apply some pressure, snap. I wonder how many times Joseph had to do this throughout the year. Or maybe it was an end-of-year ritual. Or something he did for the hell of it. It's so satisfying, I approach Blake's locker and remove that padlock, too.

I've shut the classroom door, but it's not locked—I don't have the key. I hurry, in case a teacher or student barges in, grab a garbage bag from a roll on top of the lockers and swish it open. I go to Joseph's locker first. On first glance, it doesn't look like it holds any mysteries. Just random stuff: a change of clothes, deodorant, books, a pencil case and loose stationery. I grab and throw it all in the garbage bag, anyway. I grab another bag, move to Blake's locker. It's almost empty except for a stack of paper and a clear plastic lunchbox that has some toxic mould growing in it. I pull out the stack of paper, rifle through it. Just unfinished worksheets and random doodling. Would Blake know I took this? The kid's not coming back to class, and he's got other things on his mind. At least, that's what I tell myself as I place the pile into the garbage bag. The lunchbox stays put.

I close the locker doors and bring the bags back to Joseph's desk. Taking a seat, I pull a handful out of the bag from Joseph's locker—a pair of shorts and the pencil case. Nothing in the pockets around the shorts. I open the pencil case. No pencils, just slips of folder paper. I shake these out onto the desk, unfold one.

You have to tell the truth

The handwriting looks like it belongs to one of the Year Five students. It's in blue pen, a morphed mix of print and cursive. I'm not going to assume anything, though. A huge proportion of adult handwriting looks like its ten-year-old counterpart.

I unfold the other slips of paper.

I know your secret

You can't hide what you did

Do the right thing

I'll tell everyone soon

It's not right what you did

You got one more day

Jesus. This reads like blackmail. Was Joseph being black-mailed? By a student or parent? Or had he confiscated these notes? Was another student giving these to someone else in class?

I return the notes to the pencil case, my hands shaking. I need to meet with Joseph again, see what he can offer about this discovery. It could be unrelated to Heath Hallid's murder, or it could have everything to do with it.

'What are you doing?'

Trevor's standing at the end of the classroom, just inside the now open doorway.

I pull the bag closed, shove it beneath the desk, stand. 'Ah, we've just been giving the class a good old end-of-year clean.'

Trevor seems to accept the lie, gestures to the door. 'You're missing your break. Come on, I want to introduce you to everyone.'

We head downstairs. The courtyard's pretty empty, most kids running around in an adjacent playground.

'Enjoying your day?' Trevor asks.

'It's been great so far,' I try to say with as much enthusiasm as possible, so I'm called back tomorrow.

We enter the staffroom, the same way we came in this morning. Trevor gets the attention of the staff, introduces me as promised.

Except there are only five teachers in the room, and I met three of them during recess duty.

'End of year madness,' Trevor explains. 'Everyone's cleaning their room like you had the initiative to do, or helping on duty, or hiding.' He laughs, pats me on the shoulder, and leaves me to it, retreating to his office.

'Grab a seat,' says one of the teachers from duty.

I remove my lunch from the fridge, put it in the microwave. Take a seat at the end of the table, so I can look at everyone.

'You all been teaching here long?' I ask.

There are two males, three females. The males have both been at the school two years. They don't offer their names. There is one older female, Amanda, who has been at the school eleven years. There are two younger teachers who don't look a day out of university. Emma, whose wide smile and bright clothes tells me she's teaching Early Years, and Ashlee, who has a green streak through her dark hair and a rolled-up shirtsleeve revealing a tattooed upper arm. They confirm it's their first year. I congratulate them for surviving. The first year of teaching is often the hardest, if not the most daunting. Especially when the principal gives you the hardest students to teach, another rite of passage. If you survive the first year, you can make at least another four.

The microwave dings, my lunch ready.

'I've been hearing a lot of conflicting things about this Joseph guy I'm relieving,' I try. I hadn't told the duty teachers Joseph had been my mentor.

Both men are on their mobile phones. They look up from their screen in unison.

'What's it matter to you?' one of them barks.

'The kids are asking a lot of questions; I just want to reassure them everything's okay.'

'Everything's okay.'

'Someone died here.'

'And someone's in jail.'

The men go back to their phones. A moment later, they pretend they've received a message and leave the room.

'Bit of toxic masculinity going on here,' I try to joke.

Emma waves it off. 'Don't mind them. They've checked out for the year. They'll be better at Friday drinks.'

A vision of Andy and Russell flies through my mind. Two males teachers from Lucy's school, semi-friends of Sarah's absent husband, Desmond. I'd first met them with beers in hand. Two gamblers, one of which got caught up in my last Margaret River fiasco. I wonder how similar these two males are to Andy and Russell. Maybe they were both placing bets on their phones. Maybe I'm the only male who's resisted the lure of quick win, quick lose apps.

I realise everyone's been staring at me for a while. 'They didn't like Joseph, I take it?'

'They loved Joseph,' Ashlee says. 'They're disappointed in him, I guess.'

'They think he's guilty?'

'I'd say staff are fifty-fifty.'

'But everyone loved him?'

'He stood up for us.'

'You can never tell everything about a person, I guess.' I dig through my food with a plastic fork, think about the notes I found. 'He must have had his secrets?'

Emma glances at Amanda, then connects eyes with Ashlee, grins.

'Don't,' Amanda says.

Emma and Ashlee giggle.

'What?' I ask.

'Just a few rumours about who he was sleeping with,' Emma divulges.

'Rumours is the key word,' Amanda says. 'Stop right there, we don't give everything to the relief on the first day.' She holds up a hand. 'No offence.'

I shrug, pretend I don't care. 'None taken.'

The door to the passageway opens and the principal strides in. She heads straight for the fridge, takes out a tub. She glances at me, *I'll see you later* echoed with a nod. She turns and starts heading out the room again, nothing said to her staff.

Emma is grinning wider than when I arrived. She points at the principal as the door closes.

'Her?' I ask.

Emma and Ashlee break into more giggles. Amanda hangs her head, shaking it.

'And a parent,' Ashlee adds, the seal broken.

She looks like she wants to tell me more but the bell rings. I haven't eaten much food. That's okay, though. Most productive lunchtime of my career.

CHAPTER EIGHT
SUPPOSED TO INTIMIDATE

There's a twenty-minute silent reading period after lunch. Halfway through this, a line of kids march into my classroom, each carrying a book and an iPad. Trevor is right behind them, to explain that a few key staff members have been called to a meeting in the Senior School. My class has grown from seven students to thirty-one for the last hour and a bit.

I try not to look shocked. Or scared. I've handled classes of thirty before, I can do it now. But there's no way I can interview any of these kids about Blake or Heath Hallid without everyone overhearing; spreading rumours about the substitute who asked way too many questions about the dead man.

Sticking to the plan, I use the relief iPad to find something on Kahoot, a website where a community makes quizzes on just about every topic imaginable. So many suitable topics, from video games to famous landmarks; even a quiz on the *Behind the News* episode everyone has now watched. I get it up on the interactive whiteboard and everyone finds their own spot around the room, friends bunching together, several boys choosing to isolate themselves should anyone look at their screen. I start the quiz, a loud countdown prompting them to get ready, and everyone's noisy and excited and cheering after each answer and I don't care if it's disturbing other classes.

Time flies by. Before I know it, the other teachers return to pick up their students and we're packing up. The bell rings. I say goodbye to my seven students, wish them a fantastic holiday if I don't see them again, because I'm pretty sure I won't.

When they're gone, there's a peaceful silence. I sigh so loudly it surprises me. All this time away from teaching, I didn't think I could do it again. Sure, I was just there to distract seven boys with busy work, but it required some skill keeping them on task, reducing silly behaviour, and all the other things I forgot become a routine part of the teaching day.

I pack my backpack and grab the garbage bags, iPad and notes, then head down to the carpark. I pass a duty teacher who looks at the garbage bags but says nothing. I throw those and the backpack in my boot, then hurry back to admin. Thankfully, Trevor isn't wandering around looking for me. I find him in his office, give him a quick debrief and return the iPad and notes. He thanks me again for coming in and *saving them.*

'Any time,' I offer.

I hope he gets the hint, extends my relief window. But he doesn't say I need to save them tomorrow, just reminds me the principal wants a word. I cross the reception area and knock on her open door. Talitha pries her eyes from a large computer screen and asks for me to come in and shut the door. She's seated at a large wooden desk; behind her, a long glass wall overlooks one of the grassed playing areas. I take a seat opposite. It seems shorter than hers. Designed for kids, even though adults would often see her. I get it, the height difference makes her the ruler of her domain.

I expect her to jump in and criticise the way I'd been talking to the students about the murder. Instead, she says, 'I've made some calls about you.'

'Oh?' Surely the school made calls about me before I came in?

'Highly recommended.'

I try to smile.

'Encouraged to apply for leadership positions but content to teach in the classroom.'

'Yes, well I—'

'That was from the references in your brief CV.' Which I'd not bothered to change since applying to work in an electronics store. Talitha leans a little closer. 'But I also Googled your name.'

'Ah.'

'Which I had assumed Trevor had done. Because you've been busy in the papers.'

'My family, they—'

'We are under scrutiny from the press for hiring a potential murder. We cannot add fuel to the fire by having a replacement who's involved in similarly nefarious deeds.'

Talitha glowers. It's supposed to intimidate, but I'm just mad. Did she read the news reports at all, or just the headings? My family was involved in a murder, but I'm the one who found out and turned them in. I exposed the illegal servers they were running around the area, too. Helped the police department wrap things up.

'You can run a police check on me. You'll see that—'

'Of course we have. That's why I was happy to have you remain here the rest of the day. But if parents get wind of your name, and those reports, and choose to make their own assertions regarding your involvement in everything...' Talitha leans back, her stare softening. 'Look. I am in damage control. Moving forward, I think it's best we leave you off the roster the last three days. Trevor tells me there were only seven kids in class anyway, and two of those parents emailed me today to say their son will not be in tomorrow. We will put the five remaining boys into other classes.'

I rise from the chair. 'I understand,' I say, trying to keep the bitterness out of my voice. After all, I was expecting this, just not the delivery. 'Thank you for having me today.'

'Should things wrap up in the courts, we would be delighted to have you on our relief roster next year.'

I don't know if she means the court cases for my family or for Joseph. I hold out my hand for Talitha to shake. Her grip is weak, like I have germs she doesn't want crawling onto her.

'Have a great break,' I offer.

I leave the room, ignore the receptionist and Trevor and head down the passageway. I'd left my lunchbox in the staffroom. Better collect it and get the hell out here before I do or say something I can't take back.

Ashlee is in the room, making a tea. 'You survived?'

'Just the day,' I say. 'Won't be back tomorrow.'

She frowns, her expression seeming genuine. 'That's too bad. You got a job lined up next year?'

I almost tell her I've got to wrap this murder investigation up first before realising she means a teaching position. 'Nothing yet.'

'Keep an eye on Catholic Ed's site. I heard whispers that a few staff here might hand in their resignation before we come back.'

I almost thank her, go to leave. This is my last chance, though. I haven't been able to talk to half the teachers, or those in the Senior School who had the eldest son. Maybe I'm meant to see Ashlee for a reason. Maybe I don't need everyone else.

'You love your secrets,' I say with a mischievous grin.

She matches my expression.

I gesture behind me. 'She and Joseph didn't…'

'Oh, they'd argue in staff meetings, get heated, but we think it was just an act. They'd spend a lot of time have "meetings" of their own afterwards.'

'She's not married?'

'Could you imagine?'

'But he was with a parent, too?'

'This is a high-income school. A lot of parents pour all their time into work and it creates a lot of relationship breakdowns. A lot of divorces, plenty of separations.'

'You don't know who it is?'

Ashlee shakes her head.

My thoughts turn to Heath Hallid's wife. They'd separated. Could she be the woman Joseph was seeing?

'You've been very fun to talk to,' I say.

She raises her mug in salute. 'Good to have fresh ears to Spill the T. Although… you won't go telling anyone this, will you?'

I shake my head. But I'm already planning my meeting with Joseph, framing the questions I need to ask him. Even if he wasn't the killer, he may have done something that led to another man's death.

CHAPTER NINE
YET TO CRACK

There are two additional cars in our driveway when I return home. One of them has the markings of WA Police on it. I pull up one house down, park on the kerb. Get out my phone and check for missed calls. Just the one from my mother. So, no delaying what's inside my house, then.

I approach, hear laughter coming from within. I enter, work my way through the house to the dining area. Lucy isn't home yet, and her parents are out, but Sarah and the kids are making our guests feel right at home.

'Did you need a police escort here, mate?' I call out.

Sergeant Gary Winters takes a sip from his coffee mug, turns and takes me in.

'You look like someone did you dirty, Henry. You need to file a report?'

'Kids ran me ragged.'

Gary pulls back from his chair, comes over and pulls me in for a hug. Gary's a hugger. 'I couldn't believe it when Sarah said you were teaching. After all the bloody help I gave you with your PI licence.'

'Did she explain *why* I was teaching?' I ask as I make my way to an empty chair.

Sarah hands me a coffee, takes a seat beside our other guest. All these coffees on demand, she can stay as long as she likes.

'She did,' Gary answers. 'I was very relieved.'

I offer my hand to our other guest. She leans over the table, shakes it. 'I guess my involvement in the case won't be a secret?'

Senior Constable Paige Kirino leans back into her chair, smiles. 'I'm just part of the training unit, I don't have to let the Perth crew know everything that's going on.'

Paige trained both Gary and myself at the Police Academy in Joondalup. She's part of their furniture, one of the brightest and most challenging instructors you can hope to have. I'm happy to see her, and Gary. I just don't know why they're here.

'What's going on?' I ask, because Gary was right. I'm drained, and I'd rather get to the point. A school day can feel breezy while you're there, but your body catches up when you reach home.

'Where are the kids now?' Paige checks.

'Still out the back,' Sarah answers. 'They're fine.'

They share a look, as if deciding who'll be the first to speak.

When neither of them does, Gary says, 'I'm coming back in a couple of days, to help with Lillian.'

He already helped me watch over the Yanchep house last week until I told him to enjoy his time off.

'No need,' I offer. 'I went inside the house.'

'How?'

'The door was open.'

'Sure.' He gives me the look that he's given hundreds of guilty people claiming their innocence. 'Please tell me you found something.'

I tell him about the message, the countdown.

'What do you think it means?'

'No idea,' I say. 'Her year of birth is nineteen ninety-three. Maybe it's a song from that year? One with more clues embedded in it.'

'A lot of songs to choose from.'

'She left me a playlist of tracks from the eighties, maybe she's made another one?'

We speculate on this for a bit, Sarah and Paige offering their guesses for the perfect song, until I realise I've strayed far from getting to the point.

'Stop,' I say to Gary. 'If you were coming to help in a couple of days, why are you here now? Why is Senior Constable Kirino here?'

Gary and Paige share the same look as Paige and Sarah did.

'Is it about the case I've taken?'

Paige shakes her head. 'We need you to tell us the truth about what happened at The Ridge.'

Ah. There we go. Two weeks and Leonie still hasn't admitted to poisoning the three grand-mums. Leaders of The Ridge, a place that was supposed to be an intentional community for all, which turned out to house a huge setup of servers recording everyone in town; the grand-mums earning their share in the profits from my family's blackmails. There are only four people who know that sweet Leonie Haynes, Lillian's permanent care mother, poisoned the three women. Poisoned because they'd known that my family had killed Tiffany, another soul cared for by Leonie, and helped cover it up, fuelled by greed. One person who knows the truth is Leonie herself. Another is Carmen Campbell, who has fled across Australia and is yet to be found. The third is Senior Constable Collins, hearing Leonie's confession while she bled in his arms. The fourth is me.

If they are here, then Leonie and The Bear are yet to crack.

'A sweet old woman was stabbed,' I say, 'by a corrupt officer in Gary's department. Who then attempted to stab me. How *is* Duke, by the way? Getting preferential treatment?'

Gary sips his coffee, trying to mask his reddened face. It's not his fault, he didn't know the reach my family had in the town, didn't know it extended into the law.

'This isn't the first time someone's asked this,' I say. 'Why come to my house to do it?'

'Leonie's health has stabilised,' Gary says, putting the mug down. 'She'll be processed. There will be a trial.'

'You will be called to trial,' Paige continues. 'And if the answer you're giving us now is the same as the one you give in court, you will face perjury. Which, best case, is ten years in prison.'

I try not to look stunned. Sarah hides nothing, though. 'Jesus, Henry! What do you know about The Ridge?'

I've told my wife everything that happened in Margaret River. Either she's omitted things to her sister, or Sarah's acting skills are improving.

'The police department allowed an illegal server farm to run for years, undetected,' I answer, 'resulting in its townsfolk being bribed. That's what happened at The Ridge.'

'Goddam, Henry,' Gary mutters, shaking his head.

Paige stabs at finger against the table. 'I agreed to come with Gary today as a display of good faith. We have faith in you, Henry. Gary's done nothing but support you.'

I reach out, pat Gary on the arm. 'I know. I shouldn't have said that.'

'We know she poisoned them,' Paige continues. 'It's just a matter of processing the evidence. Look, I know you're keeping quiet because of what the three murders tie to.'

She means the other deaths they have no murderer attached to. Two more poisoned townsfolk. The Campbell brothers, who also watched Tiffany die; their deaths and a shed full of servers the reason their younger sister, Carmen, was evading authorities.

Five poisoned townsfolk.

Plus the attempted murder of one of my uncles in prison, which Leonie coerced another prisoner to try.

Plus the death of my cousin, Trent. Shot, left to tumble off a cliff into the ocean.

Which would leave an eighty-three-year-old unable to see the walls outside a prison again.

'What is Leonie being arrested for now?' I ask. 'If she's being processed, but you can't prove her involvement in the poisonings…'

Gary can't meet my eyes. 'They've traced the bullet in Trent's body to the gun Leonie had at The Ridge.'

Ah. Leonie won't be leaving prison again, anyway.

I wasn't aware of this development. I expected it. Divers found Trent's body several days after it fell into the ocean. It was only a matter of time before they'd make the connection. At The Ridge, Leonie had been about to hand herself in to the police, pointing a gun at Duke and The Bear to justify an arrest. Not knowing Duke was there for the wrong reasons, that he would stab her to protect his secrets. So, at some point she'd wanted everyone to know she'd shot Trent. To make the sting sharper for his mother, Aunty Janice, the woman responsible for Tiffany's death—one woman's child taken for another's.

'I need to talk to her,' I say.

'She continues to refuse your request.'

'Then I have nothing to add.'

Paige stands. 'Then prepare your statement for a more official visit. Which won't be from either of us.'

She turns, thanks Sarah for the hospitality, leaves.

Gary looks at me, pulls at the collar around his neck. 'I'll see you in a couple of days. I promise I won't talk about this.'

He will, though. By then, I may have figured out what I should tell him.

I reach out, shake his hand. 'See you in two days.'

He pulls me in for an awkward hug. 'You called your mum yet?'

'You know I can't.'

'Call your mum. Before…'

He trails off, but I get it. Before she turns out like Leonie. Fuelled by loneliness and anger, becoming a different version of herself, doing something she can never take back. Something worse than holding onto secrets.

CHAPTER TEN
THREE STAGES OF GRIEF

As expected, I don't receive a call to come back to Isidore College. Allowing me to sleep in, after a quiet night at home. For dinner, Aqil had cooked us fish curry, Win had provided red bean ice cream. We'd avoided talking about my police visit, or my investigation. Instead, we'd planned ahead. Looked online, snapped up tickets to Singapore. Committing to the Christmas trip.

Now I'm parked down the street of a grieving widow's house. Ahead of me, two news vans wait along a stretch of grass. Desperate to film something happening inside.

I glance at my phone. I've used the Notes app to summarise my day, and it's only by reading what I've discovered that I realise how much I didn't do. I failed to speak to the teachers of Blake Hallid's other brothers. I didn't confirm the rumour about Joseph sleeping with both the principal and a parent; and I didn't get that parent's name. Nor did I get to the bottom of who wrote the notes in the pencil case or determine if the secret related to the relationships or something else.

I type in a note about cameras. During my recess duty, I'd tried to find any security cameras, possible vision of the classrooms or courtyard. There were none, though, spying on kids off-limits. Which was great for moral decency, but another roadblock for Joseph's case.

I slip my phone into my pocket, exit the car. Start walking towards the news vans. The second I step on the lawn, doors slide open.

'You know the Hallids?' a reporter calls out.

'Just doing my daily walk.' I gesture to the house. 'This where they live?'

A reporter nods.

'The teacher-killer family? I know a parent from that school. Not those poor people, though.'

The closest reporter gestures to someone within their van. Wanting someone to bring a microphone or camera or both.

'I heard a rumour,' I say, trying not to laugh as their eyes widen. 'Yeah, the principal was sleeping with the killer-teacher.'

'Can you go on record to confirm this?'

'I think you should ask the principal. Imagine that footage. Shoving a microphone in her face and accusing her of an affair as she tries to run away.' I nod to both reporters. 'I'd better keep going with my walk. Hurts to slow down. Have a good one.'

I walk across the lawn, maintain a steady pace alongside the neighbouring houses. Twenty seconds later, both vans tear past me, no doubt heading for the Freeway. When they're out of sight, I spin round, work my way back to the Hallid house.

I'm not proud of lying, but I'm quite proud of the way I tricked the reporters. It's the balance I need to find if I'm going to succeed as a Private Investigator. Besides, the principal can deal with the fallout of sleeping with one of her teachers, negative press finding its way to her without me being there.

I walk up the driveway to the Hallid house. Robyn Hallid lives far from her sons' school, in the northern suburb of Wembley Downs. I wonder if she moved here after her separation from Heath, the house one of convenience for that reason rather than her boys' education. Perhaps next year they'll attend the school around the corner?

I pause, kick at a weed sprouting from a crack in the bitumen driveway. Ask myself, is this really what I should be doing?

Yesterday, an exhausted Lucy relaxed on the couch after dinner, fell asleep against me. The kids were running around, screaming, and it didn't phase her one bit. This morning she left so early for work I didn't even see her. I'll have to sort something special out for the weekend, to celebrate her freedom—another school year in the books.

I did tell her about this visit, though, and she was as hesitant as I'm feeling right now.

'Just gauge her reaction and go with it,' she'd said.

The house is rather old. Most are redeveloped—double-storey, tin-roofed, rendered-wall houses that look identical. This one's made of seventies red brick, rocks layered at the foundation, good old black tiles on the roof. There's a small cement balcony, steps leading up to it. I climb the steps and reach the front door, rattle its screen with my knocking.

A young boy opens it. The youngest, for sure. Reilly.

I didn't expect the kids to be home, although I should have.

'Reilly!' a woman calls out. 'I told you, no opening the—' The woman appears behind the boy, freezes as she sees the door is already open. Her shoulders slump a little. She wants to tell me to fuck off, but she's lost the spirit to.

'My name is Henry,' I offer, trying to swing her reaction. 'I'm on a team helping to make sense of Heath's passing…' I glance at Reilly, who's swaying on the door handle '…and I just need to ask a few questions. Five minutes of your time.'

'Do you have ID?' Robyn asks. 'Like a badge or something?'

'I'm a Private Investigator. I don't get a badge.'

'Reilly, away from the door, sweetie.' She sweeps her son behind her, shielding him. Her features become more prominent. Around five and a half feet tall, blonde hair tied into a ponytail, a tracksuit on even though it's another almost-forty-degree scorcher. There's an orange tint to her pale skin, the remnants of a fake tan. 'Leave now, thank you.'

As she steps back, closing the door, I blurt, 'There's a theory the teacher didn't kill your husband.'

She freezes. 'Say again?'

'Don't you want the right man to go to jail?'

She considers this, then pushes the door further. 'Police can sort that out.'

I thrust my foot into the remaining gap. The door thuds against my shoe. Not going to lie, it's far more painful than the people in movies make it look. I do everything I can to withhold a scream. Howl a little.

'Shit,' Robyn says. 'Now look what you've done to yourself.' She opens the door in sympathy. 'You're a persistent fella, I'll give you that. You got some form of ID? Driver's licence?'

I bite back the pain. Get out my wallet, show her my driver's licence with a shaky hand. She grabs it, gets her phone out, takes a photo.

'Your name seems familiar,' she says, handing the licence back.

I shrug, don't ask her if she reads the paper since she's the new flavour. 'Can I come in now? Five minutes?'

She waves me in while glancing outside. Probably checking to see I'm alone. Or wondering where the news vans disappeared to. She directs me through an entryway and into a dining room. A large wooden table has a pile of paperwork scattered across it. Most appears to be schoolwork.

'Sorry it's a mess in here,' Robyn says.

'That's fine.'

'Boys won't be at school their last week, so I've got them working from home instead. Well, two of them.' Robyn stifles a tear, then points to the adjoining kitchen. 'Tea? Coffee?'

'Coffee would be great.'

I know she was referring to her missing eldest son. That's a matter for the police, though, not me. I can't get involved. I need to ask her about Joseph.

I sit at the dining table, push a small pile of mental maths sheets aside. 'Did you know Blake's teacher much?'

'I know all my children's teachers,' she calls out, filling a kettle. 'In so much as I attend parent info evening and a few other events.'

'You never went to parent-teacher meetings?'

'Last year, yes. This year, there's just been so much going on… For Blake, I figured I wasn't hearing anything so there was no point scheduling one.'

'But didn't Joseph try to schedule one with you? The one Heath went to?'

'I'm a flight attendant. I had to work the redeye from Hong Kong the day before. I'd been sleeping when I got the call about, well…'

'I'm sorry for your loss.'

Robyn brings over two mugs, hands one to me. She's used a pod machine, but the coffee smells decent. 'I was done with Heath in my life. Intimately, I mean. But I *did* used to love him, and he was an okay father to the boys. He was around, at least. When he had to be. We'll miss him.'

'The boys are taking it hard?'

'I get to see three stages of grief with those boys. Reilly's too young to know what's going on, so he's in denial, thinking dad will come by this weekend. I think Blake's feeling guilty, since it was his classroom, his teacher. And my eldest, he's an angry teenager.' She sips her coffee for a while, wipes some foam from her upper lip. 'He ran off.'

'Do the police know?' I ask, even though I'm aware they do.

'They'll look for him, but he just needs some space. Time to process what's happening. He'll come back when he's ready. Another day or so.'

Robyn's saying this with as much strength as she can muster, but I'm sure she's filled with panic. Unless this is a common occurrence.

'Did Heath have any enemies?' I ask, trying to focus the conversation on the deceased.

'Enemies? He was an accountant, not a superhero. Unless he miscalculated something for someone and pissed them off.'

I'm surprised to hear that Heath was an accountant. My mind had pictured some huge, testosterone-fuelled tradie. All man, ready to pummel anyone who speaks ill about his kin. I've got to sit down and do my research, look up everyone's background. Earn my pay, whatever that turns out to be.

Robyn puts down her mug. 'Wait, you think Heath pissed someone off and they attacked him at the school?'

'The teacher is adamant he went downstairs to make coffees for himself and Heath. A break in their meeting. When he came out, Heath had fallen.'

'Heath did love his coffee. That's his pod machine I took with me.'

If Heath loved his coffee, he would have kept a better machine to himself. Not that it matters now. 'It might not be your cliché enemy,' I try. 'Did Heath get on with the other parents?'

'He barely saw the other parents. Except at swimming. He could be passionate about his boys' sport. I'd see him yelling a bit too much during swim meets. Bailey wasn't the best swimmer, that was Jeremy, but you'd never think it. You'd have to ask Bailey's coach about how Heath affected the other parents, though.'

Another thing I *didn't* do.

I drink some of the coffee, think about what else I need to ask Robyn. There's no tactful way to frame my crucial question, so I just blurt, 'Was he having a relationship with someone else?'

She cracks a dry laugh. 'We didn't separate cause he cheated on me. And I haven't pried into his life after our separation.'

'Are *you* seeing someone else?'

'You're not my type, honey.' She registers the shock on my face, adds, 'Just joking. I've had three dates, three different men, all fizzles. I have no idea what I'm looking for. I've kept busy with work instead. Now my boys are the most important focus.'

I nod, pretending I understand. At the very least, it probably means she was not the parent Joseph was seeing. *If* she's telling the truth, of course.

'I don't envy your job here,' Robyn says. 'You're trying to say someone other than the teacher killed my husband, but there isn't anyone else who wanted him dead.'

'I don't envy your position as a parent,' I say, then point to the paperwork on the table. 'You're doing a great job keeping them on track.'

'Some days are easier than others, and the joy often outweighs the heartbreak.' Robyn holds out a hand. 'You got a business card or something?'

'I haven't had any printed yet.'

'But… In case Bailey…'

In case Bailey doesn't come back when he's ready. I grab a pen from the table, write my name and mobile number on one of the mental maths pages. 'Here you go. Do you have a photo of your son?'

Robyn brings up a photograph of Bailey on her phone, lets me look at it. I pray she doesn't call. I can't try to defend Joseph *and* look for a missing boy. Especially when I haven't seen my own sister.

I've intruded long enough. I was going to find a way to interview the younger boys, but I'd have to speak to them in front of their mother, every answer coerced. At least now, I know a bit more about Robyn and Heath and their relationship. Enough to have a think about where this case is going.

Enough to know I need to go back to the source.

I extend my thanks to Robyn and show myself out. Little Reilly isn't hanging by the door this time.

I hop into my car, pull out my phone, call Jensen Healy. She answers on the third ring.

I cut the formalities short. 'I need to meet with Joseph again or I'm done.'

'Why?'

'He's lied to us. He was keeping secrets. I need to know them.'

CHAPTER ELEVEN
WE'RE CONSENTING ADULTS

Joseph looks even more deflated this time round. Like he's spent *years* in prison, not days in remand. There appears to be a fresh bruise under his other eye. I don't ask about it. Jensen starts the conversation, provides an update. He sinks to the table as he realises there's still no solid evidence he didn't kill Heath Hallid.

'What about Kristen?' Joseph asks.

'Who?' Jensen and I chorus.

'Year Four teacher, was in her room when it happened. She came out, saw the body, screamed.'

Jensen looks at me. I shake my head. Another person I didn't speak to, though I don't remember seeing her.

'I can arrange an interview,' Jensen says.

'My time at the school is a dead-end,' I offer. 'The principal doesn't want me there, since my own family's associated with murder.'

Joseph sighs. 'Tali is under so much pressure to maintain the school's image. Nobody gives a shit about public schools, but these private ones… I'm sure Isidore College will be in the paper every day. Someone on the editorial staff already has a grudge with it.'

'It won't help your case,' Jensen says, 'especially if the reporting's heavily opinionated.' She looks at me. 'We have to work fast.'

I nod. 'That's why we're here.'

I couldn't bring the *I know your secret* notes in, nor my phone to show photos of them. So I can only describe what I found, recite the lines I can remember. It doesn't seem possible, but Joseph slumps even further against the table, his face pallid. Defeated.

'I can't tell you about that,' he mutters.

'Every aspect of your life's going to come out in court, Joseph,' Jensen insists. 'There's another team prying into it right now. If you thought the newspaper was bad, the police and their prosecutors will accuse you of much worse.'

He sits upright, looks at Jensen then me, assessing whether we're telling him the truth. He tries to hold out as long as he can, then says, 'Fine. Tali and I… met up. We're both single. It happens.'

'She's your boss.'

'We're consenting adults. She doesn't give me any favours. You've heard how I speak up for the staff.'

I wonder if the disagreements draw them together, can't help but chuckle. Then I think about the way Talitha spoke to me yesterday. 'She sees you as a potential murderer.' I glance at Jensen. 'Trouble in paradise.'

'That's not true. She'd support me.'

'Has she visited you? Called?'

Joseph shakes his head.

'So that's your secret?' Jensen asks before I can. 'Nothing else?'

He keeps shaking his head.

I fold my arms, lean back against the hard chair. 'And what about the parent?'

He looks confused.

'The one you're having an affair with.'

'I'm not…'

I unfold my arms, make like I'm about to stand. 'I'm done, then.'

Joseph holds out a hand. 'Wait!'

I settle back against my chair.

'She's a Year Six mother,' Joseph explains. 'I taught her son last year. She was going through a messy divorce. I saw her a lot, her son wasn't taking the divorce well. When I stopped teaching him, she asked me for coffee. Then drinks. Then it took off.'

'Does Talitha know?'

'Nobody does. And it doesn't matter. Tali and I don't have some kind of traditional, exclusive relationship. '

'Is this the secret that someone knows?'

'No idea.'

'Who's been sending you the notes, then?'

'I don't know that either. Whenever I'd open the class door in the morning, a note would be there on the ground.'

'Slipped through the gap?'

'I assume so.'

'Not from the cleaners?'

Joseph shrugs.

'Someone gave you a deadline to come clean, but you don't know who, and you don't know what you have to come clean about?'

'Yes!' Joseph rocks on his chair, letting out an exasperated sigh.

'You don't recognise the handwriting?'

'No!'

After seeing and marking their students' work for a full year, teachers are pretty good at knowing who wrote what without seeing a name. So, it's not one of his students; unless this is one part of his job Joseph is still lazy at.

I look to Jensen. I don't know what else to ask.

'Would the parent's ex-husband know about your relationship?' she says.

The anger drains from Joseph's voice. 'Julian? Maybe. She could have told him. He's still involved with the kids.'

'What's her name?'

'Maria Bortoni. She's kept his last name, for now. Has a son in Year Six, Hammond, and fraternal twins in Year Nine. One's Jeremy, the other's Chloe. She goes to the sister school.'

'They both had sons in Year Nine,' I mutter.

'What?' Jensen asks.

'Heath Hallid's son is also in Year Nine,' I say. 'Let's find out if the two kids know each other. Maybe Jeremy found out about the affair and let the Hallids know?' I resist a smile, excitement coursing through me at the thought of making progress. 'The teachers were already circulating rumours, that's how I knew. It wouldn't surprise me if the kids had their own rumours.'

'I don't get it,' Joseph says. 'She's a single mother. She can see who she likes. It's not the kind of secret I should be scared about hiding.'

You didn't want to tell the principal, I think.

'Besides,' Joseph continues, 'how does that get Heath Hallid killed?' He leans forward, anger returning. 'Pry into that man's life instead of mine. Someone came and killed him, there has to be a reason why.'

We process this for a moment, puzzle pieces yet to fit together.

'I'll get as much info as I can on the Bortoni family,' Jensen says before I can ask.

'Thank you,' I offer.

'Next steps?' Joseph asks.

'Right. Well, I'll meet you again tomorrow,' Jensen says to him. 'We'll start going through responses you may need to make if this goes to court.' She glances at me. 'Which it's likely to do.'

That glance said it all. Time is running out. She doesn't think I'll find anything to save Joseph before he goes to trial. For some reason, that doesn't bother me. This is my first case since getting my PI licence, the first mystery that doesn't involve my family. I can only do so much, get so far. If she's not happy with that, she should have hired someone top of the line. Which reminds me…

'I've uncovered a fair bit in two days, and we're yet to discuss payment. If you want me to keep going…' I leave it there. Jensen understands.

We bid farewell, Joseph left unsure whether he has my continued help. Maybe that will make him more desperate, more willing to add further details to his stories. Because as much as we think we're alone in this world, people are always watching. Someone had to have suspected his affair with Maria Bortoni. Someone had to have seen him with the principal. That's how the rumours started. That's what may have led to the notes in his classroom. Surely he suspected someone? Anyone? Hiding their name wasn't helping his own case. If he had time to think about it—as if he had anything else to do in his cell—then maybe he'd be able to come up with something to move the case forward.

My phone rings late that afternoon. Lucy had messaged to say she was on her way home, so I expect to be talking to her, but it's Jensen. Confirming her firm has deposited a decent sum of money into my account. More than I made during my short stint in retail electronics. Before I can ask why she's given me so much, or who's funding such a commitment, she tells me about the progress she's made, her voice laced with panic.

'The boys from the Hallid and Bortoni family knew each other,' she explains. 'And Maria Bortoni has also been in contact with the police. Jeremy left for school this morning but he never turned up to class. So, we have a boy missing from each family.'

I think about my meeting with Robyn. How long till she looks at my number on her son's worksheet, calls me for help? 'You want me to find out where they are?'

'Maybe. Police are on that, though. For now, let's focus on *why* they disappeared.'

I thank her for the money, for the lead. Hours ago, the case seemed stalled, Joseph the gatekeeper of the truth to make it move forward. Now it has a new life, a different direction.

CHAPTER TWELVE
NOT GOOD FOR BUSINESS

'Why are you excited two kids are missing?' Lucy looks like she wants to slap me, as if I'd just tipped her scale from a tiring to shitty day.

I try to put on my serious face. 'Maybe there's more to this case than everyone thought?'

'You think the same person who killed the father has taken two kids?'

'That's one angle.' I close our bedroom door, hoping Sarah's kids haven't been listening in. 'Or they know something and are hiding together.'

'Wouldn't they go to the police if they knew something?'

'When do teenagers go to the police?'

Lucy thinks about this for a while. She drops to the bed, pats a spot beside her. 'Maybe one friend is consoling the other? His father just died. They want to be alone, away from the police and reporters.'

'That's another angle.'

'So, three angles?' We lock eyes until Lucy cracks the smallest of smiles. 'Are we overthinking this?'

I sit down, our old bedframe creaking. 'Probably.'

Lucy wriggles a little, pulls her phone out of her pocket. 'I want you to see something.' She opens a social media app, searches for *Killer teacher*. 'They may have wanted to escape from this.'

She hands the phone over. The posts about Joseph, Isidore College, Heath and his family have multiplied exponentially. Parents and their children spreading rumours, assumptions about the case, assumptions about Heath and what could have led to his death. Internet detectives, throwing every wild theory into cyberspace. Apparently, the school paid Joseph to kill Heath, the teachers wanting to send a message to all annoying parents. Apparently, the students were going to kill the teachers on the last day of school, in retaliation. Also, Joseph had threatened to kill all of his students before, and parents who'd held meetings with him were sharing their relief having survived their encounter. Other parents surmised Heath was abusing his kids and Joseph had had enough. Others said Heath was having an affair with Joseph and they'd had a lover's quarrel. Theory after theory, threads of groundless accusations. The public swayed on their own platform before Joseph's trial even began.

Joseph was already guilty. That it was all fake news didn't matter.

'Fuck,' I mumble, handing Lucy's phone back.

'It's not great,' Lucy says. 'And you and Jensen can't control it.'

'Are the teachers at your school saying the same things?'

Lucy nods. 'They've made a Top Ten list of parents they'd throw over a balcony.'

'Of course.' I take a deep breath, exhale. 'We've all thought about it, though, right? Helicopter parents who think they can push you around, who want you to respond to their queries no matter the time of day. Parents who've spent zero time helping their kids learn anything, from reading to using the toilet, expecting the teachers do it for them. The shitheads who abuse their kids, who teachers have to submit to mandatory reporting. Fuck, do you think Joseph reported Heath for that?' I stop, realise I'm shaking, add, 'Jensen's team can find out.'

'Or maybe you use the connections you've made and get some help?' Lucy squeezes my hand, trying to smile, the desire to slap me gone. 'I've got two days of school left, then a PD day, then I can finally help you. But it might be too late by then.'

She's right, of course. Lucy's always right.

'I'm sorry,' I say.

'For what?'

'I just listed everything you still have to put up with. I ran away from it, and you… You're so much stronger than me.'

Lucy squeezes my hand again, leans in and gives me a kiss. 'Aw, honey, I know.'

I pull her closer, ready to tickle her all over; frustrations talked away, light teasing ready to lead to some much-needed intimacy.

Then my phone rings.

It's Jensen.

'Fuuuuck,' I whisper.

Lucy lifts herself off the bed. 'It's okay. I need a shower anyway.' She winks at me; lets me know what I'm about to miss out on.

I groan, answer the call, put it on speaker. 'Hi, Jensen.'

'I've got some details for the Bortoni family. I've emailed them to you.'

'Are you meeting with them now?'

'I've got a friend in the media who says they've caught wind of both disappearances. Everyone's camping out front of Maria's house while she gets an appeal ready. She said she'd speak for both families.'

There's no way Jensen or I can get some one-on-one time with Maria, for now. 'What about the dad, then?'

'That's why I called. Everyone's focused on the mothers right now. Julian's all alone in his South Perth apartment. Think you could go have a word?'

'Sure. First thing in the morning.'

'No, like *right now*. Before the press think he's interesting.'

Before they realise his ex-wife was in a relationship with an accused murderer, and he might have objected to said union.

I glance at Lucy, who just shrugs. Just like teaching, this new venture isn't a nine-to-five job.

'Okay,' I say, 'I'll go visit him.'

I end the call and turn to Lucy. She blows me a kiss. 'Guess I'll have to shower alone.' She sees my dejected face, chuckles. 'I'll save you some dinner.'

It usually takes around half an hour to get to South Perth from my house. But during peak hour, there's an endless queue of cars lined up to get on Narrows Bridge, one of the few ways to cross the Swan River, so it's a bit over an hour before I reach Julian Bortoni's building.

It's a tan-coloured apartment complex named for the road it's on. A gap between low, purplish-rendered walls leads me to visitor parking. As I leave my car, I hear signs of life from the zoo across the road. I haven't been to Perth Zoo since I was a child. Before my father died. The sun is starting to set so the animals are becoming more active, thankful that enormous crowds are no longer gawking at their every move.

Smoke lingers in the air. It's just from a cigarette, though, not a bushfire. Two men are standing at the boot of a car in a nearby laneway, both puffing away. Their car, an orangey-gold Ford, is right next to a sign saying *No Parking*. One of them is skinny, the other built like a rugby player. The rugby player's face is familiar, but I can't peg him.

I note but ignore them, ascend a set of steps, reach the entrance to the tan-coloured building. I find the button for Julian's apartment, a number with his name on it. I press it. Without even asking who I am, he buzzes me through. Probably just wants to get whatever interview is coming over with; or he's ready to chase me away as a message to every other reporter and officer around. I feel the cool of the lobby's marble flooring through my shoes, take everything in as I wait for the lift. There's a staircase nearby but I'm trying to walk the shortest distance possible, letting my legs heal after the ordeal in Margaret River. Running, running, endless running—if this case has me chase someone, I might quit.

The lift dings. I step inside. There are six floors and a lower-ground level, plus another button that doesn't have a label on it. I hit the sixth-floor button. When it stops, it opens to a carpeted corridor. In no time, I'm knocking on Julian's door, its number matching the one on the buzzer. A dishevelled man answers, yawning as if he's just woken up. He's older than I expected, perhaps in his late fifties. Leather-tanned skin suggests he spends a lot of time in the sun. He's a few inches shorter than me, thin except for a pot belly pressed against a stained white shirt and pyjama shorts. Balding patches of sandy hair point to the side, yet to be combed. He's definitely been sleeping. I guess without kids to look after, he's on his own time. But with a son missing, you'd think he'd be out there doing everything he could to help.

'Who are you?' he grunts.

I introduce myself, say I'm a Private Investigator, leave out the part about representing Joseph.

'This about Jeremy?'

'His mother is helping the police,' I say. 'We thought you might give me a little insight, too.'

He waves me inside. I try to push down the pang of guilt for misrepresenting myself, but Jensen needs answers fast. This is the quickest way to gain Julian's trust, learn about his son and the Hallid family. I take in the apartment's interior. Walls lined with patterned wallpaper, expensive leather furniture spaced far apart, a long stretch of windows looking out at the Swan River. I have a feeling this place costs twice as much as my house and it's less than half the size. Envy shifts to sadness as I realise this is one of those houses set up like a showroom—absent of any family life. No photographs of his kids, his ex-wife or a new partner. No books scattered around, or packets of snack food left out. Nothing out of place, a complete contradiction to the owner in his current state.

I imagine his kids coming to visit, told off for touching things, cleaning up after their every move, existing but not really living. No wonder his son had avoided this place and run somewhere else instead.

'I represent the Hallid family in particular,' I say as Julian leads me to a white leather sofa, pointing to an empty space. 'Robyn is concerned for her son. Now that Jeremy has disappeared, that concern has doubled.'

Julian finds a robe on the couch, slides it on before sitting in its place. 'This is the third time Jeremy's gone "missing" this year. Only, he just tells a mate's mum he has permission to sleep over and crashes at their house. One or two days later, he's back with Maria or myself.'

'You're not worried?'

'I share Robyn's sentiment. Both boys missing just after Heath's death...' He wipes away an invisible tear. 'I'd like to think Jeremy's just helping his grieving mate. They'll be back for the funeral.'

'Were you there the day Heath died? At the swim meet?'

'Fuck yeah, I was cheering Jeremy on. My son cracked the college freestyle record!'

'That's great.'

'You bet it is. That kid's fast on land and water; he's gonna make me a fortune!'

'What about Bailey Hallid?'

'Bailey? He's strong, but... He was on a couple of heats later, but he placed outside the top three. Unusual swim for him; maybe he sensed something was wrong?'

'When did you know something was wrong?'

'When we heard the sirens from the pool. To be honest, I thought a kid had hurt himself. Never thought poor Bailey would get the news he did.'

'And his mother, of course.'

'Robyn? Hah! She probably started dancing the Higgy Jiggy when she found out.'

'The Higgy Jiggy?'

'That dance everyone does. No, the Hokey Pokey. You know what I mean. She was waiting for him to sign divorce papers, now it's official. She'll be celebrating.'

'Her kids just lost their father,' I say, trying to sound grim.

Julian coughs, runs a hand through his hair. 'Yeah. I know. That's callous, I apologise. I guess my views on marriage aren't exactly positive after the year I've had. You married?'

'I am.'

'Communicate. Make time for each other. Two things I stopped doing. Got caught up in my business. Told myself it was to pay bills, to look after my family and get them what they wanted. Turns out, I just needed to be *with* my family.'

I nod. 'Thanks for the advice. Do your kids get to stay here often?'

Julian gestures at the surrounding room. 'Not exactly a family place. It's a novelty for the kids when I have them, but we have no appointed dates or anything. Maria is great for them, I'm not opposing that. Having the zoo across the road is a huge drawcard for me, although they're getting a little old for it now.'

'Do you think Jeremy and Bailey will come here?'

'I wouldn't be surprised. When he's having problems, he appears.'

'But he hasn't appeared yet?'

'No. Haven't heard from him.'

'Do you mind if I ask what you do for work?'

Julian stands, make his way to the nearby kitchen. 'You want a drink?'

'I'm good,' I say as he pulls a beer from the fridge.

'Might spruce myself up later, head down to the pub. There's one a hundred and fifty metres away. Perfect for a stumble home.'

'Your work?' I ask again as he sits back down.

'Broker,' he answers.

'Stocks?'

'Wealth management services.'

'Did you work with Heath, then? He was an accountant, wasn't he?'

'We'd send some work each other's way. Didn't see him too often unless one of us was picking up our kids. Tried to get him into my fantasy basketball group. He couldn't keep up. Got real angry when he was losing.'

I think of Andy and Russell, the schoolteacher friends of Sarah's husband, Desmond. Andy had rigged a junior basketball league, taking bets on the outcome of games to fuel his gambling addiction. Andy might even be in Hakea with Joseph, now.

'You bet on the basketball, too? Like, the actual games?'

'I try to avoid most gambling. Not good for business.'

Somehow, I don't believe him. 'You said Heath got angry?' I ask instead, trying to focus, picturing Joseph's bruised eye.

'Oh yeah. Heath might have been this mild-mannered accountant to some but when he got pissed off the whole world knew. He didn't like losing, so the fantasy basketball set him off. He ranted about all these players getting injured and throwing his stat lines. Wanted his money back. It wasn't like it was a fortune, we'd only chipped in a hundred bucks each.' Julian shakes his head at the memory. 'We gave him his money back, closed his account, said we'd decided not to host fantasy basketball given all the injuries.'

'You sided with him, got on his good side?'

'On the surface. We kept the league going, just… without him.'

So much for Heath having no enemies. How many times had his anger ostracised him?

Julian leans closer. 'I tell you what, I can tell why that teacher did him in.'

'He was that bad?' I ask, trying to appear shocked.

'The teacher probably told him his kid was a dumbass and he took it as a personal attack. The older kid's smart, but they left the younger two to fend for themselves.'

Julian's introspect into what happened is spot-on. Did he know Heath that well, or was he lurking near the meeting? He'd already said he only saw Heath when they did the kid pickup thing. Was that enough to know how he'd react to someone criticising his son?

'Bailey will be alright, then?' I say, keeping to the guise of representing the Hallid family.

'Like I said, boy's smart enough. With my Jeremy, they'll be right.'

'Do they have their own bank accounts? Access to easy money?'

'Bailey's kept on a leash that way. Kid doesn't work, mum gives him money. Jeremy has his own account, though.'

'Could Bailey have squirrelled enough cash away, for—'

'Some kind of trip? Look, maybe delve into that if the boys aren't back before the funeral. But like I said, they *will* be back. They might even stay here. If that's what you have to tell Robyn, go for it. You've earned your money. I'm not panicking.' Julian rises from the couch again. 'Leave Bailey alone for now. Kid's been through enough shit without his dad dying on him.'

I rise with Julian, taking away the dominant staredown he was trying to achieve. 'What do you mean, enough shit?'

'Being gay in a Catholic school isn't met with as much tolerance as you'd think, even in this day and age.'

'Bailey was gay?' My heart flutters a little. I know sexual orientation shouldn't have anything to do with a murder, but there are people who've fixed their ideals to the past, triggered by anything that differs. Maybe the system has changed, but I'd imagine the Catholic Church is still hanging onto its rigid stance against homosexuality. Maybe someone working there made it tough for Bailey and had it out with his father? Maybe his father had had it out with a teacher? In our time together, Joseph never mentioned his views regarding sexual orientation. It couldn't be such a simple connection, could it?

'I guess Robyn didn't tell you,' Julian continues. 'Jeremy's supported him but I know the boy lost a few mates when he came out.'

'Jeremy's not—'

'Nah. Not that it would matter. But I've already caught him bringing home a few girls. Worried I'm going to be a grandpa long before my time.'

'Did it matter to Bailey's father?'

'Nah. Bailey came out to Jeremy first, who helped him talk to his parents. Bailey was worried they'd flip, disown him. Can you believe that? We have an incredibly diverse society here in Perth compared to when I was a kid and he's still worried they won't be inclusive. Because there are parents who still disown their child, as if something is wrong with them. As if they aren't the same kid they were in the first place. As if their love for them will have to be different.'

Julian's whole body is shuddering. He wipes sweat from his brow, trying to calm himself. Maybe he came out to his parents when he was Bailey's age and they didn't have the same welcoming approach. Maybe he'd forced himself into a heterosexual relationship, burying who he was. It's not the time to pry, though. I've got so much out of this man already and it's obvious I've pushed him a little too far.

'Thank you so much for your time.' I turn to the door.

'Sorry to get all worked up,' he says.

'No, it's fine. I get it.' I force a smile. 'And I'll let Robyn know her son should be home soon.'

'I'll be at the funeral,' he adds, walking with me to the entrance. 'I wish I got to know Heath better, you know. Maybe I could have helped with his anger issues.'

'Was that the reason for his separation?'

'I never pried. Robyn once said he'd changed, though. Maybe his truer self was just coming out. I guess you never really know someone, you know?'

I nod. Do I really know Joseph Pooles? Was the time during my prac enough to get to know the real man? Or had I witnessed a different persona?

I thank Julian again, head down in the lift. There's no longer the orangey-gold car blocking the adjacent laneway, the two smokers gone. I reach my own car and pause. Are my doubts about Joseph increasing? I'm trying to prove the man's innocence, not his guilt.

I shake off the thought, get in my car. Head back north but veer off at Leederville, go past Lake Monger down a long, long road that leads to the ocean. I should call Lucy, tell her I'm taking a slight detour. All I can think of, though, is that I need to get to know Joseph as soon as possible.

At the end of my prac, I'd taken a taxi to Joseph's house. We'd shared a congratulatory beer, then met the rest of the staff in the city for end of term drinks. A night that ended in a high ratio of hangovers. I would have thought that Joseph had moved closer to his new school since, but I'd checked the details Jensen first gave me and recognised the address. An old property in Karrinyup, right behind the shops.

I'm there in no time, most cars keeping to the Freeway.

I don't expect the police to be waiting outside. They would have gone through the house by now if they'd needed to. I've got my lock pick set in the car this time, so I can try use it to get inside. If it doesn't have an alarm, or a nosy neighbour. It's not breaking and entering if I'm getting into the house of the man I'm helping, is it? He would have given me a key if he could; if I'd told him I was going to rifle through his belongings.

I'm about to pull into the driveway when my foot hesitates, taps the brake.

It's his house. I recognise it.

There's a light on inside.

CHAPTER THIRTEEN
FUCK THE SILENT APPROACH

I park my car a couple of houses down, walk back to Joseph's yard. The shadow of Karrinyup Shopping Centre lingers in the distance; the old building wrapped in scaffolding, cranes everywhere. They're expanding, competing with the other ever-growing suburban centres to draw the most consumers. This is why the city's dying—no need to shop there when the same outlets are closer to home.

I shake the thought, focus on the house. It's as old as the shopping centre, red brick walls from the seventies. There's no car in the driveway. The light inside is from the front room, a lounge room. I don't see any telltale shadows within, no intruders walking by. I creep to the front door, try the handle. Locked. I look around. Surely a neighbour has spotted the light on, realised Joseph wasn't home and called the police? Although, would people care what happens to their murderous neighbour's house?

Fuck it. No need for the lock picks, yet. I knock on the door. Wait for a reaction.

The house has laminated timber floorboards. I can hear the *thump, thump, thump* of footsteps hurrying across their surface. Are they headed for the back door?

I bolt round the back. The left side of the house doesn't have a fence, just clumps of bushes I have to wriggle my way through. I half-expect the crashing sound of leaves ahead, the intruder coming my way, but I soon burst out of the greenery alone. Onto a concrete jungle. I work my way between bags of sand and rusted garden implements and round the building. There's a sensor light high on the wall, sending shadows to a backyard that's a mix of lawn and rocks. Nobody there, either. I find the rear door, a sliding door. It's not smashed but someone's pried its lock open. The glass panel is open a few centimetres. I slide it further and it squeaks. I cringe, wait for someone to appear. Nobody. So, they're either somewhere in the house or they've left via the front or other side.

I edge my way inside. The only thumping is from my own heartbeat, now.

I'm standing in some kind of entertaining area I didn't see last time. Enough light filters into the room to highlight a brick-built bar, leather couch and round table filling most of the tiny space. There's a lingering aroma in the air, the stale tang of cigarette smoke. Joseph never smoked when he mentored me. At least, that I knew of. No time to worry about that, though. I peer round the bar. Nobody hiding there, just dusty bottles of liquor and a humming fridge. There's an archway leading to a passageway. Beyond that, an adjacent archway that leads to the front lounge room. The passageway branches to the left and right. I go left first.

If anyone's hiding, I feel they're in a bedroom, a perceived place of safety. Under a bed or in a cupboard or behind a door.

Who the hell would be hiding, though, invading Joseph's house?

Nobody's in the first room. It's got a tiny single bed, a drawer and not much else. A guest room, perhaps? There's a doorway at the end of the passageway. I'm sure it leads to the main bedroom. Should I go there, or…

As I glance back, considering my options, a shadow moves across the archway opening.

I run. Fuck the silent approach. I reach the archway, turn left into the lounge room. A single bulb reveals everything in the room. I scan the area, searching, searching. A few items seem a little messed up—books tipped over on a low bookshelf, a TV remote on the floor, a Lego set scattered across the floorboards, a stack of what looks like student projects scattered across another leather couch. No human presence, though. Nobody hiding behind anything. Which seems impossible, unless they've snuck out the front door.

Unless I misread the shadow's direction.

I turn, look back through the archway. The intruder—definitely an intruder, with the back door pried open—has either gone down the opposite end of the passageway, or back into the entertaining area.

I edge under the archway, turn left. Down this side, there are two doors. One is closed. The other is open, a tiled floor and cupboard visible in the gap. A laundry, perhaps? With another door leading outside?

There's another thump; a squeak. Coming from the entertaining area. The sliding door—someone's sneaking out.

'Stop!' I yell, hoping the outburst will freeze them.

I run down the passageway, cross under the archway. There's nobody at the door. Where have they—

Something slams against me, topples my body sideways. I smack against the bar's brick wall, pain rippling down my left side. I groan, try to push back. As the weight lifts off me, I reach out, grab air. Then there's another *thump thump thump* and a thin shadow enters the room, bounds over me, heads for the door. Another figure is already sliding it open. I try to stand, drop back to the floor. Reach out to grip the bar's counter, pull myself up.

'Stop,' I try again, little energy to my voice.

It's too late. The intruders are already gone.

CHAPTER FOURTEEN
MY BRAIN WILL TELL ME WHY LATER

Alone in the house; too sore to run after the intruders, too curious to leave. How much longer until police arrive, neighbours reporting the disturbance? I shuffle back into the passageway. My left arm and side already hurts. Bruised muscles, bruised ribs. I don't know if the intruder meant to hurt me more or less; I just fell off-balanced and that was enough.

I check the laundry and toilet. Empty, no sign either room's used or ransacked. I head down the other side of the passageway. Pass the room with the single bed, stop at the end. It's a larger bedroom. Double- or queen-sized bed. Old quilt cover. Five pillows stacked atop. A rolled-up rug at the end of the mattress. A couple of paintings hanging on the wall. There's a set of drawers half-opened, cupboard doors swung out, some clothes strewn on the bedspread. Is this the work of the police or the intruders? Was there something special hidden in Joseph's room, or is it because it's one of the few rooms with signs of life?

I try to think back to my time with Joseph. He never let on that anyone was sharing the house with him. There's just not enough I know about the man. Jensen should be able to help me, rather than another prison visit. I have to confirm his family members, whether they're here in Perth. I need to confirm past relationships. Otherwise, who am I seeking the innocence of?

I return to the front lounge room. The intruders turned off the light. I find the switch but leave it. Better to make it seem like nobody's home. I could grab a few things from the room. Books? The Lego? Memory has me picture the stack of student projects on the couch. They seem important, I should grab them. My brain will tell me why later.

I use the streetlight outside to guide me through the room, find the leather couch, grab the stack of paper. Then I head for the rear sliding door, step outside. Wait for a moment, wincing, waiting for the intruders to jump me from the shadows. When they don't, I close the sliding door. Wipe the handle with my shirt. Wonder what else I should have wiped down, to hide my own intrusion. I work my way through the side jungle, head back to my car. No neighbours call out to ask what I'm doing. Nobody sits in their own car, watching. Police presence is non-existent.

Thirty minutes later, I'm home. Lucy's already in bed, asleep, rest vital for the home stretch of the schooling year. Win and Aqil are watching television at a low volume, a show about a chef travelling through France. Sarah's in the bedroom we gave her, reading to the kids, trying to get them to be as sleepy as my wife. I hope Lucy isn't as drained in a few days, when she can help me. I need her intelligence, the way she approaches things at a unique angle. And I need her to bounce my ideas off, to be honest and tell me which ones are worth pursuing and which ones are wasting my time.

She'd like the idea driving me now, I know it. My brain caught up on the car ride home, remembered the trigger that had me collect the student samples. I sit at my study desk, spread the work out. Read through a portion. Most of them are for a Humanities assignment. The impact of bushfires on the community and ways people can prepare for them. Pessimistic but necessary learning in Australia. Rather than submitting a cut-and-paste printout from Wikipedia, Joseph has had his students handwrite the majority of their work, offset by printed images. Which gives me a lot to work with.

On one edge of my writing desk, I have the notes from the pencil case. I take the first project, compare the handwriting to the style in the notes. Place it on the ground, making a *No* pile. Repeat the process with the next project. Work my way through six more samples before I have one for a *Maybe* pile, which I keep on the desk.

An hour passes. Maybe two. I lose track of time, Sarah and her parents bidding me goodnight at different points throughout my task.

In the early hours of the morning, I have five projects in the *Maybe* pile. Five out of twenty-seven is not bad. But the five are very similar, I'm not sure which one matches the notes. If I'm being honest, none of them are an exact match. Or maybe they all are—my tired eyes are blurring everything together.

A thump draws my attention, makes my heart rate spike. It's not an intruder, though. Sarah is back out of her room, grabbing some water from the fridge.

'You still going?' she whispers.

'Lost track of time.'

She downs her glass of water, approaches. 'Didn't know relief teachers had to take work home to mark.'

'Ha ha.'

'Thought all the marking was done, anyway. Lucy's reports are all in, now.'

She's right. I didn't even consider that. These are projects Joseph should have marked to finalise grades. Is this another example of his old laziness shining through? Is there such a thing as old laziness, or has he just gotten better at covering his incompetence?

I show Sarah a couple of the notes from the pencil case. 'What do you think? Any samples on the desk match these notes?'

She scoffs. 'Which student writes this weird cursive these days?'

'Maybe Joseph tried to teach them and gave up halfway? Explains the cursive-print blend.'

'My kids just do oversized printing so far.' She hands the notes back. 'No, I don't think any are the same.'

'Closest one?'

She points to a sample on the desk. 'That one, I guess. Ninety per cent similar.'

'Thanks.'

'Why are you smiling?'

'Just…' I pick up the sample, hold a note against it '…I guess most of this work is confirming hunches.'

The sample is from Blake Hallid.

If the samples match, then Heath's son was blackmailing his own teacher.

Did Heath end up killed because of it?

CHAPTER FIFTEEN
WE NEED THE STAFF

Lucy shakes me awake the next morning. It's early and I've barely slept. Everything feels like it's still part of a dream.

'Social media has taken a weird turn,' she says. 'Look at this.'

Everything on her mobile phone's blurry. I blink until a few lines are readable.

'It's a whole bunch of anonymous teachers,' she explains anyway. 'They've started a group, *Support for Joseph*. Except it's just people ranting about how awful parents from their own classes are, and how they applaud Joseph for standing up to one.'

I push myself upright, scrolling through some comments. 'Jesus, they think he's guilty and they don't care.'

'They've even written how they'd finish their own troublesome parents. The boss sent me the link. There's going to be a massive meeting at school to discuss the implications.'

I hand the phone back. I'll find the group on my device. 'They're suggesting he claims the mental illness angle?'

Lucy nods. 'And some say they'll strike if he's found guilty.'

This is not a reaction I expected, especially en masse. I wonder if Jensen did or, if not, how her team will approach this. I edge myself out of bed, bring Lucy in for a hug. 'Why would other teachers support a potential murderer? I just… I can't…'

'Maybe they're just trolls pretending to be teachers?'

That seems far more likely. At least, I want it to be.

My phone buzzes against the bedside table. 'Who else is awake at this ungodly hour?'

Lucy heads off to the bathroom, letting me take the call. I expect it to be Jensen, perhaps viewing the same social media page. Instead, it's Trevor, from Joseph's school. Asking me to come in for relief.

'We've tried everyone,' he explains, as if that makes me feel better. 'Nobody will come in.'

'You're being very honest with me, Trevor,' I reply. 'Why would I be any different?'

'You had a good day Monday, didn't you?'

'Right up until the principal told me she didn't want my type around her school. Which puzzles me why you'd even consider calling again.'

'The staff liked you. We had more kids back yesterday so we can't merge every class. One of the Year Four teachers has been absent all week, and now a Year Six teacher called in sick. I don't think they're sick at all, but I can't dispute it.'

I look at the time. Just gone six. Can my head handle a day of kids? 'Who am I covering for, Year Four or Six?'

'Year Four.'

'What's the teacher's name?'

'Kristen Silver. Don't worry, she emailed me the work. It's all time-filler stuff.'

The teacher's name rings a bell. 'Hang on a sec.'

I put the call on speaker, bring up the Notes app on my phone, scroll through some dot points. There. Kristen Silver. The teacher who was in her room when Heath Hallid fell from the balcony, diagonally to the right of Joseph's room. The one who screamed in the courtyard when she came down and saw Joseph by the body.

I hesitate, almost ask whether someone has checked on Kristen's welfare, offering emotional and psychological support given what she witnessed. I can't do that, though. Trevor doesn't know my insight into the case. 'You still there?'

'Still here.'

'Just checking something with my wife.'

I open a browser on my phone, go to the site I discovered while getting my PI certification, a way to find people if you know a name, address or suburb. The opposite of what I used to look for Lillian, when I just had a landline number. Like that method, it's not invasion of privacy. At all. I type in **Silver K** and narrow the search to Western Australia. Less than fifty results show up. From a quick glance, there are only a few near the school.

'Trevor?'

'Please say you'll do it.'

'I've one thing to do first, then a long drive in traffic. I can start second period. You'll have to cover the start of the day.'

'I can manage that.'

'But I get paid a full day's pay.'

'I'll shift someone's DOTT around so it looks like you didn't miss a thing.'

'And Talitha won't send me straight back home?'

'We need the staff, or the school will close when everyone's expecting us to.'

There were lots of things I didn't do during my first day at Isidore College, but I don't need to go back to move the case forward. Still, it wouldn't hurt to cross more things off my list.

'Okay. I'll see you second period.'

Trevor extends his thanks as I write the three possible Kristen Silver addresses close to the school. I end the call, hurry to the shower. One of things I didn't do was speak to the only other teacher at school when the murder occurred. Now I know she's home and trying to stay away from everyone.

Perfect time to interview her, before I go teach her class.

Two of the results from the lookup site have phone numbers. They both belong to men. So, by the process of elimination, the third listing must belong to Kristen Silver; unless she lives miles away from school. Either way, I'm about to find out. I've driven to the address. It's a couple of minutes from a university, half the houses redeveloped or brand-spanking new, the other half in desperate need of repair. True uni student dwellings, shared by as many people as they can fit. Kristen's address is one of the latter houses. Weeds waist-high out the front. Windows covered in dust and grime. Tiled roof loose and faded. Timber beams weathered away, threatening to collapse. The type of home owned by someone who gives all their time to their job.

I park in her driveway, a broken mess of bitumen. Hesitate. Is it vital that I question her? The police would have taken her statement, we can access that. She's been through a lot, seeing a body crushed in her school's courtyard, a place she assumed was safe. It's obvious she wants to avoid thinking about it, talking about, hence the reluctance to return to school. What will she do if one more prying person visits? I push away any hesitation, knock on her screen door. Of course I need to speak to her. She's the one person who could help Joseph's case. She was there. She could have heard something, seen someone. If she's repressed the memory, I need to help her bring it out.

While checking that she's safe.

There's no answer.

'Kristen?' I yell.

She has to be here. She'd called in another sick day, sent her work to Trevor.

'Hello?'

Nothing from inside, not even the echo of footsteps.

'It's Detective Winters,' I try. Gary will kill me for using his surname, but if Kristen thinks it's the police, she might open up.

Still nothing from inside, though.

I leave the front doorstep, round the house. There's an open carport, a strip of metal sheeting sticking out the side of the house. Concrete slabs where a car would sit, oil stains marking the spot. No car today, though.

So, Kristen has gone out, someone else is using her car, or she no longer has the vehicle. If this is her house.

I walk through the carport, open the latch on a chest-heigh gate and let myself into the backyard. The weeds here are even taller. There's a shed with a missing door, the gap filled with vines. It reminds me of the one on Uncle Graham's property, where he'd hidden a vital clue to help piece together my family's secret. Kristen could have hidden things in her shed without anybody else knowing. There's a timber-decked patio at the back of the house, leading to a rear door. I give the door a try. It rattles in the frame, won't budge. I could kick it hard and it might break apart, but I'm not that desperate. Yet. Plus, then I'd be trespassing. Not quite what I'm allowed to do as a Private Investigator, if I want to remain known as a law-abiding one; forgetting the visit to Joseph's house, of course.

So, sit and wait in my car? Maybe Kristen's just getting something from the shops? A quick trip for a coffee? Maybe I could find the local café, join her there?

My stomach rumbles, hating me for missing meals. I've done this before, skipping routines when a case is pulling me in. I could stand to lose a few kilos, but it's not the way to do it. It'll start messing with my mind soon, making me jump to preposterous conclusions that lead me down wrong paths.

I head for my car. I can always come back after my day of relief teaching, put my mind at rest. Along the way, I stop by the letterbox. It's stuffed with a pile of junk mail. Ads for supermarkets, liquor stores and auto parts. I pull it out and check for letters. Just an electricity bill. No reason to open that. It *is* addressed to Kristen, so it's the right house. I get back in my car, pull out of her driveway and position my vehicle by the edge of a park, four or five houses down. I'll give it ten more minutes, then I have to get to school. Ten minutes to watch Kristen's place, pray she comes home. I keep the engine running, let the air-conditioner chase away the morning heat. Find the bottle of water on the side of my backpack, down half the liquid in a few gulps. All that's missing in my car is the typical PI's set of spy equipment. Binoculars, camera, snacks. There's going to be a lot of watching in the years to come. A lot of waiting. Can I cope with that? Is there anything I can do to pass the time? Podcasts are swinging for a second golden age; maybe I can find a few appealing ones, listen to them? Audiobooks have a growing following, too. Maybe I can work through some fiction that way?

A few minutes pass before anything happens. Then, in the distance, I spot an orangey-gold vehicle turning into the street. It glides along, passes me, pulls into Kristen's driveway. I wiggle myself upright against my seat, get out my phone and start recording, zooming in as far as the lens lets me. The two smokers from South Perth exit the vehicle, the skinny guy and his rugby player mate. The Perth versions of Duke and The Bear. They hurry to Kristen's door, bang on it, wait. After no response, the tall one gets out his phone, calls somebody. Nudges rugby player and gives him an order. Rugby player gets something out of his pants pocket, a card, and slips it in the mesh of the screen door. The men hurry back to their car. Reverse, drive away. In and out in less than a minute.

I stop recording. Get out my car. Run over to Kristen's front door. Grab the card the men left behind. Examine it. There's no message, just a symbol and a phone number. The symbol is from a playing card. Jack of Spades. It doesn't ring a bell, but it reeks of something gambling-related. There are a couple of people I can call to confirm this. Sarah's husband, for one. Like Lucy said, use my contacts.

I use my phone to photograph the card, then return it to the mesh. I would love to stay behind at the park, wait for Kristen to return, see her face when she finds it. Will she be confused, shocked, scared? Does it have anything to do with what happened at her school, or is it an unrelated manner? Gamblers anonymous? Some way to get in touch with her bookie?

I can only think of a gambling outcome. Which means I can't ignore the connection borne from coincidence. The two men who left their card at a teacher's house were also outside the apartment of a parent from the same school. A parent who deals in wealth management. Sure, the men weren't with Julian at the time, but maybe they'd visited him before I'd arrived, or came back later. Do they funnel their gambling money through some kind of brokerage deal? Is a group of parents and teachers from the school all part of King of Spades' operation?

I can ask someone all about this on my way home this afternoon. Pay them a visit in City Beach. For now, I've got to hurry to the school. Add to my second source of income and throw more questions at the teachers.

Maybe Joseph's innocent after all. Maybe a loan shark is making an example out of people who don't pay.

CHAPTER SIXTEEN
PARENTAL REMORSE

I walk in to a math lesson, kids bunched into different groups. I work my way around the room to figure out what's going on. Most seem bored with their task. When Trevor sees me, he can't hide his relief. He gives a quick summary of the day, then thanks me profusely and leaves the room. I gain everyone's attention, bring them back to the mat. Lucy packed a small container of relief teacher material for me: some books, worksheets and game instructions for activities that aren't a standard part of the curriculum. I pull out a bundle of coloured A3 paper. Each one has a set of numbers in a grid. It's a cool trick Joseph showed me, many years ago.

'I need a volunteer,' I say.

Every hand goes up.

I pick the kid who's almost bouncing off the carpet. 'What's your name?'

'Bodi.'

I ask Bodi to pick a number between one and a hundred, but to keep the number to himself. Then I show him each piece of A3 paper and ask if the number appears on its grid. With each *Yes*, I make a mental note, then at the end add up everything and call out the resulting number. Bodi's jaw hangs open, a good sign I guessed correctly. Except it's not guessing. To an eight-year-old, it's magic, but the numbers in each grid have something to do with the binary system, and all I did was add up the first number on each page Bodi said he saw his number on.

Now I have a wave of hands rising to ask if they can have a turn. I do a headcount; thirty-two kids in the class. It doesn't look like there are enough tables and chairs for that many. The combined classes means another teacher besides Kristen is sick or having a break. I choose another kid, and another, and dangle the carrot that if we can get enough work done by recess, I'll choose one more. We go through the activities they were working on when I arrived and I get a few students to share some tips. Then I send everyone back to complete the work.

A few minutes of their time and I've gained their attention and trust. Just like the adults who make me a coffee even when I'm prying into their lives.

I head over to the teacher's desk at the side of the room and find the iPad Trevor left me, go through the notes for the day. I'm with this class the whole time, no specialist lessons, except we combine with the remaining Year Four students in the last hour for basketball training. I'll hopefully have a chance to talk with the other teacher then. If they're not a substitute, too.

Time moves fast as I circle around the classroom, helping those still puzzled by the Escape-the-Room style tasks their usual teacher has left for them. Math can be hard to explain as an adult, even if you're good at it, but most of the concepts here I can demonstrate verbally or on the whiteboard. Before I know it, a kid reminds me it's almost recess and everyone hurries to get their food and hats; the number grid trick forgotten.

The bell rings. Trevor didn't give me a duty until lunch, wanting to keep me happy.

I wait until everyone leaves and take the classroom in for the first time. It's quite different to Joseph's. Whilst he had his stuff in his desk and his own private locker, there wasn't much else around the room that gave it character. This room is different. Kristen loves memes, or her students do. She's stuck laminated memes on every stretch of wall, about school, teachers, friends, work ethic and other silly stuff. Work samples flap from cord strung across the room. There are notes and keywords on the windows, written with liquid chalk. These students don't have a locker, perhaps because they are younger. Instead, there's a large set of boxed shelving, a bag hanging out of each compartment. Work and other supplies must be in their desk tray instead.

I open the set of drawers under Kristen's desk. They're pretty full, but with stationery. Extra pencils, pens, sticky notes in one draw; rubber bands, notepads and sleeve protectors in another; personal items like deodorant and sanitary pads in the largest one. No pencil cases full of secret notes. No business cards for shady gambling contacts. School and private life separated.

There's a *thump* from someone doing something upstairs. Even with the silence, that's all I can hear. How muffled would yelling or screaming be?

From the teacher's desk, I look at the windows facing the courtyard. It's a pretty narrow view. I can see the staff building straight across—well, the library and other specialist rooms above it—connected by a covered bridge. There's not much of an angle to see anything that could have fallen diagonally to the right. You can't see the courtyard itself. Even if Kristen was looking this way when Heath fell, I'm not sure she would have seen more than a blur. Something I would have mistaken for a bird swooping past.

I exit the room and look up. It's a bloody high drop. It's a miracle this is the first time somebody has ever fallen over the railing, especially when kids run and push and bump.

I can't think like that. There's just the one death, no need to suggest there would be more. I head down to the staffroom, the call of coffee too strong. I pass one of the teachers I saw last time, Emma, in her fluorescent duty vest. She waves hello before someone runs to her with a problem. Before I enter the staff building, I glance around at the buildings, searching for cameras once more. Unless they're hidden, it doesn't look like there are any around the courtyard area. More must be elsewhere on the grounds, though; at least at the front gate.

There are a lot more teachers in the staffroom this time. Cackling, yelling out, joyous—the year's end in sight. Someone's made a cake, a few slices remaining. There are packets of biscuits scattered around and a bowl full of Lindt chocolate balls. Presents to share.

I make a coffee before anyone acknowledges me. Ashlee calls out, asks me to take a seat beside her.

'Good to see you again.'

'I needed more gossip,' I say. May as well be direct.

Ashlee laughs, then introduces me to the teachers surrounding us. The woman beside me, Marisa, is the Year Two teacher. My thoughts focus on the best way to talk to her about Heath Hallid. I almost miss Ashlee's question.

'I thought you weren't going to be in again. Did Trevor realise how good you are?'

Even though I'd love to keep the rumour mill going, it would be better to avoid talking negatively about their boss. 'He was pretty desperate to call me in today. Another school is trying to poach me, so I'm not sure which one I'll be at tomorrow.'

'Which school is that?' Marisa asks.

I give them a name of a school in my suburb. It's so far north, they won't know anyone there. 'I live close to it,' I explain.

'You drove all that way to get here?' Ashlee says.

'I'll take the work wherever I can. Besides, this school is interesting. It's in the news!'

Marisa groans. 'Thank goodness the reporters have lost interest in us.'

'You knew the father?' I ask, trying to hide my smile.

'I taught his son this year. His youngest. He has three. *Had* three?' Marisa shuffles in her seat, looks at her coffee mug and realises it is empty. 'Taught the middle child, too, a few years ago. Blake. So, I've had two of his kids. You know how many times I saw him.'

'Twice?'

'Four times!'

We've drawn more teachers to our conversation. They're chuckling away.

'First day,' Marisa continues, 'he's there at the drop-off. "Any problems, swing 'em his mother's way," he has the nerve to say. And then at the end of the year, he comes in and complains we never got him in enough, that he could have helped his son succeed more.'

'Parental remorse,' another teacher adds.

'Constant communication is sent to mother and father,' Marisa continues. '*And* we have an open door policy. He could have contacted me at any point of the year.'

'Too busy at the TAB,' Ashlee says.

'Oh God, yes. Took Blake there for the boy's birthday. When he was seven. Most kids want to go bowling or play laser tag or go to that trampoline place, but he takes poor Blake to the bookies. That sums things up right there.'

'Does anyone believe Joseph had had enough and pushed him?' I ask.

Everyone mutters to themselves, shaking their head.

'We can't imagine Joe doing that,' Marisa says.

'Then who pushed him?' I ask. 'Or did he fall by himself?'

'That's the million-dollar question, isn't it?' another teacher says.

The door to the passageway opens and the principal appears. She looks over at the sea of teachers, trying to find someone. She spies me and double takes. The expression says it all—she did not know I was here. She retreats from the room, the door snapping shut behind her.

'Anyone catch that look she just gave me?' Marisa says, thinking the double take was for her.

'Well, you only told her this morning,' Ashlee replies.

'Told her what?' I ask.

'I put in my resignation,' Marisa says.

The bell rings. Recess over. Teachers shuffle to the sink to wash their mugs.

'You know what,' she continues when we're alone. 'Come find me at lunch and I'll tell you why I'm resigning. Talitha might ask you to work here and I think it's fair you know everything.'

'I'd love to know everything,' I say.
This time, I don't hide my smile.

CHAPTER SEVENTEEN
TECHNICALLY IT'S NOT AN AFFAIR

For the next hour, the students have a Christmas booklet filled with all sorts of activities designed to keep them busy. Crosswords. Word searches. Writing prompts. Colouring activities. Budgeting tasks for Christmas presents. Designing an ad for a Christmas toy everyone wants. I just have to monitor them, make sure they're doing something and not just talking off task. It's the relief teacher's dream.

Which means I can have another snoop around Kristen's classroom.

I hover around the wet area near the door, which has the pigeon hole shelving for bags instead of lockers. The shelving that isn't stuffed with backpacks is full of files, books and boxes. I was like this for the first few years of my teaching career, hoarding every available resource because you didn't know what you might need. It didn't take long to realise there were favourites you liked to use and other things you'd never touch, no matter how good they seemed. I gave a lot of my resources away long before I left teaching and digitally scanned most of the paperwork. It doesn't look like Kristen is ready to make that commitment yet. There are lesson plans for outdated curriculum, books on disputed theories from the seventies, and box upon box of untouched art supplies.

The students are getting loud. I pop my head around and talk to a few of them, get them to demonstrate their Christmas toy ideas. There are a few that are so good, they surprise me. If I had no integrity, I'd steal them and go running to Hasbro.

Before I know it, the hour is almost gone. I've found nothing more than teaching paraphernalia that's starting to bring up repressed memories.

Time to go outside. It's a hot, sunny day. Mid-thirties. We can survive ten minutes out on the grass. Well, *I* can survive ten minutes. Kids don't seem to care until it hits the forties. I introduce the game, a version of British Bulldog called Fruit Salad. I line everyone up along one side of the stretch of grass. Give a rundown of the rules, take a few questions, hurry them into the first round. Truth is, kids learn best by doing. They might stuff up the first couple of goes, but they'll see how most people are playing and learn from there.

Five minutes in, the game is loud and crazy and the kids are having so much fun that another group comes out to join us. The teacher is from Year Five. They worked with Joseph. Perfect.

As the kids keep playing, my only involvement is changing who's it and making sure they aren't running into each other. I ask the teacher how long they've been at the school. How long they taught with Joseph. His name is Tim. My height, extremely tanned, brown curly hair hanging to his shoulders. I'm pretty sure he was one of the male teachers who were passively aggressive when I asked about Heath's death last time round, but this time he's full of that end-of-year energy and eager to talk. Especially when I tell him that Joseph was my mentor.

'Great guy,' he says. 'Kids love him. His behaviour management was much better than most teachers here.'

'But how was he to work in a team?'

'I mean, he worked with us when he had to. Got lesson plans done. Gave us lots of brilliant resources. But the rest of the time he was pretty happy to stick to himself. Me and George, the other Year Five teacher, we get our classes to do a lot of stuff together, like this, but Joseph didn't always join in.'

'You believe he's innocent?'

'I mean, I bloody hope he is. But at the same time, I can imagine getting so frustrated with a parent that something like that could happen. Pure accident, I'd think.'

'Are the parents here intense?'

'They pay through the roof to send their kids to the College, then think that the money fixes all their problems, gets them A's. When reality sets in, it's us who gets blamed. Nothing to do with parents who'd rather spend time at work than with their kids.'

'Sounds like you're looking forward to some time off.'

'I mean, don't get me wrong, the good outweighs the bad. But yeah, it's nice to be done with one group and hand them off to someone else.'

I point to the Junior School buildings. 'Pity there were no cameras to catch what happened. Prove Joseph innocent.'

'God, they monitor us enough without video surveillance.'

'I thought there weren't any cameras on ground,' I say with as much innocence as possible.

'Some at the entrance, more throughout the Senior School, but we're largely left alone here.'

I shake my head. 'So, grabbing some cups of coffee is the only alibi Joseph's got.'

Tim points to an eight-foot high wall on the opposite edge of the grass. 'Swim meet was in there, and nobody heard or saw anything. But Joseph'll be okay. Someone will investigate, find the right clues.' He cups his hands around his mouth to make a pseudo-megaphone. 'Nathan, when you're tagged you stand still!'

I glance at the wall hiding the College's swimming pool. It's so close to the Junior School, but Tim's right; nobody could see over the wall; from this angle, it was unlikely they could see someone up at Joseph's room. Could they have made it from poolside to classroom and back again in less than five minutes? Maybe. If they were running. And if they left the second Joseph went downstairs. And knew where they were going. And if they pushed Heath almost instantly.

A lot of *ifs*.

I should end things now, take my class inside for some actual work, but Tim's willingness to talk has me begging to act on a hunch.

'If someone investigates, will they find out about the affair he's having?'

Tim looks at me wide-eyed.

'With the parent,' I continue.

'You know about that?'

'We caught up a while ago and he told me. A Year Six parent.'

'The mum's divorced,' Tim says, 'although she's kept the ex's name for now. I guess, cause they're divorced, technically it's not an affair.'

'But what would happen if other parents found out? Or your principal?'

'Beside it being all over the socials in half a second? Joseph would be told to look for a job elsewhere.'

'And what if your principal found out you guys knew the secret?'

'We'd have to sit through hours of meetings about appropriate standards and behaviour. Protocols and bullshit.'

'That's all?'

'She'd split the teams up. Give us the most challenging kids next year. Make sure we had little support.'

I wonder if Talitha would be angry enough to murder someone, or have Joseph framed for murder. I shouldn't ignore scorned lovers as suspects. I've already ignored a scorned mother, and Leonie went on a killing spree.

'Mario, you got tagged,' Tim yells. 'I swear, these kids cheat every chance they get.'

I look at my watch. A quick activity to shake off some excess energy has become a twenty-minute game. 'I'd better get my class back inside,' I say.

'Nice to meet you, mate,' Tim replies.

Trevor designated the rest of the time before lunch to math games, which consist of iPad apps that look far more like video games than anything math related. I cycle through my conversation with Tim, then double-check the timetable Trevor gave me. I'm on lunch duty first up but have twenty minutes to spare afterwards. Maybe I should use that time to have another chat with Talitha. Be direct. Get some answers that way. She seems to dislike me already, what is there to lose?

I wonder how she'll react when I tell her I know what she's been up to with Joseph.

CHAPTER EIGHTEEN
ON TO THE NEXT BIG THING

The door to Talitha's office is closed, the reception desk unmanned. Trevor's office is empty, too. I knock on Talitha's door. Wait. There's a shuffle within the room, but no response. I knock again. The door finally opens. Talitha sees it's me, sighs. Steps back and waves me in.

'You had no idea Trevor called me today, did you?'

'Not until it was too late.'

'It's that hard to get relief teachers?'

Talitha sits back at her desk, gestures for me to take an empty chair. 'We have three others in, and that's after scraping the bottom of our list. The rest don't want to be seen in a murder school.'

I don't mention the social media buzz about revenge-seeking students.

'Glad Trevor found me at the bottom, then,' I say instead.

Talitha ignores the jibe, asks, 'Were there any reporters camped outside the grounds this morning?'

'None that I saw.'

She nods. 'Good.' Her rigid postures deflates, her arms flopping against her desk. 'I'm scared to even look now.'

'I know a thing or two about reporters camped outside.'

Talitha nods. I don't need to explain.

'But they move away pretty quick,' I continue. 'On to the next big thing.'

She flickers the briefest smile. 'Thank you. Everyone's telling me there are only a couple of days left, to hang on. Isidore College doesn't close for the holidays, though. Only for five days over Christmas. I'm going to be fielding calls from every concerned parent and it's nothing but a nightmare to think about.'

I don't point out that it's something her position calls for, and why she's paid far more than teachers. 'What if something else happened, though, and it wasn't Joseph?'

Talitha settles back against her chair. 'What do you mean?'

'I'm sure there's a secret someone might crack.'

'What are you…?'

I lean forward. 'I have a confession to make.'

'Yes?'

'I know Joseph. He was my mentor. I had him on a prac when I was earning my chalk. I visited him in prison yesterday, to see how he's doing. When you wouldn't hire me back. And he told me about the two of you.'

Talitha rises from her seat, her face reddened, her hands clenched into fists. She rounds her desk and I swear she's about to strike me. But she strides past, to the door, and slams it shut. She spins around and stabs a finger towards me. 'You are not to tell anyone!' The venom is back in her voice. 'And what we do is none of your concern!'

'You're ready to sell him out as a murderer. Do you really believe it's true?'

'It has to be! Nothing else makes sense.'

'There aren't any cameras that would've recorded everything?'

'Not in the Junior School.'

'But was Joseph down in the courtyard when you saw the body?'

Talitha pulls up the chair beside me, sits far too close. 'I was here, in my office, and I heard a horrible scream. Not a playful one like you hear from the kids. A *something-fucking-awful-has-happened* scream. It was Kristen. I ran out to the courtyard, saw her. Saw the body. Saw Joseph.'

'Was he carrying two coffee mugs?'

'Yes. I took them out of his hands. He looked like he was about to drop them. He was on auto-pilot. Standing there, not responding.'

'What happened to the mugs?'

'Police photographed them, took them.'

'You called the police?'

'Yes.'

'And when they arrived, did you stick by Joseph's side?'

'They kept us apart, took statements.' Talitha pauses, takes a deep breath. Trying not to lose control again. 'I didn't see him after that.'

'You haven't visited him?'

'I have been living here. Literally. I've been to so many meetings I've lost count.' She gestures to something behind me. 'Lucky I've got a wardrobe full of clothes.'

'And you're adamant he killed the father?'

'The police will sort that out.'

'So, your relationship meant nothing?'

Talitha grips the sides of her chair, tenses a little, then lets go. 'We both got what we wanted out of our time together. What happened between us doesn't change what he did.'

'If the police are as adamant as you, what if they ignore any evidence that causes doubt?'

'Like what?'

'Like the fact that he was down in the courtyard carrying two cups of coffee. Coffee he was bringing back to the room.'

Talitha reaches out, places a hand over mine. I try not to flinch. 'Look,' she says, 'I get that he was your mentor. And it's lovely you've kept in touch, because most mentees don't. But can we ever truly know someone?'

She pulls back, stares at me, knows how my family guides my answer.

'In light of that, I would be happy for you to return tomorrow. If you're needed. Now, I've got to call another parent who's threatening to pull their boys unless we offer a substantial discount.'

There's so much more I need to ask, and this meeting didn't go the way I'd thought. I could go the low road, reveal Talitha wasn't the only one Joseph was sleeping with. But I don't think that will do anything more than anger her, and she'll retract her invitation to return. Deflated, I leave her office. I think about grabbing a coffee but the siren rings. End of lunch. A quick burst of silent reading and then some sport with the other Year Fours. I should feel relieved that it's a relatively easy way to end the day. Instead, every step towards the courtyard requires effort, my brain working against my body.

I feel like I've missed something. A question I should have asked. An answer I didn't get. For the life of me, I can't figure it out.

Through the glass door, I can see a wave of children returning from the playground. Maybe I can get something out of the other Year Four teachers? The thought is enough to get me moving.

Then my brain catches up. Tells me what I missed. My chat with the Year Two teacher, Marisa. To find out why she's resigning. I slap my forehead. Idiot.

Silent reading, sport, dismiss the kids. Run over and catch Marisa before she flees. It *can* be done. The thought puts a spring back into my step.

Q

A parent is hovering outside Marisa's classroom. She has a potted plant and a bottle of wine. As the last of the kids leave her room, Marisa appears by the door. The parent hands over the gifts and brings Marisa in for a big hug. As an upper primary teacher, in a far less opulent school, I rarely got that kind of warm thanks. If I did, I wonder if I would have continued teaching.

The parent leaves with her son and walks past me with a knowing nod. Marisa catches my eye and gestures for me to come inside. I got nothing from the other teachers during the sport session. It was too hard, anyway. The session consisted of a rotating set of sports—Ultimate Frisbee, Soccer and Basketball—my attention occupied while keeping everything running. Marisa, on the other hand, should be able to dish a little gossip. I shut the door behind us and we sink into some beanbags.

'You enjoying it here?' Marisa asks.

'It's hard to gauge the kids since it's the last week,' I admit, trying not to think of all the germs and assorted grossness on the beanbags. 'At least I don't feel bad that no real learning is taking place under my watch.'

She laughs. 'It's a nice week to get that relief teacher money.'

I haven't checked how much the school is paying me. That, on top of Jensen's payout, will get us through the Christmas drought, pay for those last-minute Singapore tickets.

'So, this is your last week?' I ask.

'I haven't given enough notice, so they'll cut some of my long service pay. But yeah, I don't care. I'm done.'

'You worked here long?'

'Ten years.'

'I stopped after ten years, too. Well, nine and a bit.'

'The old principal said he was always happy if he got a teacher for five years. He expected them to move on after seven.'

'Has Talitha been the principal for long?'

Marisa shakes her head. 'Her ideals have rubbed a lot of us long-standing teachers the wrong way. She doesn't want to listen to our experience. Don't get me wrong, she's come up with a lot of good initiatives. But they're not for me.'

'Will you teach somewhere else?'

'I haven't got anything lined up. I'm going to take a break.' She looks around the classroom. 'This becomes your whole life until you forget there's so much more out there.'

'I hear that.'

Marisa shuffles in her beanbag, trying to get comfortable. 'If Talitha tries to employ you, ask about the programs she's implemented. Especially for English and Math. It's this whole scripted nonsense designed for supporting smaller groups, not an entire class. But if you're okay to handle that, then good for you.' She sniggers. 'Then ask about the expectations of your workload. Cause next year she wants to have us all running clubs before and after school, like some kind of extended daycare. Completely removing our time with family and friends. For those who have any.'

I shake my head at the thought. 'Don't worry, I won't be going back to teaching.'

'No?'

Do I tell Marisa I'm investigating Joseph's death? No, if I break the relief teacher charade, there's no telling who she might tell. 'I'll stay casual, at most. I wanted to relieve here cause I know Joseph. He was my mentor when I was at uni. Although I'm older than him.'

'That would have been funny.'

'It was interesting. But I saw what happened in the paper and I just… I guess I wanted to know where he ended up. I don't think a murderer trained me. I can't accept that.'

'We can't accept it, either.'

'Did Heath Hallid ever get angry with you? Yell at you, stuff like that?'

'During one of the four times I saw him?'

'Yeah.'

'He was angry his kids weren't progressing to standard, and he had his little rants, but he never yelled.'

'You think he yelled at Joseph?'

'Male testosterone thrown into one room? Of course.'

'Joseph said that Heath punched him. That's why he left the meeting, to get coffee and diffuse the situation.'

'I'm not surprised he punched him. Heath punched another parent once. In the car park.'

'Who?'

'I don't… Let me think. It was a year or two ago.'

I reach for the stars. 'I wasn't Julian Bortoni, was it?'

'You know what, I think it was. Their sons are friends.'

I'd picked Julian's name because it was the only other parent connected to Heath. At least, the only one I'd talked to. I wonder if the altercation was around the time Julian kicked Heath out of their fantasy basketball group.

'You said Heath took his kid to the TAB. Did he like to gamble?'

'I mean, it's the TAB. You don't go in there to just watch the races, do you?'

I take out my phone. Notifications fill my screen. I ignore them for a moment, unlock the phone and bring up the photo of the business card from Kristen's house. 'You ever seen this company? It's not owned by a parent from here, is it?'

'Not that I know of, sorry.'

We trade a couple more stories about Joseph, some small talk about teaching. When the conversation dries, I thank Marisa for her time and wander back to the staffroom. My phone vibrates, reminding me of the myriad of messages awaiting. I unlock it again and scroll through the notifications. I've had my phone on silent all day and haven't glanced at it. If I had, I would have realised that Jensen wants to give me an update. She's tried calling four times, without leaving a message. Lucy has called and left a message. I listen to it. She lets me know that the whole family is going to Hillarys Boat Harbour again to watch the sunset and have dinner. If I'm not exhausted, they'd love to see me there. The boat harbour will be crowded on a hot day like this, half of the northern suburbs basking on its adjoining beaches.

My finger hovers over my contacts, ready to call Lucy back. But there are two things I need to do before I commit. First, I need to check on Kristen, see if she's home. See if she'll talk to me about what she saw. Second, I need to take Lucy's advice and get help from someone I know. Someone who's knows the gambling world more than me. Who's been seeking help for their gambling addiction. I can see them on my way home, since they live close to the coast.

I find Trevor, return the notes and iPad, thank him for bringing me in. I check on the pay. It comes through next Tuesday. Over four hundred a day. When I get to my car, the car park is almost empty. No after school sport or clubs today. It doesn't take long to get to Kristen's house. It must be nice, living close to your place of work. I turn into her street and pray I'll see her car in the driveway. As I get closer, my heart skips a beat. There *is* a car in the driveway! An old Mazda, its blue paint faded from years in the sun. I pull up behind it, hurry out.

My mind races through the questions it needs to ask, trying to focus on the ones that will help establish Joseph's innocence. I'm so preoccupied, it takes a moment to catch up as I reach the front door. To realise the screen is wide open. To see the objects in the front room, smashed and scattered to the ground.

'Kristen?' I call out.

There's no reply.

CHAPTER NINETEEN
REPORT A SUSPICIOUS INCIDENT

Given the car outside, the smashed items inside, I expect to be walking into a crime scene. I get my phone out, ready to call the police. At some point, I need to tell myself I should wait outside, let forensics handle things. But I'm curious, and I'm uncertain that something *has* happened to Kristen.

I don't call out for her. I don't know if there's anyone else lurking within, and I'm not about to get smacked down again.

Things appear scattered in a random order, someone traipsing through the room in a whirlwind of anger, grabbing everything they could and wrenching it to the ground. Books and DVDs are pulled from the shelves, framed photographs smashed on the floor, dust-free patches the only reminder of their position.

I creep through the front room and round the corner into a small passageway. Off this are three doors and an archway. Two of the doors are wide open, one is closed. The one at the end of the passageway, of course. I need to assess whether I'm alone before I take in more detail. I peer through the first open doorway. A bedroom. Nobody's there, unless they're hiding in the tall wooden cupboard that looks like it belongs to the world of Narnia. I shuffle down the passageway, cautious of my feet creaking against exposed floorboards. The rooms have carpeting, but this area is like lava for each misplaced step. The open archway is first on my right. It leads to a kitchen area and another archway. It looks like a laundry is beyond that. Lots of areas to hide.

I focus on the doors back in the passageway. The last open one is just beyond the archway, also to the right. It leads to a bathroom. I edge into it, glance behind the door then the shower curtain. The room smells damp, mould growing in the walls. I hurry out, reach for the closed door at the end of the passageway. If someone's in the room beyond, they'll watch the handle turn, prepare to strike. I stop, reach back into the bathroom and grab the lone towel hanging on a rusted rack. I bundle it up in one hand, keep turning the door handle with the other. My back is flat against the wall, doing what it can to avoid the blast of a gun, should that be the weapon of choice. When I've turned the handle enough, I push the door open and throw in the towel. It unravels and thumps to the ground in a wet heap. Nobody attacks it; no shots fired. Which either means the room's empty or someone can distinguish between the blur of a towel and a person.

I abandon stealth and hurry into the room. There's stuff scattered everywhere but I don't know if it's from someone searching or Kristen being untidy. I check under the bed, pull open another wooden cupboard. There's nobody lurking in the shadows. Which means I've just got the kitchen and laundry area to inspect. The car has to belong to someone, right? Surely they're somewhere here?

I leave the bedroom, walk beneath the archway into the kitchen. There's a bowl in the sink, full of water and the remnants of cereal. The rest of the area is clean, nothing smashed here. Come to think of it, the front room and a bit of Kristen's bedroom were the only areas disturbed. Maybe the intruder knew where to look? For whatever they needed to find?

I should grab a kitchen knife. A pan. Anything. But the light shifts in front of me, beyond the archway to the laundry, and urgency takes hold. I hurry through the kitchen, round a small table and chair set, reach the archway. There's a door to the right, leading to the unmistakable odour of a toilet. There's a screen door to the left, leading to the backyard. The shift in light must have been from someone opening and closing the screen.

I'm not going to follow. No need to be led into another trap. This time, I sprint back through the house and use the front door to exit. I'll round the house, surprise whoever's in the backyard. But as I step outside, there's a *thunk* of a car door. Someone's sitting in the faded blue Mazda. They turn on the ignition, which clicks over with a wheeze and shudder.

'Wait!' I run to the car. 'I know Joseph!'

I get a better look at the person in the car. Young woman, mid- to late-twenties. Pale skin, amber hair, freckles across a terrified face. The woman is panicking and all I can think of is that she looks like an older Ginny Weasley from the *Harry Potter* series.

Her car lurches into reverse. Smacks straight into my car.

I cry out. It must sound awful, because she yells at me to get away.

'I just want to help!' I scream, waving my arms for her to stop.

There's an awful screech of metal and her car pushes off mine. She swings it around and out the driveway.

'I don't want to hurt you!'

She doesn't stop to consider my words. I reach the end of the driveway as her car roars past.

I hurry back to my car, check the front. The damage sounded far worse than it looks, a smear of paint left behind. I get in, start the engine. Begin reversing.

Wait! What am I doing? I can't start chasing this person. I don't know if it's Kristen or someone else. Just like in my efforts to find other people, including my sister, I failed to get a photograph straight away. Or a description, at the very least. If it *is* her, she's spooked. She probably came home to a ransacked house and then heard and saw this tall man walk in, inspecting everything, shouting at her to stop. If it wasn't her, it was most likely a relative or friend. Likewise, they'd seen the messed-up house, seen a big man yelling at them, assumed their life was in danger. If I drive after them, I might heighten their panic, make them take stupid risks. Like pulling out in front of a truck.

I call the police, report a suspicious incident I just witnessed. As I do so, I try to think about my trip through the house. What did I touch? Can anyone connect me to the place if something has happened to Kristen? A nosy neighbour may have noted my licence plate, but I think that's about it.

'We'll send someone out to look as soon as possible, sir.'

I give my details and end the call. Then I remember the door handle to Kristen's bedroom. I had to touch that to turn it. If my prints are amongst the jumble on it, and I made the phone call to the police, they'll think something is suspicious. I'll be in the same circumstance as Joseph—my word against theirs, guilty until proven innocent.

I kill the engine, hurry out the car, head back to Kristen's front door. I look around the doorway. The King of Spades card isn't in the screen, nor does it appear to be on the ground. So, someone saw it, took it; or it's buried deep in the mess further inside. I step inside, examine the mess. Someone might have conducted a more precise search first—key areas hit—the mess just created to cover up the items inspected. Without knowing what those items were, though, a mess is just a mess.

I head towards Kristen's room. Stop. Consider key differences between the two teachers' houses I've now invaded. In Joseph's house, his spare rooms were so bland, it was pretty clear he lived alone. In this house, though, the spare bedroom might not be a spare.

I use my shirt to wipe the door handle of the back bedroom, then find some paper towels in the kitchen. I take them to the first bedroom, with the giant cupboard. Look around again. Try the cupboard, opening the doors with sheets of paper towel in my hand. Anything to mask my prints. There are lots of clothes hanging inside the cupboard, but no path to Narnia. I look around some more. There's a bedside table, atop it a framed photo of an old couple. Somebody's parents? I use my phone to capture their image. In the table's two drawers is an assortment of boxes for things like jewellery, hair accessories, and toys Lucy swears she's never used.

Kristen had a housemate. Maybe it was the woman who just drove off, if that wasn't Kristen. If she saw the business card, and the mess inside, it was enough to get her to run. I need to know why.

It's time to call for help. I head outside to my car, get out my phone, and dial the number.

CHAPTER TWENTY
MORE FAMILIAR TERRITORY

The inside of Desmond's house is the epitome of a man cast out on his own, the cliché mess of a separated husband. Dirty dishes stacked beside the sink. Clothes scattered everywhere, a pile on the floor. Beer bottles on the remaining surfaces, all empty.

'Did you never learn how to look after yourself?' I ask as Desmond leads me back into the lounge room, two beers in hand.

'I'm just… Well, this sums it up. I'm a mess.'

He hands me a beer. After the long day I've had, I need it. I look out the window, towards the ocean that lies a block away. Several big houses obscure most of the view, but the sunset still looks amazing. He's lucky to have bought a house in City Beach years back, when it wasn't worth a million or two; or more.

I find a seat on a couch, pushing aside some clothes and a newspaper. 'You probably need to get this cleaned up. If you want Sarah and the kids to come back.'

Desmond shakes his head. 'I fucked up. I don't think Sarah's coming back.'

'The kids will want to see you.'

'I know. Are they doing okay? Is there enough stuff to do at your house?'

Because my house is half the size of yours? I shake the thought away, say, 'Their grandparents are spoiling them rotten, diverting their attention.'

'I think Sarah will go back to Singapore with them. Like, stay there.'

'Do you want that to happen?'

'Of course not! But it's all about broken trust, Henry. I don't know how you come back from that.'

Desmond has hidden a gambling addiction from his wife for their entire relationship. A separate, secret bank account helped hide that for a long time; until debt mounted, and collectors started taking their frustrations out on his limbs.

'I *am* making a lot of progress, though,' Desmond adds. He's talking about the support group Carina introduced him to. Carina's an AUSTRAC agent involved with money laundering. She helped him avoid prison time for everything that went down with Trent and my family's affairs.

'That's great to hear,' I say. 'Don't give up on yourself, or your wife. Keep showing her you're trying.' I don't tell him about the trip we're all taking to Singapore for Christmas, since he thinks she's going there anyway. I just hope he can prove his worth before then, join us for much-needed family time.

Desmond nods, downs his beer. Rises to go get another one. 'What brings you here, anyway? I know it's more than a pep talk.'

'Lucy told me to reach out to people who could help me.'

'You think she meant the man who's causing her sister grief?'

I ignore the comment. Pull out my mobile, bring up the photograph of the business card. 'You seen this before?'

Desmond leans over, snatches my phone. Grimaces. Yeah, he's seen that symbol before.

'What is it?' I ask.

He swipes my phone, stops on the video of the two men leaving the card at Kristen's house.

'What are you involved in this time?'

He hands the phone back, gets out his own.

'You heard about the teacher who murdered a parent?'

'Of course. It's all over my feeds.'

'I'm looking into things for him. Trying to prove he's innocent.'

'You're a detective now? You working for Gary?'

'No. I got my PI licence.'

Desmond chuckles. 'Didn't want to join his department?'

'I get to stay in Perth, for now. Lucy's deputy next year.'

'I heard. Good for her.' He waves his mobile. 'I'm going to make a call.'

'Who?'

'Someone who can help us. You might wanna phone Lucy, tell her you'll be late.'

Thirty minutes after the call's made, the doorbell rings. Carina Outridge enters the house, looks around, harrumphs in disapproval.

'Love what you've done here. A real alcoholic hobo vibe.' She shakes Desmond's hand. 'You *are* going to the group I referred you too, right?'

'I'm drinking, but I haven't gambled.'

'One can lead to the other, but we should celebrate the first step.'

Carina turns to me, shakes my hand. She's cut her auburn bob, now shaved down one side and dyed with streaks of green and purple. She's got a nose ring, too. Never noticed that before. She's dressed for whatever job she's on, another piece of undercover work. We met when she'd worked her way inside my cousin Trent's gambling house operation, a test of the waters while waiting to be assigned to a casino-related case.

'Did we drag you away from something?' I pry.

'It can wait till tomorrow. Desmond mentioned you had a gambling-related issue?'

I show her the image, then the footage of the two men at Kristen's house. They stare at each other as the video ends.

'Who wants to tell him?' Carina asks.

'You do it.'

'Grab a beer.'

Desmond disappears and Carina clears another part of the couch; sits. 'Back in the days, and this is decades ago, old gangs used to leave business cards, but often as they pulled a job. I have an uncle who got some for me from Chicago, but I've rarely seen any from Perth. Not a group with this symbol, anyway. I bet they're literally named King of Spades. Pretty fucking brazen to put your phone number on there, though it'd link to a time-sensitive burner.'

'Do you know who they are?'

'I do not. Which means they're a new outfit. Your cousin ran the last one I took down, now you're here for this one. Anything to tell me?'

'Just that it might relate to a murder I'm investigating. Both things have nothing to do with my family this time, though, I swear.'

Desmond reappears with the drinks, hands one to each of us. 'You remember when you found me at the casino, and those two guys took me back up to my room?'

I hold the bottle in my hand. Stare at a bead of moisture working its way down the glass, try to picture Desmond at the casino. 'I thought they were going to beat you up, but you worked a number on them instead.'

'Because they thought I was still wheelchair bound.'

'We *all* thought you were wheelchair bound.'

'Well, anyway, one of those guys I worked a number on was in your video there.'

'His name's Viktor,' Carina adds.

'Just Viktor?' I ask.

'I forget his last name. The other guy is Silas. We are aware of these guys. Viktor works for a group of men we've spent a long time trailing. Men who have their fingers in assorted operations here.'

'You think they've branded themselves now?' I ask.

'That, or King of Spades, or whatever they're called, have hired them. Which means they're enforcing debts, cause that's what Viktor and Silas usually help with.'

'Then Kristen, the teacher whose house is in the video, she owes this group?' I look to Desmond. 'How much would she owe if people like that visit her?'

Desmond shrugs. 'Could be ten dollars, could be ten thousand. Depends if the group wants to make an example.'

'I saw them out the front of a parent's apartment, too.'

I detail the sighting outside Julian Bortoni's residence.

'Sounds like they'd already paid him a visit,' Carina says. 'He wasn't shaken when you saw him? Roughed up?'

'Not at all.'

'So, maybe it wasn't to warn him at all. It's either a huge coincidence they were outside his apartment, or he's got them running errands.'

'Because he's part of the Spades group?'

Had Julian's fantasy basketball league been one outlet for his gambling, the legal side to an otherwise shady operation? Desmond started by betting on sports, then moved to betting at gambling houses.

I look at him. 'This sounds very familiar.'

Desmond holds his hands up. 'Not going undercover or anything on this one. The temptation would be too great.'

'I know,' I say. 'I wouldn't ask that of you.' I glance at Carina. 'Would you be able to get permission to look into this group?'

'I can try.' She places her beer bottle on the floor beside the couch. 'But it will take a while, and it sounds like you don't have long till the teacher's sentenced.'

No, I don't have long. Joseph's already faced immediate imprisonment. The police and prosecutors will be in a hurry to make an example of him, given the escalation of people supporting his actions online.

'Look into it anyway,' I say. 'I'll go back and have a word with Julian.'

Carina nods. 'You remind me of myself, you know.'

'How so?'

'I started in law enforcement, moved into consultancy, drifted to AUSTRAC.'

'So, there's a career path after this?' I smile.

'I have another way to help,' Desmond chips in. As we both turn to him, he adds, 'It wasn't luck the big guy in your video found me at the casino. He spends half his time there. He'll be there tomorrow night.'

'How are you so sure?' I ask.

'He goes around collecting debts. Lots of gamblers in the one place.' Desmond's brown skin reddens as he says this. *He* was one of the gamblers.

'Tomorrow night, then,' I say. 'I'll meet you there.'

'No,' Carina says. 'You just said you weren't going to surround yourself with gambling, now you're going to meet at the casino?'

'Henry will help me,' Desmond says, looking at me expectantly.

Shit. The last time I babysat Desmond, I took him for a drive down to Margaret River, to get away from everything, and I said something stupid and he punched me in the face.

'Looking forward to it,' I say, rubbing my cheek.

Remembering the sting.

Wondering how the hell a murder investigation has led back to more familiar territory.

I walk Carina to the door, make sure she has my number. 'Can I ask for one more favour?'

'Sure.'

'I need a PI.'

She chuckles. 'Looking to hire someone to solve your own case?'

'No, it's not that. You said you were a consultant; did you make any contacts with international investigators? I need someone overseas to help me.'

'With what?'

'I have a hunch, think maybe they can help find my half-sister.'

'I'll look into it for you. They might charge a bit, though. Couple of thousand dollars. More if you need things done quicker.'

I don't know how I'm going to get the money. It depends on how much I'll make from this case. 'I'll manage,' I say. Because I'll find a way. Anything, to find Lillian.

CHAPTER TWENTY-ONE
GET TO THE ROOT OF THE PROBLEM

The buzz of my phone wakes me from a deep sleep. Lucy walks past, fresh out of the shower, a towel wrapped around her body.

'Mmm, come here,' I mumble.

'Answer the phone,' she says.

'What time is it?'

'Quarter to six.'

I guess it's Trevor. Realising he never booked me for today, desperate for a relief teacher yet again. I find my phone on the bedside table and look at the screen. Not Trevor.

'Jensen?'

'Henry. I—'

'I'm sorry I didn't call with an update.'

'Never mind. We need to go see Joseph. Can I pick you up at six-thirty?'

'They won't allow us in so early.'

Jensen sighs. 'They'll make an exception. He's in a crisis care unit.'

'Why?'

'Allegedly, he tried to kill himself.'

Jensen pulls up outside my house. I kiss Lucy goodbye, wish her luck on her last day of teaching for the year. I can't wait until Saturday, when we can finally spend time together. I tell her as much and she agrees.

'I can help with your case, too,' Lucy adds.

'You'll solve it by Monday.'

'Monday? More like Sunday.'

I open the front door just as Jensen's about to knock. She looks as tired as I feel. 'You okay?' I ask.

'Just lacking a whole lot of sleep.'

'You're not responsible for whatever Joseph did.'

'I know, but there have been a lot of calls to field.'

Lucy appears behind me, introduces herself. I give her another kiss goodbye, then Jensen and I head to the car. The first few minutes' drive is in silence. It's not until we join the heavy queue on the Freeway, rolling forward at a snail pace, that Jensen opens up.

'First few days in prison are always the worst. Especially for someone who's never been there. But Joseph was so sure we'd prove his innocence, I can't understand why he'd slip like this.'

'Is he in a bad way?'

'He tried to hang himself on the bunk bed. Guards were on to him right away. Barely any physical damage but they have to observe him now.'

'Was anyone in his room? The other half of the bunk bed?'

'The first two days, then they were transferred. He's been on his own, but that wouldn't have lasted long. Beds are scarce, the floor has to make do sometimes.'

I feel a ripple of anger through my body. Put someone in a cage and treat them like an animal before sentencing? That'll work out swell.

As we continue to work our way through the crawling traffic, I update Jensen on everything I've accomplished since our last talk.

'You've been busy,' she says.

I tell her about the gambling connection with the parents and teachers, the plan Desmond made for tonight.

'You don't have to put yourself at risk. Just find what you can on Joseph.'

There's only so much I could find from Joseph's school. I'm not sure what else Jensen expects me to do, then realise what she *doesn't* want me to do. 'Are you afraid I'll connect him to the gambling outfit?'

'I just... You know what, see what you can find. If he's connected, the prosecution might work the same angle. Best to be prepared. Besides, if some debt collectors were after him, we can spin that. Maybe they thought Heath Hallid was Joseph, and they came to settle things?'

'Or maybe they were after Heath Hallid all along. He tried to be part of a fantasy basketball group. He could have been gambling in other ways.'

Jensen beams. 'That's a great angle. We'll go with that if things get ugly.'

I glance at my phone. Almost seven, no call from Trevor. 'Looks like the school's not going to ask me in on the last day. So, there's not much else I can find out there. I tied up most loose ends, but I never got to speak to the swimming coach or teachers in the Senior School. Or the headmaster of the whole place.'

Jensen beeps the horn as someone cuts in front of her. 'No signal, idiot!' She takes a deep breath, loosens her grip on the steering wheel. 'I have a friend who's been filtering any findings. Forensics, etcetera. Most surfaces were too contaminated to get good prints from any third party in Joseph's classroom. They examined the feed of a few cameras around the College. Unfortunately, it just shows people arriving and leaving at the front gate, for the swim meet. Nothing to show anyone entering or leaving the Junior School itself. They did a headcount, matched faces and all that. Nobody extra turns up. Nobody extra leaves.'

'I guess that's good,' I say. 'In a way.'

'How so?'

'Well, it narrows the field. Of all the faces they saw coming and going, one of them could belong to the killer.'

Jensen talks to one of the medical staff while I peer in at Joseph. He's asleep on a hospital cot, any trauma removed by the look of peace on his face.

Jensen brings the staff member over to me. 'This is Amanda Miller, PCS psychologist.'

Amanda brushes a grey hair back, a stray from her ponytail. She has a thin face with sharp features, but when she smiles it's warm, her green eyes drawing a sense of calm. We shake hands.

'PCS?' I ask.

'Prisoner Counselling Services,' she says. 'I was telling Jensen we did an eval on Joseph when he first arrived and he seemed fine. Nervous of course, first time in the system. Nothing to raise the usual risk assessment flags, though.'

I gesture to the sleeping teacher. 'Why do you think he tried to hang himself?'

'He hasn't explained that at all.'

'Maybe I can get him to tell us?'

'He's out at the moment. Pain killers.'

'How long will he be here?'

'He'll go back soon. Under hourly watch until it's okay to scale back. Two-hourly, four-hourly, until we're convinced he won't repeat.'

'You're convinced he won't repeat?'

'Not until I know why he did it in the first place. If it's through trouble adjusting to custody, we have programs in place that might help. Jensen tells me you were a teacher, too? I'm sure you filled in your share of behaviour management plans?'

'A fair few.'

'Think of it like that. One's called a Support and Management System.'

'You think it will help?'

'It makes everyone accountable, at least. As we try to get to the root of the problem.'

Jensen walks closer to Joseph's bed, hovers by his feet. 'He must feel like he's not going to win this case. That he's going to spend a long time in prison.'

'He was on his own at the time, right?' I ask, thinking about Jensen's comment.

'Yes,' Amanda confirms.

'But he was sharing before?'

'They shuffle a lot of men around, brought in and out for trial or transfer.'

'The person he was with wouldn't have suggested anything?'

'It's too hard to say.'

'And he was getting another roommate?'

'Today. Although that will change.'

'Would he have known who was about to fill the extra bed?'

'I don't see how.'

I had thought that if Joseph was part of the gambling group somehow, then someone tied to it—another enforcer like Viktor— might have worked their way into the prison system. A messenger from behind bars, ready to make a terrible time worse. But if Joseph didn't know who was joining him, there was no need to panic. If someone had threatened him, he would have told Jensen. So maybe she was right. Maybe Joseph felt he wasn't going to win the case. Even with his story of going down to get coffee, with the fact that the principal saw him with the mugs, *took them out of his hands*, he knew it wasn't enough. No cameras, no witnesses; Joseph doomed through lack of evidence.

We wait a while but he doesn't wake. It's a wasted trip in a way, but at least the counsellor has reassured us, and we know he's being monitored. It's almost nine by the time we get back out into the parking lot.

'You want to get a coffee somewhere?' Jensen asks.

'I wouldn't refuse a coffee.'

We head back towards the coast. For a moment, I stare at the side mirror and swear I see an orangey-gold vehicle a few cars behind us. When I turn to get a better look, I no longer see it. Paranoia. Maybe that's what got to Joseph. He imagined what was coming. Imagined the absolute worst, and it consumed him.

'Shit!' I pull out my phone.

'What's the matter? You want me to pull over?'

'No…' I check my contacts. No, I gave her *my* number, hoping she'd call with more information, but I never got hers. 'What if Joseph was paranoid about a secret he'd been keeping?'

'You mean the notes?'

'I've put this off for long enough. We've got to go see Robyn Hallid. Find out the truth from her son.'

CHAPTER TWENTY-TWO
GAVE EVERYTHING TO THE JOB

The second we arrive near Robyn Hallid's house, it's obvious we won't be talking to her or Blake. It's a media circus, vans from every station parked on her front lawn. A police car is between the vans and the house, an officer standing post at the door.

'She's only going to let us in if we've got something about her oldest son,' I tell Jensen.

'What do we do, then?'

'Find her oldest son.'

Jensen drives me home, the offer of coffee forgotten. When she reaches my driveway, the house looks empty for the first time in ages. The doors are closed, curtains drawn. Maybe everyone's taking advantage of the last day before school holidays. The last day before staycationers swarm every tourist attraction.

'You received our firm's payment, right?' Jensen asks before I leave her car.

'I did.' A ten thousand dollar deposit. Far more than I'd been expecting. Enough to afford the overseas PI that Carina is going to arrange for me. 'Was the amount a mistake?'

'It isn't.' She reaches over, squeezes my free hand. 'Thanks for all your help so far. It's making us aware of the angles we need to work through.'

I slide my hand away, almost ask whether the money will put Joseph in debt if he's ever released. I'm sure my fee is a small fraction of what they're charging him. Maybe it's another pressure that tipped Joseph over the edge. Teachers are paid on a scale, increasing with each year they're in the game. A long-standing teacher like Joseph would earn just over a hundred thousand per year. He doesn't have family to provide for, has owned the Karrinyup house for so long I'm sure the mortgage remains minimal. Still, would there be enough salary left over for weeks or months or years of legal fees?

I should feel guilty taking so much, but a pay day is a pay day. I've just started as a PI—who knows when my next case will be, especially if this one doesn't go the way we hope. It's enough to keep me going for several months. With something left over to take Lucy for a dinner I'm always owing her. Somewhere nice; a fancy restaurant she deserves to visit.

'I'll see if I can convince my boss to give you more for finding the boys,' Jensen says, interrupting my thoughts.

'Sure,' I say. As if I'm going to argue. Getting paid more for something I was already going to do? It's an easy decision. 'Although the police will be all over it.'

'You might find a different angle, though?'

'I'll see what I can do.'

I exit the vehicle, open the front door to my house, wave goodbye. Enter a silent cave. I call out anyway, get nothing back. All the lights are out, curtains closed. I turn on the air con, remove the humidity. Make that coffee I promised myself. Then sit at my desk and devote some brain cells to catching up with the case. Wondering when the hell everything went south.

Joseph's under crisis care. Two teenagers are missing. A teacher, too, maybe her housemate, perhaps threatened by a gambling operation. All connected in a way I don't quite understand. All too much for me to handle.

I need Lucy here. She helps me through doubt, gives me ideas when I struggle to visualise any connections. But she's spending her last day as a full-time classroom teacher. Next year, she'll only be in the classroom a couple of days a week, the rest in a leadership role. I can't ruin her memories with my insecurities. Ten thousand dollars worth of insecurities.

I grab my phone, call Gary. I know he said he'd be back in another day or two, but I need to pick his brain now. He might have a contact in the police department who can help me. Except Gary doesn't answer. I leave a message, ask him to call me back as soon as possible. I make another coffee, sit back at my desk, look at the paperwork from Joseph's house I'd sorted into piles, marked work pointing to Blake Hallid as the sender of the secret notes.

Blake's work is on the top of one pile. I grab it again, examine the written answers. Grab the notes and compare again. The writing is so similar but… there's something about it that bugs me. It's similar, but not identical. Between each sample, the weird print-cursive hybrid doesn't have the same loops and joins on the same letters.

My phone rings, dragging me from my confusion. Gary. He didn't take long.

'You busy?' I ask.

'Helping Paige plan a new training program. Unofficially, of course. You rang? You got something on Lillian?'

'No. It's the case I'm working on.' I go through everything, answer the occasional question. Express my doubt at my current level of abilities, my fear that Joseph will rot in prison because I missed an obvious lead.

'Well, you think you're handling it on your own,' Gary replies, 'but you're not the only one on the case. I'm sure there's an entire unit on it. Detectives, forensics. You know all this, though, you're just not able to see it happening. Plus, this Jensen and her legal firm, they should've found out more than they have. They're just using you to do their dirty work.'

'They're paying me well to do it.'

'As long as the pay doesn't come with a caveat. Like, you don't *have* to prove the teacher innocent, right?'

'I believe he's innocent.'

'Why? Cause he was your mentor?'

'Yeah. Hey, you believed in me because we went to high school together.'

'But you also had an impressive record from your brief stint on the force. What was Joseph like as your mentor?'

'Lazy. Unorganised. I never thought he'd still be teaching, to be honest.'

'And what is he like now?'

'From what everyone's told me, far more professional. Far more dedicated to his job *and* always sticking up for the other teachers.'

'You think it's all an image, or that he's changed?'

'I'd like to think he got older, matured.'

'I see. Let me have a think about this, okay? You want to meet up tomorrow?'

'I'll be around.'

We say our goodbyes and I'm left to ponder his last question about Joseph. One I'd already asked myself. Has my mentor changed? That long into a teaching career, you can't survive being as nonchalant as he was during my prac. Yearly reviews, parental feedback, student accountability... You'd get called out, put on notice. Fired or seconded elsewhere. Especially from the prestigious school he'd ended up at.

Unless the college overlooked things because he was fucking the principal.

No. The teachers were adamant he worked hard to stick up for them. The students loved him, too. So, Joseph had evolved as a teacher. Gave everything to the job.

And now he's in prison for it.

I have to focus on that aspect. Joseph is about to lose it all for something we can't disprove.

I take that heavy thought to the couch, ready to lie down for a moment, to rest my weary eyes; a week of early morning starts taking their toll.

I wake around noon, several pings on my phone begging for attention. I lift my head off the couch, check my surroundings. Everything's still dark. Silent, bar the phone. I swing myself upright, stretch, check the screen. It's Jensen, sending me two newsfeeds.

I click on the first link. A report on Joseph's attempted suicide, media already taking it as another sign of his guilt. Non-biased journalism at its best in Perth. The kicker is, the report ends with a statement about how people who need mental support can reach the relevant authorities. As long as you're not an accused murderer, I guess.

The other newsfeed is on the two teenagers who've run away, their extended absence leading to the appeal from Maria Bortoni, their faces plastered at the top of the report. The report itself focuses on the general concern for the boys' welfare; no opinionated statements linking their disappearance to a possible part in the murder.

I reply to Jensen's messages, let her know I've read them. Then I listen to my growling stomach, make myself some brunch. A toastie, molten cheese defying the heat outside.

By the time I've eaten, freshened myself, hopped in my car and made my way to Julian Bortoni's South Perth apartment, it's just gone two in the afternoon. I think about Lucy, counting down her last hour. Hopefully, the parent group and students have organised a nice gift for her.

The car in front of me pulls into the same apartment complex I'm headed for. I follow, but they jag the last spot. I swing the car around, cross over into the car park of the adjacent zoo. No spots here, either, one of Perth's premier tourist destinations a very busy place. I find a free space on a grassed verge a block down from the zoo. By the time I walk to Julian's apartment, it's two-thirty. I've slept half the day and the rest of it is draining fast.

At least I don't have to wait at the entrance door to get buzzed in. Someone's propped it open with a milk crate. I head up, knock on Julian's door, announce my visit. There's no answer, though. I just assumed the man would be in. He could be working or searching for his son or maybe he's at the pub down the road?

I try the door handle. It clicks with a little push, the door creaking open.

'Julian?'

I edge my way into the apartment. The silence that invaded my house feels worse here. There's so much life outside, a bustling city going about its business, but in here there's a void. I resist the urge to shout out again, as if any interruption will make things worse. I work my way to the lounge room, sunlight streaming through clear glass windows. Pause. Take in the scene before me. A white leather sofa stained red with blood.

CHAPTER TWENTY-THREE
AN ELABORATE SERIES OF HAND SLAPS

There's not as much blood as my brain exaggerated, but still… it's a sprawling patch right at chest height, the width of a tennis ball. There's no body, but it's hard to imagine someone skipped away from this.

I need to leave. Call the police. But I should check the apartment first, see if Julian's somewhere else. He could have made his way to the bathroom, trying to staunch his wound. *If* it's his blood. I find his bedroom first, though. Nothing on the bed, the floor, the cupboard. The bathroom is an attached ensuite. Nothing there, either. No trails of blood leading from the couch, nothing to give me a clue. Images of Leonie Haynes flash through my mind; the moment I stumbled upon her in The Bear's arms, bleeding out from the knife wound Duke inflicted. A gaping wound I had to seal. Do I have it in me if I have to do something like that again?

Too much time has elapsed. If there was a commotion before I arrived; a tenant may have already phoned emergency services. If

I want to clear my involvement in this, I can't have someone see me here. I head back to the entrance. Pause at the lounge room. There's so little in the area, it's hard to tell if anything's out of place. Over at the open kitchen, there's a large canvas bag on the bench. Some food shopping? I hurry over, unable to resist a peek.

The bag is bulging, stacked to its limits. Fingerprints be damned, I rifle through the contents. It contains a loaf of bread on top. Below that, chips, soft drink and energy drinks, biscuits and instant coffee. Frozen pizzas and hot pockets thawing beside them. Instant noodles and Mac and Cheese packets deeper down. A six-pack of eggs on its side. Two rolls of toilet paper holding the weight of everything above.

This doesn't seem like the shopping of a man of around fifty. Maybe a divorced, mid-life crisis-suffering male, but it's still a stretch. This seems like food that younger people would eat. Was Julian buying it for his son and friend?

I leave the shopping, exit the apartment just as the lift dings. I sprint to the next apartment door in the carpeted corridor. Hold my hand on the handle, pretend to be closing it. Two officers walk out of the lift. I turn and pretend to be shocked. I ask if everything's okay, but one of them holds a finger to his lips, motions to Julian's door.

'You going down?' his partner asks.

He says it as a question, not a threat. I nod and he gestures to the lift.

'You hear any yelling from inside?' the other asks.

I shake my head. Get into the lift. Hold my breath until the doors slide shut, wait for them to call out, ask for my details in case they need to follow up on things. But they don't know what awaits in Julian's apartment, and I guess they figure they can knock next-door at a later point. I shrink back against the lift's wall and sigh so heavily I almost start sobbing. When the doors open again on the ground floor, I can't hurry out fast enough. They've parked the police car where the orangey-gold Ford once lurked. I walk out the driveway, cross the road, take the footpath through Perth Zoo's front area in a line for my car. Try not to think of all the cameras in and around the building, the ways someone could tie me to Julian's disappearance. The time it will take before those officers knock at my door.

I near a small crowd outside the zoo's entrance. Most are teenagers, their uniforms walking adverts for their schools. The school year finished early for them, the first minutes of freedom spent outside a tourist spot. I watch as two teens approach a seated counterpart, all three already out of their uniform. There's a bit of nervous glancing, the teens checking their surroundings, then one of them reaches out, hands the seated one a folded note. Money. A fucking drug deal right outside this busy place? No. Unless I missed some sleight of hand, the seated teen has palmed nothing back. It's a one-sided transaction.

The teens all give each other an elaborate series of hand slaps and dabs, then the two turn and leave the seated one alone. Allowing me to get a better look at his face.

A face I've committed to memory, since it's related to my case. And has been all over this morning's newsfeed.

Bailey Hallid glances at his phone, looks around yet avoids eye contact with me. He shrugs, dismissing a thought, stands. Puts a baseball cap on, tilting it to shade his eyes, hurries off. Veers to a bus stop, holds out a hand. There's a bus down the road; has Bailey memorised the timetable, or was that just luck?

I've got a choice to make, seconds to make it. Head back to my car, return to my case, let Jensen know about Julian and follow up things through legal channels? Or hop on the same bus as Bailey, find out where he goes, see if he joins the Bortoni kid somewhere, if they learn about his father's fate or even meet up with him?

Who am I kidding? Bailey Hallid *is* part of my case, and I'd be an absolute idiot to let him get away. Especially when the police and media are on the lookout for him.

I hurry to the bus stop just as the long green vehicle squeaks to a halt.

We don't go far. I look up the bus route, see that it rounds past Isidore College, wonder if that's where we're headed. But no more than three minutes later, Bailey presses the button to stop the bus. It hisses to a halt. He takes the front exit. I wait, see him hurry down the street, then jump off via the middle doorway. Bailey is already a good thirty metres ahead. He rounds a corner, disappears. Does he know I'm following him?

I pick up the pace. Round the corner to see Bailey jogging ahead. He reaches another corner, turns.

He knows he's being followed.

Fuck it. I take off, try to shorten the gap between us. But my legs are not as youthful as his and I've been running so fucking much lately around Margaret River and my body won't coordinate. My sprint becomes a jog becomes a hobble. I pass a row of tall apartment buildings all new to the area. Beside the apartments are two tiny houses. Single storey, remnants of an early-nineties era. Bailey hasn't entered any of these, he rounded the corner just past the smaller house. I take the same path. The Freeway sounds close, the roadway noise a constant *whoosh whoosh whoosh*.

On the next lot, backed against the old house, there's a new building. Three storeys tall, one half a stretch of ten-foot-high window frames, the other half still covered with scaffolding. The window frames seem absent of glass panels, covered with blue sheeting. There's a skip bin near the front door, full of rubble. A new building still under construction; almost completed. No real estate or developer sign, though. Maybe a private renovation?

Bailey could have run past this building, too. Down the street, rounding another corner, heading back to the bus stop. But instinct tells me he's gone inside this house. It has a wrought-iron fence along its front border, a matching gate chained shut; but open just enough for a thinner body to squeeze through.

I wait a minute. Listen for something other than the whoosh of cars.

There. The bang of a door, deep within the house.

So, what do I do now? Barge my way in there, demanding Bailey talk to me? Call the police, let them know I've found one of the missing kids on the news? Maybe even both teens, if Jeremy Bortoni is waiting inside; a few blocks down from where something's happened to his own father.

No. In both scenarios, Bailey will retreat. Hide elsewhere, put himself in danger. If he's hiding in this fancy house, he's not exactly slumming it, although there might not be any electricity. Another kid just gave him money, which he might use to buy food. Resourceful shit to look after himself. Not to buy drugs and alcohol and throw a party in someone's dream home.

I snap a photo of the house then type another bullet point in the Notes app, remind myself to look up the owner of the property.

Then I keep walking, already having lingered for too long. I round the block, glance back, fail to see anyone looking for me. I keep going. I'll catch the bus, find my car, drive to the one person who has the power to say what we should do with Bailey's sighting.

Lucy would tell me this is a stupid decision, that I should call the police, wait outside the front gate, make sure Bailey doesn't leave. But she'll be out late, the first round of nights celebrating the end of the teaching year. So, she can't be the voice of reason, for now. And I'm supposed to meet Desmond tonight, at the casino, but it's far too early for that.

With time to kill, it's time to try Robyn Hallid again. Hopefully, her home is no longer swarmed with reporters.

CHAPTER TWENTY-FOUR
DEVIOUS BASTARD

School's out means peak hour has already started; especially given it's the last day, more children needing a lift with their heavy bags. Which means I sit in traffic for around fifty minutes instead of fifteen. Trying not to stew over the parking ticket I just received, for being half an hour over my paid limit.

I try to focus on the positives, such as the almost-empty driveway at the Hallids. There's only one van near its entrance. I park down the road, wait to see if the reporters react to my appearance. While I sit there, I check my messages. There's an email from Carina, the details of a PI she still keeps in contact with. I compose my own email with the thoughts I've surmised regarding Lillian's whereabouts. I want the PI to check a location for me. If Lillian appears there, I need the PI to follow at a distance, record her home address. I offer extra money if they can do it before the end of the week.

I exit my vehicle, approach the house, walk past the van. A reporter I gave a tip to last time leans out the window, sees me and retreats inside. I smile, reach Robyn's door and knock. She opens it herself this time, no kids hanging off her. Doesn't remember me for a moment, then mirrors my smile, invites me inside.

'Any luck with your case, Mister Herbert?' She heads to the kitchen to grab some drinks, pulls out two beers.

'Not too much,' I answer, waving off the beer. Best not to drink in front of a grieving mother; although, what are wakes for?

She hands over a bottle, anyway. 'What brings you back here, then? Is it Bailey?'

Her voice carries so much hope, I can't drag this out. 'I've seen him.'

She grips the table with her free hand. 'Where?'

I give her the address, show her the photo I took of the building.

'Are the police talking to him now?'

'I didn't call them.'

'You didn't…' Now Robyn's grip tightens on the beer bottle. '*Why* wouldn't you call the police?'

Lucy's voice echoes with her question. How do I articulate my selfish decision? Because I exposed corrupt cops in what looked like a well-run unit? Because my father's family is a bunch of murderers and manipulators and the police will now be itching to prove I'm the same? They'll say I had something to do with my mentor teacher's actions, Julian's disappearance, two runaway teens; connections made on loose threads.

'I wanted you to make that call,' I say, the first reason I drove here. 'Or go visit him yourself.'

Robyn shakes her head, reaches out and grabs her phone from the kitchen bench. 'Wait here.'

She retreats down a passageway, out of sight.

It's not long before footsteps patter back, only they belong to someone much smaller. A boy the spitting image of Bailey. Same facial features, same hair. Only, half the size; a lot smaller than I'd peg for someone in Year Five. A boy due for a growth spurt.

'You must be Blake,' I say.

Blake gives me the scowl his mother was working towards.

'I'm a Private Investigator,' I add. 'I've found your brother.'

'Good for you,' Blake says. He walks past me to the fridge, opens the door. 'Probably didn't want to be found, though.'

I place my beer bottle on the kitchen counter. 'Why not?'

Blake hides behind the fridge door. Doesn't respond.

'Is it to do with the notes he left at Mister Pooles' classroom?'

Blake peers around the door.

'I know about the notes,' I say.

Blake closes the door. 'You're not a good Private Investigator.'

I take the bait. 'Why not?'

But he doesn't answer me. We stand in silence for ten, twenty, thirty seconds. Then there's another set of padding footsteps and Robyn Hallid returns to the room.

'They're sending some officers to the house.' She points her phone at Blake. 'Everything okay?'

Blake nods, but his face is red, his body shaking.

Robyn turns to me. 'What did you do?'

'I asked him about the notes.'

'What notes?' She turns to Blake. 'What notes?'

When he doesn't answer, I tell Robyn about the notes left under Joseph's classroom door. 'I think Bailey knew a secret about Mister Pooles. It's why he's hiding now.'

Blake gives a slight shake of the head.

'If I knew what the secret is, maybe I'd have a better idea of what was going on in Mister Pooles' head. Why things happened the way they did.'

Blake stares at the floor.

Robyn catches the avoidance. 'You know about the notes?'

He tenses.

'Blakey?'

Blake lets out a deep breath, his body loosening. Then he pushes past his mother, sprints through the room, retreats down the passageway. A few seconds later, there's the telltale slam of a bedroom door.

Robyn stares at me, dumbfounded, then takes off after her son. Leaving me alone.

I give it a minute, don't hear any shouting. I text Lucy, congratulate her on another year done and dusted. Look at the time, wonder whether I should go home first and catch her before heading to the casino. Lucy replies, says that her and three other teachers are already taking the train into the city, the celebrations starting early. No point in going home, then.

I should have a quick peek around the house, work out what I'm looking for. I wander through the kitchen into an adjoining dining area. Paperwork and photographs cover the surface of the dining table. Most images are of Heath, posed with various people. Robyn must be getting a montage ready for the funeral. I hope she doesn't discover any torn photographs like I did, after

Uncle Graham passed. She's got enough on her plate without revelations of an affair, even if the couple were separated.

I could look at the paperwork, or snap images of it with my phone. See if there's anything untoward going on—debts she or Heath owed, another relationship *she* was covering up, restraining orders or other summons for things I'm yet to hear about.

I can't, though. Maybe when I'm years-deep into this new profession, I'll be hardened enough to snap away. I can't be that invasive now, though.

There's another slam of a door, deep in the house. Blake in defiance as his mum leaves the room? Or Reilly Hallid, who answered the door last time? He's exceptionally quiet for a seven or eight-year-old boy. Maybe he's out the back, running around, lost in his own imaginary world; avoiding the drama unfolding inside.

Along one wall, beyond the dining table, is a thin writing desk covered with plastic In trays; each labelled with the name of the three boys. Inside the trays are stacks of paper, plus a few books. Blake's stack is tiny, Bailey's is threatening to spill to the floor. It must be Robyn's attempt to home school them, to stick to some sort of routine to end the term. Honestly, I'm amazed she didn't just throw the television on and declare an early start to the holidays.

Robyn enters the room with a reddened face. 'I apologise.'

'No need to.'

'But I have something. It's amazing what the threat of no video games does.'

Television, video games. It had to be one of the two. 'What did he say?' I ask, trying to mask the excitement.

She holds out a metal tin. It has cartoon creatures all over it, a glossy shine on them.

I recognise the creatures, part of pop culture for the past twenty-plus years. 'Pokémon?'

She nods. 'His father bribed him. Devious bastard.'

'Bribed him, how?'

'His father wrote the notes. Paid Blakey in Pokémon cards to slip them under his teacher's door in the mornings, when they were there early for swim meets.'

'Heath wrote the notes?'

As Robyn nods again, I struggle to voice another question. Heath Hallid was more connected to Joseph than anyone thought. He knew something about Joseph, was threatening to expose the secret. And now he's dead.

'Did… Did Blake know what they meant?'

'He didn't even read them. Or so he says.'

'Thank you,' I croak out. 'Can you keep this between us for now? Until I figure out what's going on?'

I stand, make my way to the front door.

'I'm sorry,' I say at the threshold, 'for failing to call the police, when…'

Robyn touches my arm. 'Don't. I understand your intentions.'

I almost tell her that if things go south, and Bailey runs from the police, she can call me to keep looking. But why put that thought into her head?

'Take care,' I offer instead.

I leave her house, make my way to the car. I was ready to head to the casino, but now I'm wondering whether it's worth pursuing that lead. I'd fallen for the narrative that there may be a gambling group hiring people to hurt everyone connected at a school, but maybe that's just a cover someone wanted me to fall for. So, I'd give doubt to the case and help make a murderous teacher look innocent.

CHAPTER TWENTY-FIVE
DON'T FOLLOW

If I go home to change or shower or eat, I might get stuck helping Sarah with the kids or entertaining my in-laws. Which has been fine most days, but right now I'm in the wrong headspace. So, I drive straight to the casino. Even if the night's a dead end, it will close off a lead from the case. Professionalism, and all that.

I sit in the casino car park, glance at the time. I'm about two hours too early. I message Desmond, tell him I'm already here. Maybe we can get this over with before dinner?

I think about the last time I was in this very car park. Sent to find the man I'm working with tonight. Back then, we didn't know the extent of his addiction. I'd found him at the gambling tables, in his wheelchair—a message to his body from the debt collectors, disguised as a work injury—but hadn't reached him in time. Two large men had swooped in on him, taken him for a ride back up to his hotel room, where a pay-off was waiting. Only, Desmond had recovered from his injury and he'd surprised the men, knocking them out. I wonder how much Viktor remembers from that night, and how he'll react when he sees us.

I should have taken some martial arts lessons by now. Sure, I've been hitting the gym more, but building muscle is different to the combat skills and stamina I've been lacking.

My phone rings. I assume it's Desmond arranging a meeting spot, answer it without looking. Swear as I hear the voice on the other end.

'Is that really you, Henry?'

My mother.

'You know it is, you called me,' I say, looking out at the car park, wishing for a passing stranger to hand my phone to.

'I'm so glad I caught you.'

'I have an important meeting in a minute.'

'But I have to talk to you about—'

'I've gotta go.'

'Henry, please. Don't be like this.'

'Don't be like…' I scrunch my eyes tight, bite back the words that want to escape. 'I'll call you later.'

'But I have an appointment tomorrow. I need you there with me.'

An appointment? Probably with her lawyer, to discuss her involvement in upcoming trials. Maybe she wants me to speak on her behalf, be a character witness? As if I'd say nice things about the woman who'd instigated the death of Charlotte Harris, Lillian's mother, and refused to check what happened to the pregnant woman's child, ignoring Lillian's existence.

'Have a good appointment,' I say, hanging up before my mother can get another word in.

My phone rings as I'm climbing out the car. I ignore it, follow a group of twentysomethings through a pedestrian tunnel, up an escalator, emerging at one of the casino's entrances. I turn right, head to the older hotel. To the bar. Because now I need to pass the time with a drink.

I take a seat on one of the armchairs near a long stretch of windows, watch as two parking attendants play paper-scissors-rock to decide who gets to take a bright yellow Lamborghini.

'Drink, sir?'

A member of staff zeroed in on me as I sat down. I haven't even looked at a menu yet.

'Coffee,' I say, forcing a smile. 'No. Espresso martini, please.'

'Won't be long.'

There's a cheer outside that gains my attention. I watch as one of the attendants snatches keys from the other, skipping towards the expensive car. I turn back to order picks—bar nuts or olives or something—but I'm alone again.

My phone pings. I ignore it a moment, then remember I'd texted Desmond to tell him I'm early.

He's responded with: *Heading your way now.*

My phone pings again. This time it's Lucy. She's taken a photo of a garden gnome next to a tall glass of cider. Apparently, the teachers are going to take the gnome to every location, documenting its imaginary inebriation. I text her back with a *Have lots of fun* message, wonder how hungover she's going to be for her day of professional development. At least everyone will be in the same boat.

The person who served me returns, places my drink on a coaster and departs before I can ask for those picks. Ah well, at least I can join Lucy in spirit now. I down the martini a little too quickly, let the taste linger on my tongue,.

Shrill laughter slices through the ambience, drawing my attention. I turn to see a rake-thin woman hanging off a large man, playfully slapping his arm before bursting into laughter again. The guy doesn't look as jovial, lost in his own thoughts. He's at least twice her age. Which would disgust me if his face didn't draw my focus; make me search my memories.

Viktor. The man I'm supposed to find with Desmond.

As they pass by, I leave some cash for the drink, get up, start following. Pretend I'm lost in my phone, which I sort of am, since I've started stabbing a text to Desmond, telling him the guy's right here in front of me. I keep following, waiting for Desmond's response. The couple's heading for a lift. If it's like the one in the more expensive hotel, which branches off another section of the casino, then you need a card to access the floors above. I swap my phone for my wallet, get out a black loyalty card from a liquor store that looks similar enough to the hotel card I last used. I keep that out and get my phone back just as it pings.

Don't follow

Too late, Desmond. Viktor's dropped the serious demeanour, laughing along with the woman now. Sharing a joke, as if they've known each other for years. I can't imagine someone being with a guy like this, though. Surely she's someone he's paying for by the hour?

The woman pushes the button for the lift. I catch up, wait behind them. The man glances back at me and I flicker a smile; trying to hide my nerves. He looks back at the woman as if I don't register on his radar, which is comforting, for now. He doesn't recognise me from last time.

We get in the lift together. I let the woman press the button for her floor first as I head to the corner of the tiny box, looking through its glass panels to the wall beyond.

'What floor, mate?' the guy says.

'Huh?' I say, turning around, pretending to be in a daze. Which is great for hiding my nerves. 'Oh, fifth floor, too.'

I turn back and stare out the glass as the lift rises, the wall disappearing and the hotel lobby coming into view. Everyone becomes ants as we reach the fifth floor. The lift pings and I hear the man and woman get out. I turn to see him pinch her bottom. She giggles, the sound forced. I try to keep up the smiling act as I exit and follow, allowing a few metres between us. They stop about five doors down and the man swipes them inside. I pick up my pace. They step into their hotel room. The door starts swinging shut. I'm not thinking about what I'm doing, just acting on impulse. I sprint to close the gap, reach out for dear life and touch the door just before it clicks closed. I hold it open a fraction of a millimetre, trying to work out my next move. Let it close, or burst inside?

I can hear the man telling the woman to get on the bed; things moving fast between them. If I wait a minute or two, I can spring into the room and literally catch him with his pants down.

There's a ping from the phone in my free hand. I stare at the screen.

Stuck in traffic wait in lobby don't follow

I look up. Did someone hear that ping? They're going to open the door any second. I just need to back away and—

No. I make myself wait, my hand resting on the door.

Ten seconds. Twenty seconds. A minute? Two?

Nobody opens it.

I text Desmond the room number, push its door open an inch. Listen for approaching footsteps. I can hear a soft grunt, nothing more.

I can do this.

I can rush inside, take the man by surprise, knock him out. Tie him up and get some answers. Desmond bashed him and a mate last time we were at the casino. He had the element of surprise, too, since they thought his legs weren't working, and he had a giant vase. I don't have a vase, but I could grab something as I burst inside. Viktor may be huge, but I *can* take him on. I've bested giants like him before.

I can do this.

I push the door open, step inside the room. Stare at the scene before me and immediately want to retreat.

I've caught the man with his pants down, all right. But not in the way I expected. I take one more step into the room, see more of the bed. The woman's lying on it, dressed in nothing but black lingerie. She's on her side, reading a magazine. Disinterested in the man at the foot of the bed. Who's standing there looking at her. Pants down. Grunting. Trying to masturbate his half-erect penis. Really putting some effort into it. Looking like he's losing the struggle.

The woman flicks a page of the magazine, looks up and registers my presence. Shudders a little, trying not to appear too alarmed. The man catches the expression, though, turns and sees me.

'What the fuck!'

He whirls round, one hand shaking in the air, the other still grasping his penis. His pants twist around his ankles, snap tight and send him twirling to the ground. His head smacks against a wooden desk and he drops with a thud that's far from comical. He's out, pants still down, everything on show.

The woman starts to scream; stops herself.

I gesture to the door behind me. 'You don't need to be here.'

She nods, hurries over to a chair with her clothes on it, throws everything back on. I could ask her name, how she knows the man, if she's going to tell anyone about my visit. But I can tell from the look on her face that she doesn't want any part of what's about to happen next. So, I let her leave the room without asking her to make sense of what I just saw.

The door clicks behind me. I'm alone with a guy with his pants down. If only Lucy could see me now. I search the hotel room, trying to find something to tie him up. I settle for the bedsheets. I rip them off the mattress, then bring the room's sole chair to the man and lift him up from behind. Work his body onto the chair, roll up the sheets and wrap them around him. As I get near his arms, I catch the edge of a tattoo peeking out his left shirtsleeve. It's of a deck of cards. Branding 101? I keep wrapping, tighten the sheets around his chest so he doesn't slump forward; then tie it all up in the best knot I can manage. Then I step round the chair and inspect my work. It's crude, but it might contain him. Or not, since he's going to be pissed when he wakes, full of an embarrassed rage and ready to take me out.

I message Desmond again: *Had to handle things. Hurry.*

Since the man's pants are near the ground, I reach out and feel around in their pockets. From the left side, I take out a lighter, a switchblade, and a wallet. I pocket the lighter and switchblade, open the wallet and look inside.

'You don't look like a Silas Raymond. I thought you were Viktor.' I'm sure Carina had pointed to his image, said he was Viktor. Must have mixed up the names.

There's a stack of cash inside the wallet. Over five hundred dollars. I remove it, fold it and slide it into my pocket. Something I got from one of Lucy's favourite book series.

'No more hookers today, buddy.'

I feel around in the right pocket. There's a mobile phone and some balled-up tissues. I get out the phone, remind myself to wash my hands soon. The phone needs a thumb print to unlock it, so I use what I remember being Silas's free hand. Thankfully, the Home Screen appears. I go into the phone's settings, try changing things to a new password, but I need the old password to do that. I go into the Messages section before the phone locks itself, but there are only three there. One to the woman he was just with, confirming a time to meet up. One to someone who's either his brother or a mate he calls bro, telling him to go buy three cases of Crown for the weekend. Classy. I use my phone to photograph the number, just in case. The third message is to a number that hasn't had a name assigned to it. The message reads: *Where the fuck are you?*

I photograph that number, too. Then sit on the bed and wait for Silas to wake up.

He stirs after another minute. He's been out a while, everything's going to hurt.

'Fuck, my head,' he groans.

He tries to move, rocking against the chair.

'The fuck, bro?'

He looks around, sees me, figures out what's going on.

'You don't want to be doing this,' he says, his slurred voice less threatening than the words.

'Julian Bortoni,' I say, standing up.

'You're fucked, Julian.'

'No. Julian's the man whose apartment you went into today. Opposite the zoo. Ring any bells?'

Silas squirms against the sheets, trying to get something loose. When he realises I've tied them tighter than he expected, he looks back at me, shakes his head. 'You want to get yourself killed for that, *perdant*?'

'Perdant?'

'Loser. Are you a loser, too?'

'I'm not the one tied up. After I couldn't even get it up.'

Silas's face balloons into a fiery ball. '*Putain de bâtard!*' He rocks back and forth on the chair, dangerously close to tipping over. I can see the sheets loosening a little. If he can force his arms up and out, I'm in trouble.

'Stop!' I stomp down on his legs, halting the rocking, then take a deep breath, trying to remove the shakiness from my voice. 'What did you do to Julian?'

'He owed money,' Silas confesses. 'We were paid to collect.'

'You shot him?'

Silas shakes his head. 'No. He shot my partner, Viktor. Then he took the money he owed us and ran.'

CHAPTER TWENTY-SIX
TU ES TOTALEMENT INCONSCIENTE

Not for the first time, I wonder what the job title *Wealth Management Services* entails. For Julian to have a gun, to be able to shoot an imposing intruder, to make off with money he owed… well, it probably doesn't just involve buying and selling shares.

'Is your friend alive?' I ask Silas.

'He'll be fine.'

'Where was he shot?'

'Right shoulder.'

So, not his chest. Maybe he'll live, after all. 'What did Julian owe money for?'

Silas shakes his head. 'Who are you, anyway?'

'Someone asked to investigate.'

'Federal?'

'An outsider.'

'I'm still not telling you shit.'

I look around the room. There's a mini-bar fridge full of mini bottles, a television bolted to the wall, a framed print of the Swan River looking less algae-filled than usual. And an alarm clock on a bedside table. Not too much to use if Silas breaks free from his binding. Which he's trying to do right now.

I message Desmond again. Wait.

Parking

Okay. Just me and Silas for a few more minutes. That's better than I thought. I walk over to the fridge, grab two tiny bottles of wine.

'We celebrating?' Silas asks.

'You've already given your head a good knock. I figure a tap from one of these is all I need to put you back to sleep.'

He stops wriggling. Stares at me with genuine concern. 'Look, I'm a debt collector. A third party paid me to collect a debt. I went to Julian's apartment with my partner, it went south. That's it. Nothing involving you.'

'You said you were going to kill me.'

'I was angry. You interrupted my time with Sandy, then tied me up.' He glances to the ground. 'Can I at least pull up my pants?'

I grab a pillow from the bed, lay it on his lap. 'There.'

'You're making me angry again.'

I hold a wine bottle high. 'Don't be.'

He sighs, mutters what I guess is a curse in his native language. Which I think is French, even though I'd assumed the duo were Italian or Croatian or some other slice of Europe I should know more about.

'Where do you think Julian ran off to?' I ask.

'Not my problem. I was paid for the collection. They can pay more for the hunt.'

I wave my hand at the room. 'In no hurry to find him, then?'

'Today was stressful; I was due some personal leave.'

A debt collector stressed after a collection gone wrong. Hilarious.

'How much money did Julian take off with?' I try.

'Forty K.'

'That's a lot.'

'You'd think so, but money never lasts.'

'And then he'll owe more?'

'Not my decision. Because of his actions today, there may be no money the man can pay.'

'He'll pay with his life, you mean?'

Silas nods.

'If the third party decides to go that way?'

'Correct.'

'The name Heath Hallid ring a bell to you?'

Silas considers it a moment. 'Perhaps.'

'Did he owe money, too?'

'Are you here for Julian or Heath?'

'I'm here for someone else,' I say, thinking of multiple people entrapped by King of Spades.

'Someone else?'

'Whose life may have been effected by those men.'

'How?'

'It's why I'm here.'

Silas squints at me a little, then leans back in his seat, chuckling. '*Tu es totalement inconsciente.* You have stepped into something you have no grasp on.'

There's a light knock at the door.

'If that's room service,' Silas says, 'ask for another pillow.'

I back my way to the door, eyes still on Silas. 'Hello?'

'It's me.'

I turn, open the door a fraction.

Desmond flutters a smile. 'Miss me?'

'Thank God. You—'

My body is wrenched backwards. I fall hard against the carpet. Look up at Silas. He's standing there sans pants, pillow in hand. He brings the pillow down against my face, pushes hard. I struggle beneath him, the air smothered from my lungs. I can't see anything, my world shrouded by goose down. I try to strike out, swing my arms against something, but the pressure isn't relieved. I can't gasp any more air. I don't have long. Killed by a half-naked man using a pillow? Fuck that. I kick up, buck my body. Try to twist it. But Silas has a vice-like grip on me, my upper half stuck to the carpet. Where the hell is Desmond? Why isn't he—

The pressure eases against my face, the pillow dropping off; relief as air rushes into my lungs. I gasp, sputter, choke on the sensation.

'You good?'

I look up to see Desmond standing over me, a cord dangling from his hand.

'Is that…' I struggle to voice '…a clock?'

'Had to grab something. Guy didn't even notice me, he was hellbent on hurting you.'

'That's… great.'

Desmond offers a hand, pulls me up. I turn to see Silas spread-eagled on the carpet. Out cold.

'At least, I hope he didn't notice me,' Desmond says. 'I don't want him to remember my face.'

Shit. Silas is going to remember my face. He could choose to let this go, or use what he remembers to track me down and finish the suffocation.

'We have to go,' I say, looking round, making sure I've left nothing of mine in the room.

I get the wine bottles, rub them against the remaining bedsheet, trying to erase any hint of my existence. There would be so many prints on the mini-bar fridge it wouldn't matter, so I leave that. I go into the bathroom, grab a small face towel. Wet it, rub the tap, then bring it over to the door and wipe down the areas I might have touched.

'You done there, Sherlock?'

I pretend to wipe Desmond with the towel. 'I was never here.'

We head to the lift. Thankfully, you don't need a card to get down. It pings open for us and we hurry in.

'You think he's coming?' I ask.

'He's not going to remember where he is when he wakes,' Desmond says. 'I hit him pretty hard.'

'We've got to stop hitting people in the head.'

'Where else would you hit them?'

The lift carries us downward.

'You want to tell me why his pants were down?' Desmond asks.

'No.'

'Did you at least get what you needed?'

'Sort of. But not really.'

'I could have helped if you'd have waited.'

'I kind of had to act then and there. Besides, you just said you didn't want him to remember you.'

'This wasn't what I had in mind for tonight, though.'

'What did you have in mind?'

The lift lurches to a halt. The doors ping open, revealing the ground floor.

'Never mind,' Desmond says. 'But I know that if you want to be a PI long-term, you can't just go rushing into rooms and taking charge.'

He's right. Being a PI is ninety-nine percent watching, waiting. Taking photos and notes. Presenting said photos and notes to the client.

'Well,' I say, trying not to envisage a life of boredom, 'the good news is, a person I thought is dead is probably still alive.'

'Which means?'

'We've got a teacher missing, a parent from the same school dead, another parent missing, fleeing with money they owed. That'd be one hell of a coincidence if it isn't all related.'

'Does it prove your teacher innocent?'

'I don't know. I *hope* it does. Do you think so?'

Desmond shakes his head. 'Honestly, Henry, what if he's behind the whole thing?'

Desmond's right. Joseph's involvement in this still isn't clear; although it *is* clear that there's more than one lead on this case.

'Then I guess he's ended up where he belongs.'

CHAPTER TWENTY-SEVEN
CHEEKY MALEEKY

After thanking Desmond for his help, and turning down an offer of drinks and dinner, I almost head home. Almost. But I'm halfway down the Freeway and know this case has a time limit and can't in all good conscience end the day without trying to speak to the one person who's eluded my attention so far.

So, I keep driving, and end up outside Maria Bortoni's house. Except, I'm not the only one still wanting a word with her, an entire fleet of news vans camped on its lawn. No doubt they're preparing to ask where Julian has fled to, a man making off with money on par with a murder. I wonder how long it will take the angle of the reporting to change, till the reporters make assumptions, connect the disappearance to the murder. Till I'm asked in for questioning, since I was outside Julian's apartment.

I try not to think about that, drive to the next destination in mind.

Unlike Maria's house, Robyn Hallid's no longer has any vans outside it. Strange, since it was her husband who was killed. I park, head to the house, knock on the front door. It opens a fraction, warm orange light spilling out at me.

'Mister Herbert?'

Robyn looks like she's given up trying to sleep, a new brand of beer bottle in one hand.

'I have one last question for today,' I try.

She opens the door wider. 'Why not. Though the neighbours might start making up stories about you.'

'It wouldn't be the first time.' I gesture to the silent room behind her. 'Is Bailey back now, or…'

'Wasn't where you said, although they found evidence to suggest someone had been staying there.' She taps the door.

'I'm sorry.'

'He'll come home soon.'

'Your other boys are asleep?'

'They've had a long week. And they're heavy sleepers. I could play some booming nineties gangsta rap and they wouldn't stir.' Robyn taps the door again. 'Wish I was the same. Was that it for your questions, or…'

I shake my head. 'You said Heath was an accountant.'

'He was.'

'Well, there are people from your kids' school—teachers, parents—who seem to owe someone money. Gambling, by the look of it.'

'You think he was involved?'

I think about the notes passed to Joseph; perhaps not about an affair at all. 'He may have known what was going on; maybe he was going to blow the lid on it?'

Robyn takes a swig of her beer, stares at me. Trying to look stoic until her eyes betray her, welling with tears.

'P and F,' she whispers.

'What?'

She takes another swig, wipes an eye. 'P and F.'

'Like the school group? Parents and Friends?'

She gives me an awkward smile. 'We thought it was funny, naming it after an official body. A group of parents wanting to extend the social meeting.'

'Which parents?'

'Well, Maria and Julian, even though they were divorcing. Heath and myself. A couple more that've since left the college.'

'And you gambled?'

Robyn chuckles. 'Julian and Heath wanted to. We didn't. It didn't stop them. Until money was owed and the two got in a big fight.'

'Heath owed Julian money?'

'The other way round. It was all paid up, though, things squared. Far as I know, the group stopped then. But if there's gambling involved, maybe someone started it up again? They always talked about making the group bigger. And if Julian's already run off owing more money, I'd say he got a lot more people involved.'

Because he expanded the group to involve teachers. I wonder how many he owed.

'You think they had another falling out between members?'

'You're asking the wrong person,' Robyn says. 'But if Heath found out what they were doing, he would've tried to stop it. Stubborn bastard.'

I picture Heath being excluded from outlets such as Fantasy Basketball, furious when he found out the club he helped start was running without him. Before I can pursue this lead further, a phone rings deep in the house, its shrill tune echoing to us. A landline. The only people who call my house on the landline are telemarketers and—

'That'll be Heath's mum,' Robyn says. 'Or Maria with another update.'

'Heath's mum's helping with the funeral?'

'They're flying in from St Kilda. Other side of the bloody country.' Robyn swigs the last of her beer, winks. 'See you at my doorstep tomorrow, I guess.'

She clicks the door shut, leaving me outside with more questions than I came with.

When I near home, there's a taxi in our driveway. Lucy's getting out of it. Well, stumbling out. Laughing with the other passengers. I let the taxi leave, waving at the inebriated teachers inside, then flash my high beams at Lucy as she tries to find the house keys in her handbag.

'Husband!'

I pull up beside her. As I get out, she launches into me, pins me against the car door.

'Had a good night?' I squeeze out.

'Just what we needed.'

Lucy kisses me. Passionately. Sloppily. And I ruin it by chuckling.

She pulls back. 'What?'

'Nothing. This is nice. But… you're so drunk.'

She reaches down, squeezes my crotch. 'Guess I'm too drunk for a little hanky panky cheeky maleeky, then.'

Shit. 'Let's go inside.'

I unlock and open the door for us. Try to shush Lucy so we don't wake everyone up. The house feels as empty as it did earlier today, which seems like a week ago. Will it feel this empty when everyone goes back to their respective homes?

'Yo, you with me, Henry?' Lucy's waving a hand in front of my face. 'Sure you're not drunk, too?'

'Not me.' I grab Lucy's hand, let her lead us to the bedroom.

She disappears into the bathroom first, starts calling out through the closed door: 'All night the teachers have been trading memes. Teachers killing parents is trending. So, so crazy.'

'Tell me when you get out,' I say. So much for being quiet for everyone. Maybe under the alcohol-haze, Lucy's forgotten our house is now a shared space.

Lucy comes out and we trade places. By the time I've brushed my teeth, I've thought of something to ask Lucy about the memes: whether they're from Joseph's school or all over the place. When I walk out the bathroom, though, Lucy's already wrapped up in the bedsheets. Snoring.

'No hanky panky cheeky maleeky, then,' I whisper.

As if that was ever going to happen.

CHAPTER TWENTY-EIGHT
COMPASSIONATE GROUNDS

Lucy is gone when I wake. I don't know how she managed to get up so early. Some kind of miracle hangover cure she's hiding from the rest of the world? My head throbs as if I'd joined her last night. Maybe it's from a week of disjointed sleep, or lack of essentials in my body. Like water. And food. Did I even eat dinner? My rumbling stomach says no.

I get up, head to the kitchen. Time to make myself a big breakfast. Toast, eggs, avocado, halloumi. Maybe some baked beans. A hash brown or two. Just the thought of it all makes my stomach gurgle away.

There's a note on the kitchen counter. Sarah has taken the kids down to the beach. She'll be back mid-morning. As I get the ingredients out, the rear door slides open. Lucy's father steps inside, sees me, waves.

'Morning, Mister Morais,' I call out.

'Please. Aqil. Dad's good, too.'

I smile. 'Have a good day yesterday?'

'We went to Fremantle for the day,' Aqil replies. 'I feel like I've walked enough for a week. Told Sarah I'd stay home this morning.'

'Everyone else went?'

'Yes. Just me here. Thought I'd give your cricket a try on the tele. See how your locals stack up to the Singaporeans.'

'A nice, slow day.'

Aqil joins me in the kitchen. 'What are we getting ready here? You need help?'

'I'm throwing in a bit of everything. Super hungry.'

'Got enough for two?'

'Sure. If you put the toast in for me.'

We cook up a feast. Lucy's father leans over, observing each dish I'm preparing, adding his own touch to them. Adding coriander and cayenne to the baked beans, a dash of light soy to the eggs. When the hash browns finish baking in the oven, we plate it all up, sit together and devour everything in a quarter of the time it took to make.

'It's good you can cook, too,' Aqil says, wiping some toast into leftover baked bean sauce. 'I always try share with Win.'

'Your wife's a superb cook,' I say, because it's true.

'Yes, but the food is better when we make it together. Like this breakfast.'

I crunch the last shred of hash brown. 'I think you're onto something.'

'Are you home today?' Aqil frowns. 'We haven't seen you much this week. You and my daughter.'

'Last week of school is crazy for her,' I explain. 'But she'll be free from this afternoon. And I think because of that, I've been trying to finish up this case I got. So I can spend time with you all, get ready for our trip together.'

'Are you liking your new job?'

'I'm not sure. I got paid a good chunk of money, but I don't know if it's worth it.'

Before I explain further, there's a knock at the door.

'I'll get that,' I say. I point at our plates as I stand. 'Don't do the dishes. I'll get to them after this.'

'What dishes?' Aqil says, rising with me and grabbing the plates.

I hurry to the door as I hear another knock; grab my phone from my room on the way, pocket it after checking the time. It's nine-thirty. Maybe Lucy or Sarah are getting a package delivered?

I open the door. It's Senior Constable Kirino. She tucks a long black hair beneath her cap, looks lost for where to start.

I help her out. 'Did Gary send you to check up on me? Or to have another talk about The Ridge?'

She shakes her head. 'Still working the Hallid case?'

'Digging up more questions than I can answer. I can't stop yet, though. I—'

She holds out a hand. 'It's not about that. I was trying… small talk. I'm here about your mother.'

I crane my neck to see Paige's vehicle. My mother's not inside. My mind races, tells me one of the main reasons a member of the police will visit a relative. 'What's happened?'

Paige holds out her hands, trying to calm me. 'She had an appointment this morning.'

I remember my mother's phone call. 'With her lawyers, right?'

Paige shakes her head. 'With her doctors. They need to speak with you. I volunteered to bring you in.' When Paige senses my confusion, she adds, 'We'll talk about it on the way.'

I look down at myself. Still in my house clothes. Breath stinking of a buffet breakfast. Not in any condition to see my mother. Which feels perfect. I almost step outside with Senior Constable Kirino, then stop myself. No. I've got a big day ahead, time running out on Joseph's case. I should be prepared. And presentable.

'I'll need twenty minutes,' I say, waving her inside. 'You can help my father-in-law with the dishes.' I think about another mother I've already let down. 'Or you can look up an address for me, find out who owns it.'

Joondalup Hospital has public and private sides, a separate entrance for each. To get to the parking for the public side, or *Health Campus*, you need to queue at a roundabout which filters traffic into a one-lane entrance. Sometimes that queue extends for hundreds of metres down the adjoining road. This is one of those days.

'For goodness' sake,' Paige mutters. 'Even the ambos are stuck waiting.'

She swings her police vehicle around and finds a side entrance to the hospital, where most of the staff park. Jags a spot in the shade of a struggling tree.

'I appreciate the ride,' I say as we enter the private hospital, 'but shouldn't you be at the Police Academy?'

'You want to know why you've got someone escorting you to your mother?'

Despite saying we'd talk about things on the way, Senior Constable Kirino remained silent in the car. So yes, I'd love to know why she showed up at my door and drove me here instead of just calling over the phone.

'Your mum's not well,' she explains.

I gesture around us. 'Really?'

We enter a long corridor connecting the private side to the public.

'It's one reason she's not deemed a flight risk.'

'And why she's not in prison like she should be?'

'The judge delayed her trial on compassionate grounds.'

'My mum tricked a judge?'

Paige whips round, grabs my arm, halts us in the corridor. 'Henry, your mother has been ill for some time. You never noticed she forgets things, repeats others? I've picked it up in our short time together.'

'She's been like that for years.'

Paige loosens her grip, strokes my arm, waits for me to get it.

'For years,' I murmur.

'Come on,' Paige says, 'let's get to her room.'

'Henry? Why are you here? Have you called Roland?'

My mother's made her half of the two-person hospital room her own. A knitted throw rug on the end of the bed. Vases and flowers behind her. Some butterflies tacked to the wall around her bedhead. A framed photo of my father, propped atop a food tray on wheels.

I thought her appointment was this morning; how long has she been in here?

'Uncle Roland won't talk to me, mum.' Since he knows I was there when his son perished over a cliff.

'Make sure you tell him he's in our prayers.'

'I can't talk to...' When the hell did my mother start praying? I look out at the hospital corridor, then back at my mother. Am I in the right room?

'Paige has been so kind to me,' my mother says, calling Senior Constable Kirino over and squeezing her hand. 'You know her father and I went to the same high school?'

I didn't know that at all.

'Year Eleven,' Paige explains, 'his family had just migrated from Japan. Osaka.'

'He got angry when everyone called him the new Chinese student.'

My mother and Paige share a chuckle. I give my head a little tap. Definitely awake. I've missed something. How often has Paige been seeing my mother? How long has she known something is wrong with her?

Paige excuses herself, leaves my mother and I alone. I can't think of what to say. This is the first time we've been together since she told me the story of my father's affair, since she confessed to being there the night everyone murdered Charlotte Harris, keeping the secret her own. I stand a few feet from her bed, stare at the curtain separating her from her roommate.

'They're not here,' my mother explains. 'They love to walk laps around the ward.'

'How long have you been here?' I ask.

'Since yesterday.'

I gesture to her possessions. 'You knew this was going to happen?'

'I'm booked in for surgery.'

I steel myself. 'For?'

'My headaches, my memory… I had a scan. Before Graham's funeral. There's a growth.'

I shudder. 'On your brain?'

My mother nods.

'You never told me,' I murmur.

'I was going to tell you after the funeral, but then things happened.'

'Yeah, things happened,' I echo.

'I've been taking medication, but it's not enough.'

'What do you mean?'

'They scanned me yesterday, confirmed things this morning. It's spread.'

'It's malignant?'

'Yes.'

'Fuck.' I step closer to my mother's bed. 'They're operating?'

'Tomorrow morning.' My mother tries to smile. 'Surgeon's taking a weekend off golf.'

'Why not today?'

'Something about monitoring me, waiting for me to come off the medication… I don't know.'

'They're just making you sit here the whole time?'

'Where else am I going to go? And it's not like I have a whole line of visitors waiting to see me.'

I cringe. No, we don't have much family. I'm the closest, in both blood and proximity, and I've refused to see her since I learned about Lillian's mother. Surely she has friends, though? I almost ask her, then stop myself. Maybe she lost them when the police arrested her.

I take another step closer, bump against the bedrail. 'I'm sorry.'

'For?'

I don't know. 'Everything?' I suggest.

'So am I,' she whimpers.

I look into my mother's eyes. Deeply, the first time I've done so since I was a child. In happier times, when it was her, my father and myself. One big drama-free family. Then my vision pulls back, and it sees her as she is now. Older than a woman in her mid-sixties. Aged by grief, guilt, loneliness. So small and frail and looking so very unlikely to survive any kind of operation.

What do I do?

I lean in for a hug but can't bring myself to touch her. All I can think of is the way she deceived me, the way she changed the life of my half-sister. Even with the prospect of death, it's a gesture I can't make.

I rest a hand on her arm. Try to keep the silence from feeling uncomfortable.

My phone rings. Thank God.

'It might be Roland,' my mother says as I pull away and fish out my mobile.

It's Jensen, though.

'Henry?' The excitement rolls off her tongue. 'I've got some news that'll make your day.'

I glance at my mother again. 'Not likely.'

'Can we meet? I did it.'

'Did what?'

'I know Joseph's secret.'

There's a knock on the door, Paige arriving with a nurse. 'Send me the address, give me an hour.'

CHAPTER TWENTY-NINE
IT'S JUST A STORY

I park on the kerb alongside Joseph's house. Jensen texted, said she's a minute or two away, just heading off the Freeway. I glance through my emails again while I wait. There's a standout I click on: a reply from the overseas PI. They've agreed to follow up on Lillian. They've already started.

I'm beaming as Jensen pulls into the driveway. She hops out, waves with enough energy for the both of us. She wouldn't tell me everything over the phone. Had to show me. A huge reason to leave my mother, but one I found far harder than I'd imagined. I know it's the heavy weight of guilt. I've ignored my mother for so long, distanced myself, and it's time I can't get back. Time she no longer has.

Thinking about that makes my smile drift away.

'You okay?' Jensen asks as I approach. 'You look half-happy, half-sad.'

'I'm good,' I say, although that's exactly how I feel. 'Does this help your case? Or make it worse?'

She can't help but grin. 'It helps. Well, it helps his innocence, not his character.' She wriggles a keyring around a fingertip. 'He hid a spare. I'll show you inside.'

I haven't told her someone already pried the rear door open. I let her go the proper way, show me inside.

'It's neater than I thought,' she says, looking into the lounge room, seeing only a few things out of place.

'You haven't been in yet?'

'I wanted to wait for you.'

'Then how do you—'

'Joseph caved. I said we'd stop representing him if he didn't tell us the secret.'

'Which is?'

Jensen keeps moving through the house. 'Follow me. He said there's a bedroom near the back.'

'Wait!' I call out. Jensen pauses. 'If you're about to gather some kind of evidence Joseph's told you about, it's tampering with the case. We need to call the police.'

'We're paying you to gather evidence. We can say you found it after we were given permission to search the house.' Jensen shakes the house keys in her hand. 'Besides, if it's not here, we'd look like fools calling the police.'

'You mean, if Joseph lied to us again?'

Jensen grimaces, turns and works her way to the guest bedroom with the tiny bed. I hurry after her.

I don't need the suspense, the game of *follow-the-lawyer-to-the-secret*. But I feed off Jensen's excitement with the thought that maybe this will mark the end of the case. I can feed the police the trickle of information I have on King of Spades and P and F, start looking for my next meal ticket.

Jensen heads straight for the bedside drawer. Pulls the wooden drawer right out and dumps it on the mattress. Expects to see something, except the drawer is empty.

'What?' She turns to me, excitement drained, bewilderment flowing in. 'He told me it'd be here.'

'What would be here, Jensen?'

She rounds the bed, bends down and scans the floor.

'Please,' I plead, 'just tell me what's going on.'

Jensen rises, catches the anger laced in my voice. 'There's supposed to be some old retro video game controller in here. One that needs batteries. And inside the battery compartment is a microSD card. On the card's a whole lot of evidence suggesting there were people who may have had a reason to kill Joseph or Heath. Or both.' Jensen sighs. 'Did you know Joseph's old cellmate tried to strike a deal during his hearing yesterday? Said he had news about another prisoner. A teacher, bragging about how he'd killed a parent. Prosecution wants to use his word as testimony. The jury will eat it up, even though we all know someone bribed the cellmate.'

What if he wasn't, though, I almost say.

'Which is what Joseph found ironic this morning, leading him to confess.' Jensen picks up the drawer, flips it over; as if the controller is somehow taped to the bottom.

I'm pretty sure the reason it's gone is the two people who were in here earlier have already found it. I won't tell Jensen this now, though, and wreck her train of thought.

'What was on the card?' I ask instead.

Jensen throws the drawer on the mattress again. 'Come on, let's check the rest of the house while I tell you.' She rounds the bed, shoulders hunched, body deflated. As we look in the entertaining area, around the bar, she says, 'Joseph was big on bribes, too. Well, I'd say blackmail.'

'He was blackmailing people?'

'He knew about some group that had a whole lot of parents and teachers involved.'

P and F. How did he hear about it? Maria Bortoni? Principal Hills? Bedside chatter exposing secrets. 'But why was the group worthy of blackmail?'

We wander into the main bedroom, which is just as scarce as the guest one. 'Apparently, they were making some under-the-table investments.'

'In?'

'He said everything will be on the microSD.'

Jensen heads for the laundry. I wonder if that was the reason Joseph was with those women, knowing their connection to P and F, using them to create a network of blackmail. A get-rich-quick scheme that fell apart when Heath Hallid found out about it.

Jensen opens a dryer door, peers inside, sighs. She turns back to me, more animated. 'Joseph found out the people in this group weren't just putting their own money into their endeavours. A few bad eggs were also siphoning the school's money, fudging the budget.'

I think back to my relief days at the school. There were small signs of strained budget money: the missing air-conditioner remote, the shortage of markers and other stationery, Joseph keeping his own stash in a drawer. I'd put this down to a drain of stock at the end of the year, though, something replenished before Term One. Maybe entire programs had been cut?

'So, he started blackmailing the parents and teachers involved?'

'Blackmail, yes. But not with money.' Jensen looks inside a top load washing machine, shakes her head. 'Teachers were doing his work for him—planning, photocopying, marking work. And parents were leaving him alone with all the trivial shit the other teachers were being constantly asked.'

'He was getting an easy ride.'

I want to laugh and cry at the same time. Here I was, thinking that Joseph had changed, had matured as a teacher. Instead, the man had found a way to care less about his job, to do the bare minimum while having everyone say he was fantastic.

'Is that why all the teachers stuck up for him?' I wonder. 'He was blackmailing them?'

Jensen heads back to the front lounge room. 'I don't know. I'm not sure how many parents and teachers are involved. The microSD has a list of names; lots of people would want to get their hands on that.'

'Joseph won't give you the names?' I ask, even though I know a few who might be on the list.

'The one thing he's being quiet about, even though it would help him. He said he recorded evidence, too. Video footage of some people admitting they were in the group.'

'How was he recording everyone?' I check near the television for a video game system. There's an absence of dust, suggesting devices were on the cabinet; again, the police could have removed these as evidence. 'There aren't any cameras in the classrooms.'

'Joseph said if he knew someone was from the group, he'd leave his laptop on his desk and record their meeting.'

'Without them noticing?'

Jensen checks a bookshelf. 'I don't know how he did it. I know he took photos in the principal's office, though.'

'Of banking details?'

'Among other things.'

'Did he record the meeting with Heath?'

'Not that he'll say. If he did, police have the laptop. He wouldn't have had time to back it up.'

'He won't say? It could save him.'

Jensen shrugs. 'Then my bet is he didn't record the meeting, or we wouldn't be here. I've tried everywhere. I can't find it.'

She's right. There are no video game controllers or anything resembling video games. If the police haven't seized the controller, then whoever had entered his house before me had known what they were looking for.

We meet back at the front door. Jensen can't help but look disappointed.

'Why didn't Joseph tell us all this before?' I ask, thinking of the extra ammunition I would have had when interviewing people like Robyn Hallid.

Thinking of how little I found out compared to the info-dump Joseph gave Jensen. This might be my first case as a PI, but I should have gathered this information myself. It's what Jensen paid me to do.

Jensen opens the front door. 'Like I said, it makes the prospect of his innocence a little more convincing, but it hurts his character.'

'He lied so we'd take the case?'

'We are going to be defending him for manslaughter, at least. He was just focused on proving he was innocent for that.'

'But you can take what he said to the police, right? Get them to look into it?'

'We're seeing what we can do. Without evidence, it's just a story. Just like the one about Joseph going to get coffees. Some people will believe it, some people won't. We can't have doubt.' Jensen waves us outside, locks the house. We walk to her car before she asks, 'Are you wanting off this case now?'

They're going to hide Joseph's revelation from the police; at least, until it's clear it won't hurt his case. How long will it be till the detectives on his case drag out the same confession, though? Make his blackmail attempts more conclusive proof that he covered a murder?

Now it's my turn to shrug. 'I don't know, especially since he won't give you the names of people in the group. Maybe he's on the list himself? Blackmailing everyone from within?'

Jensen opens her car door, sadness in her eyes. 'Give me the weekend to sort things out. Give yourself that time to think things through. I'll call you Monday.'

I tell her about my family's trip to Singapore, which is booked for tomorrow night; leaving out the cloud of my mother's operation.

Jensen powers down the driver's window, lets the heat out of the car. 'Then you've done what you can. We could have been looking into this days ago. Now, what he said was here isn't, so… Honestly, I don't know if I want to represent him.'

She starts the ignition. I hold out a hand. 'Wait.'

She leans out the window. 'Go on.'

'This was Joseph's secret? Not the affairs he was having, the fact that he knew of a secret group and he was blackmailing them?'

'Pretty much.'

'So, if the notes were from Heath Hallid, he was giving Joseph an ultimatum. Confess what he was doing, or everyone would know the truth.'

Jensen thinks about this. 'So, who had the most to lose from that?'

'Exactly. One teacher or parent, or a group of them?'

CHAPTER THIRTY
ONE MORE ATTEMPT

I could go to Hakea, drag more of the truth out of Joseph. But I'd have to schedule an appointment, and I can't look at his face right now. I could drive back to Joondalup Hospital, be with my mother. But I'm trying to process that one, work out how I can look at her face with the empathy needed. So, I could go home, relax, start packing for the impending trip to Singapore. Spend time with Lucy's family, since I've been absent so much.

Instead, I drive to a place I tried to visit last night. One surrounded by media desperate for news of a missing ex-husband and child. I figure this is my last day on Joseph's case; whatever happens next will be up to a jury to decide. For whatever reason, Joseph refused to give any names on his supposed list on his supposed microSD. The good thing is, Robyn Hallid already gave me a starting point.

There's no longer the maelstrom of media outside Maria Bortoni's house. I'm sure there will be an unmarked police car somewhere, eyes on the property should Julian appear. I don't bother looking for them, hurry straight to Maria's front door, bang on the screen. A dog barks somewhere out the back. I wait but there's no approaching patter of nails on flooring, no guard lurking behind the door.

'Maria?' I call out.

A long time passes before the door opens. A teenage girl peers out from behind the screen. 'Mum's not here.'

I can't remember the girl's name but know she's Jeremy's fraternal twin. Her face is quite similar in shape, but she's got a lighter hair colour. 'Oh,' I say, 'do you know where she is? Only, it's an urgent matter. P and F stuff.'

The girl looks at me like she wants to remember my face but can't. Would she know everyone in her mother's group? She shrugs, not caring if she does. 'Dunno where she is.'

'You know when she'll be back?'

The girl shakes her head.

I'm never going to speak to Maria. I need to accept that it's part of the job. If I was still with the police, I could get an interview with the click of my fingers, but as a PI, I have no authoritative reason to demand her time.

I resist asking if the young girl knows where her brother is; that would only put them on alert, provoke another move from their current hiding spot. Instead, I offer her thanks and tell her to have a good day.

She shuts the door without a response.

Leaving me to retreat home. At least I have a window to pack for Singapore now, while I wait to hear from the few people who might help me on this case.

Except, when I pull into the driveway, there's another car waiting. This one isn't a marked police vehicle, but it's driven by a cop.

Gary. Probably here to drag me back to the hospital, give my mother a hug.

Gary and I stand before a familiar, thick wooden door. I peer through its thin slat of frosted glass, can't make out any sign of life beyond. I reach out, knock anyway.

'She won't be here,' I offer.

'I said I'd help you look,' Gary says. 'We've got to try.'

'I tried for two weeks.'

'One more attempt might be all you need.'

'Fucking inspiring, that is.'

'I know.'

We wait a long, silent minute. 'I could pick the lock.'

'Is *that* how you got in last time?'

'Well, Lillian didn't exactly let me in.'

Gary thinks about this a moment. 'We could go get a coffee, come back, wait down the street?'

I throw my hands up in the air. 'We've done that, Gary. Besides, the note in there said something will happen tomorrow, not today.'

'But she's got to come back to plant the next clue, right?'

'Listen to my year of birth. That's all I've been told to do.'

I pull away from the house, start heading back to the car.

'Wait, Henry.'

I keep walking, though. To hide the shudder my body's making, the welling tears on my face. I have poured myself into Joseph's case because it's detracted from thinking about the last time I was at this house, the message I found within. I allowed Gary to take me to Yanchep, to help, because there was no reason to refuse a nice gesture. But it's all for nothing. Lillian's playing a game with me now, just like Uncle Graham. Scattering clues, leading me to the truth in frustrating fashion, instead of being straightforward with me. What happens tomorrow, even if I figure out her clue? Will it lead to another step in her game, another puzzle to keep me occupied while she continues to ignore my existence?

A hand clasps my shoulder. 'Stop, mate.' I freeze. Gary rounds me, catches the distress washed across my face. 'What's going on?'

'What do you mean?' I murmur.

'Lillian's been missing a long time; the empty house can't be the only thing upsetting you this much.'

Do I tell Gary the truth? He's the only genuine friend I have these days; my youthful core of mates parted ways when I became an officer, their way of life conflicting with my new respect for the law. Gary's stuck up for me, though, even after exposing the rest of my family for their crimes. He believed in me, knew I wasn't like them, since he came from a broken family, too. He's already put his career on the line to help me track down Lillian, and that hasn't stopped him.

I motion to the distant ocean. 'Let's go grab a coffee.'

I've been to the café by the ocean so much, I don't have to tell them my order—they simply bring it. Over my triple-strength brew, I tell Gary everything. About my mother; something I should have seen coming but chose to ignore. About the case; too hard to crack, proving I'm not ready to be an investigator.

Gary listens at first, refraining from offering his opinion. By the time we've got to our second coffee, he reaches out, pats my arm, gets me ready to receive the lecture I deserve.

'Shit happens,' he says instead. He laughs at my puzzled look, adds, 'You can't control everything, Henry. We just proved that back at the house. With your mother, it's about what you do next. Go back to the hospital soon. Be there when she goes in for the operation. With the case, well, you've done what you were paid to do. I'll forward your details to one of my department sources. When they call, tell them everything you've told me, add to the case they've already built.'

'And end my involvement?'

'You can do that, you know. The lawyer can hire someone else if they need more.'

I sigh. Gary's right. After what Joseph admitted to Jensen, I can't speak to the man again, can't trust what I'm helping prove. Curiosity has its claws in me, though. I need to keep piecing the mystery together—I don't want to read about it in the news. The reporting on Heath Hallid's death has already been all over the shop, swayed by public opinion more than fact.

'I'm close to solving it, though,' I say. 'I'd given myself this last day.'

Gary knows he's not going to win, smiles. 'Then give yourself this last day. Five pm, though, and I'm coming back for a drink. Work week over.'

'Done.'

He takes a bite of the pastry he spied by the counter. A cruffin or some other Frankenstein creation. 'Now,' he says, wiping his lips, 'have you talked to Lucy about all this?'

'Everything that's happened this week?' I shake my head. 'Bits and pieces, but it's the final days of school, she's occupied. I want her to enjoy this last moment as a full-time classroom teacher.'

Aside from the emotional rollercoaster my wife is on right now, she's had to pack everything in her classroom, get her students through less structured lessons, tie up reporting and communication with families and teachers—a month of work in a week, before she gets time off.

'But isn't it a PD day today, or whatever?' Gary says. 'Maybe you can go visit her, have another coffee?'

I think back to the nine end-of-year stretches I participated in. Some were a single day, most were over three or four days, depending on the calendar. Often, the school tried to bring in a specialist in a designated field. Someone spruiking a writing program that'd already failed in the US, or a mathematician who introduced fun, hands-on learning activities the school couldn't afford to buy. More often than not, though, the teachers had already checked out, using the day to message each other, plan the drinking night ahead. So yes, Gary's right, I could go visit Lucy and get everything off my chest.

'There'll be plenty of time for that tomorrow,' I answer, anyway.

He nods, devours the rest of his pastry. 'You know, I might get a holiday unit up here next time I'm in Perth. Beautiful area. Better than the hustle and bustle of the city.'

'Uncle Graham took us to the Inn in the national park once. The place used to be full of people picnicking, out on the lake with boat hires, exploring caves on tours. The lake's receded now, the boat hire gone. Caves are still there, of course.'

'Always caves with you, Henry.' Gary catches his own words, winces. 'Sorry.'

My phone rings, giving Gary a reprieve.

'Henry?' It's Senior Constable Kirino. 'You free to talk?'

I let Gary know who's on the line. 'I'm with Gary. Is this the part where you start teaming up on me again?'

She laughs. 'You asked me to look up an address?'

'That was fast.'

'Well, I had to explain my interest, but that's okay.'

'Explain to who?'

'The address was flagged to the Hallid case.'

I clear my throat, try to bury my shock. 'Why?'

'There's a forensic accountant looking into the finances of a few people involved. Heath, Joseph, their spouses or exes, and several more educators listed as witnesses.'

I picture the address I'd asked Paige to investigate, the South Perth house Bailey had disappeared into. 'Did Julian Bortoni own it?' Since the property was so close to Julian's apartment, it wouldn't surprise me.

'Interesting you say that. He doesn't—a shell corporation does—but there's correspondence to suggest Julian helped start it up. Then a lot of receipts and so on then go through Heath Hallid's accountancy business.'

'Who owns the shell corporation?'

'They're still figuring that out.'

'But they think it's connected to Heath or Joseph?'

'You reported Heath's kid hiding in it. You believe in coincidences?'

'More than I should.' There's a moment of silence over the line, which I take to mean the end of our conversation. 'Thanks for looking into the address for me.'

'Oh. That's not the only one.'

'The only what?'

'House. Owned by the corporation. Three were purchased in the last six months. Two under construction, one of them almost finished. Another is an old property marked for demolition.'

'Can you text me the addresses?'

'Your mother's surgeon wants to see you first thing tomorrow morning. You'll be there, right?'

'Yes.'

'Doctor Aaron Theodore. He'll come to your mother's room as early as possible.'

'I'll be there.'

'Then I'll send the addresses.'

We end the call. Gary's been leaning close the whole time, trying to catch every word of the conversation.

I jiggle my car keys. 'Feel like going house-hunting some more?'

CHAPTER THIRTY-ONE
LOTS OF BANGERS IN HERE

Back in the car, we search up the three addresses Paige sent me. The first is the South Perth house I'm sure Bailey went into. Since the police couldn't find him there, I doubt he'd return. So, if he's hiding at another of what potentially might be his father's properties, we have a fifty per cent chance of driving to the right one. That's if he's hiding at one of these properties and not a mate's house, or on the streets—some secret location with Jeremy.

The two remaining properties are contrasting. One is in Willetton. A good old fashioned, single-storey, brown brick, black tile home. A product of the seventies or eighties. It's near a basketball stadium, a bus stop, some shops and heaps of takeaway food. A place perfect for two runaway, teenage boys. The other house is in a historically rich suburb. It overlooks the Swan River, three storeys in height, gated to keep everyone out. All rendered walls and steel-framed windows; whites and greys that scream *this home isn't for children.* Neighbouring houses are just as large. It's easily worth a couple of million. Maybe more.

'That one,' I say, pointing to the picture of the Swan River house on my phone.

'Why that one?' Gary asks, humouring me.

'It's the opposite of what you'd expect. Plus, if I was a teenager, I'd give anything to crash in some fancy mansion, pretend it was mine.'

'Good enough.'

I start the car. We've got a long drive ahead, almost an hour. In that time, Paige's source may ask officers to look at the properties, too. Hopefully, they'll start with the more obvious Willetton choice.

Music from my phone kicks in over Bluetooth, Whitesnake's power ballad, *Here I Go Again.* Gary taps his fingers against the window sill. As the song ends, kicks into a tune by A Flock of Seagulls, he asks, 'Why is finding these boys so important?'

'Huh?'

'I know they're missing, but why do we need to find them before my people in blue?'

I can't tell Gary I've been in Joseph's house, can't tell him someone else was in there, too. My gut tells me the intruders were Bailey and Jeremy. I don't know *why* they were in the teacher's house; my guess, to trash the home of the man who killed Bailey's father. My gut tells me I interrupted that retribution, but before they fled, they helped themselves to a few possessions. One of them being the controller that Jensen was trying to find. Allegedly hiding a microSD that will answer everything.

Like how a group of teachers and parents—or one teacher or parent in particular—raised enough money to buy houses worth millions.

'I think they saw something,' I answer, another thing my gut's telling me. 'When Heath was pushed.'

'I read the report,' Gary says, 'they were at the swim meet.'

'The swim meet was right next to the Junior School.'

'Did you walk it out when you were there, make sure there was enough time to get from one location to another without being noticed?'

I sigh. 'No. But my class played next to the area, and I made a few guesstimations. It has an eight-foot wall that's impossible to see over. So, if someone snuck out of the swim meet, nobody would have seen them.'

'Worth questioning, then.'

The song changes to a power ballad.

'Didn't know you liked these kinds of songs.'

'I'm more of a nineties hip-hop person,' I say. 'Want to hear that playlist?'

'No, keep this going. What is it?'

After Uncle Graham's funeral, I tracked down my half-sister's last location: The Ridge. Only, Lillian had already gone, leaving behind a shoebox full of clues to keep me looking. Clues that led to a phone number which dialled a pre-recorded message, a series of song samples. I created a playlist, the full versions of the songs in the order they'd played in the message; though I wasn't sure what the eighties tracks represented.

I unlock my phone, hand it to Gary so he can see the playlist:

Here I Go Again – Whitesnake
I Ran (So Far Away) – A Flock of Seagulls
The Lucky One – Laura Branigan
Free Fallin – Tom Petty
With or Without You – U2
Controversy – Prince
Teen Age Riot – Sonic Youth
How Soon Is Now? – The Smiths
Swap Meet – Nirvana
The Message – Grandmaster Flash and The Furious Five
Disappearing Act – Shalamar
Fast Car – Tracy Chapman
Don't You (Forget About Me) – Simple Minds
In the Air Tonight – Phil Collins
Burning Down the House – Talking Heads
No More The Fool – Elkie Brooks
Fight the Power – Public Enemy
What's Love Got to Do With It – Tina Turner
Pesta Muzik – Sweet Charity
Round and Round – Ratt
One Thing Leads to Another – The Fixx
Call Me – Blondie
Forget Me Nots – Patrice Rushen
Close to Me – The Cure
Modern Love – David Bowie
Just Like Heaven – The Cure
Why Worry? – Dire Straits
Hallelujah – Leonard Cohen

'Share this with me,' Gary says. 'Lots of bangers in here.'

'I don't think I'd call these bangers, Gary,' I laugh. 'Maybe you should see my nineties playlist?'

'Nah, mate. The eighties have made a comeback.'

'You think that's why Lillian left the list?'

'She just wanted you to listen to good music.'

We pull up at the Swan River house. Its online images don't do it justice. The unobstructed views of the city, running alongside the river, add another million to the price, easy.

We get out the car, examine the wrought-iron fence and its matching gate blocking our way in. The gate is electronic, but it's got a large chain and padlock on it, too. Just in case.

'No cameras, from what I can tell,' Gary says.

'House like this, they'd have microscopic ones,' I say, shuddering as I picture the countless cameras Aunty Janice scattered throughout Margaret River. 'Or they're hidden in a tree or something.'

'If nobody's living here, you think someone will appear if we climb over the gate? A nosy neighbour?'

'We only need a few minutes to check for the boys.'

'True.' Gary grabs the gate's bars. 'Give me a boost.'

With a bit of effort and a fair amount of swearing, I push my friend up onto the flat top of the gate. He rolls over it, drops to the driveway on the other side.

'Easy.' He reaches through the bars, cups his hands. 'Here, I'll lift you now.'

'How about you just go up to those gigantic front windows, have a quick look for signs of life?'

'The second I hear sirens, I'm running.'

'You're serving your badge with honour.'

Gary chuckles, hurries to the stretch of seven-foot high tinted windows. He shuffles from one pane to the other, peering through. A lounge room is in there, or dining room—some kind of entertainment area. House like this, the bedrooms are probably upstairs. Above the home office or theatre.

Gary disappears for a moment, rounding the house. When he reappears, he lets me know there's a solid gate blocking the path, set within a wall as tall as the windows. He scans the rest of the front area, considers something. Walks to the other side of the driveway, pulls aside some ferns, exposing a garbage bin. He lifts the lid, reaches in and pulls out a box.

'Pizza,' he calls out. He opens the box. 'Some cheese still stuck on the lid.'

'Gross,' I yell in reply.

He peers into the bin again. 'Five of six boxes in here. Plus soft drink bottles.'

'How about that boost, then?' I say.

Because I understand the connection he's made. Discarded food means someone's living here. Pizza and soft drink are often the staple of teenagers.

We are at the right house.

CHAPTER THIRTY-TWO
A TOXIC RELATIONSHIP

Turns out, the gate on the side wall is unlocked. And if the boys are home, they're asleep or deaf. Because I've thrown a rock through the rear door's glass panel, and the resulting crash is far louder than I'd hoped.

No boys, though. No alarm, either, unless it's silent. Although, if a nosey neighbour hasn't reported us yet, they will soon. Unless the surrounding houses are empty, too, owned by overseas investors; kept as holiday or business premises, only rented when needed.

'Thought you were a whizz with a lock pick set,' Gary whispers as we enter the house.

'This door was shattered when we got here, remember,' I grin.

At some point, Gary will arrest me, a line truly crossed. Thankfully, this isn't that moment. Perhaps the thought of helping runaway teenagers is more important than protocol?

'Should we try upstairs?' Gary whispers.

We're in a huge laundry area. It's full of benches, cupboards and washing machines, all never used. There's a staircase to the left, wrapping round to an unseen landing. One of many staircases, I'm sure. It wouldn't shock me if there was a lift.

I nod.

What do you need in three storeys? More rooms or bigger rooms? Areas for the whole extended family to live in, or hobby rooms for a solitary owner? Imagine the space I'd have to fit Win and Aqil, Sarah and the kids. But take them away and I wouldn't know how to furnish a house this size. Home theatre? Library? Bowling alley? Video arcade? Bar? Café? With all of that, you'd never have to leave home. Except this place is empty.

We reach the landing to the next floor. Gary puts a finger to his lips, motions to the passageway. He's heard something. Not empty, then. There's a light on in the passageway, guiding us down its length. We tread on white carpeted flooring, heading for a closed door. Behind it, the sound of gunfire. A movie?

I edge round Gary, get to the door handle first. Turn it. The door is heavy. As it swings inward, loud sounds rush at me, a screech and crash and more gunfire. I hesitate, then step forward. It's a huge room—at least six or seven metres wide and long. Sparsely furnished. A three-seater leather couch in the middle, an enormous television hung on the distant wall, a cabinet beneath that. There's a small round table to the side of the couch, covered with soft drink bottles. Packets of chips litter the ground.

Bailey and Jeremy are on the couch, engrossed in the video game they're playing, the characters almost life-size on the gigantic television. It's *Call of Duty* or something similar—one in the myriad of games making war seem terrifying while also glorifying it. I saw a poster for this game on Blake Hallid's locker. Maybe the brothers bond over it?

The teenagers are so captivated by their mission, they don't register our presence. Their presence is everywhere, though. From the sweat-laden funk in the room to the empty packets of chips on the ground. It seems like they've holed themselves in this one room even though they have a mini-mansion to run riot in. Maybe the smaller dimensions remind them of their own houses?

I clap. The boys mistake it for something in their game. I clap again. And again. Until Bailey turns, sees me. Smacks Jeremy on the arm.

'Aw, shit.' Jeremy pauses the game. Blissful quietness creeps in. 'How did you find us?'

'It's my job.'

Jeremy stands, folds his arms. He's one teen to have already had a growth spurt, almost six foot in height. His body mass hasn't caught up, though. He's a mess of gangly limbs, but he's trying to use his frame to look intimidating. I don't have the heart to tell him it's not working.

'People have been looking for you,' I say.

'No shit.'

I gesture to the game on the television, the discarded food. 'This is what you've been doing all week?'

'Pretty much.'

'Nice escape from reality.'

'What'd you mean?'

I gesture to Bailey, who still hasn't risen from the couch. 'Someone murdered his dad, and instead of being with his family to help them grieve, he's here playing games with you?'

Jeremy glances at Bailey. 'He wants to be here.'

'Can't he just play online, from home?'

'It's better with a friend. You have any?'

I glance at Gary. 'The mouth on this one.'

He nods, leans close. 'Already called this in,' he whispers. 'Whatever you've got to get out of them, do it soon.'

'Bailey,' I say, ignoring his mate, 'I think someone came to that parent meeting to kill your dad.'

'Yeah,' Jeremy says, 'his teacher.'

'Or someone else.'

Jeremy shakes his head. 'Cops can sort all that out.'

'I'm a PI. Name's Henry.' I gesture to Gary. 'He's a cop. Gary.'

Bailey's eyes widen. 'Jez.'

Jeremy swings round. 'Shut it.'

'Your friend isn't helping you here,' I say to Bailey. 'He thinks he's protecting you, or something, and that's nice, but things are still happening out there in the real world.'

'Let it happen,' Jeremy says.

I step further into the room, glare at Jeremy. 'Jesus, I don't know if this is all an act to look tough in front of two strange adults, or if you're just an arsehole.'

'Fuck you, old man.'

'Fuck me? *Your* old man has run off with forty thousand dollars, after shooting a debt collector.'

Jeremy's arms unfold. I can hear him gulp. This was unexpected news.

'He didn't include you in his plans?' I add.

'You think we're hiding his money in here?' Jeremy tries, as defiant as possible.

'You're in a million-dollar house, so it's possible.' May as well go for gold, ask what I need to. 'Maybe the two of you have been busy stealing your own things, though?' I point to the television. 'Found any extra controllers lately?'

Jeremy swings back to Bailey. 'Don't.'

'You think they sent them?' Bailey murmurs.

'No. Quiet.'

'But what if—'

'I said I'd take care of this, okay!'

'Toxic,' Gary murmurs.

'What?' Jeremy snaps.

Gary chuckles, folds his arms. Looks far more menacing than the teenager, even if he's a puppy. 'It's what you kids call it, right? A toxic relationship. That's what you two have.'

'Bailey's my best mate,' Jeremy says, his face reddening.

'And you're treating him like garbage,' Gary replies. 'Telling him what he can and can't say. Speaking for him, telling him to shut up. That's not a healthy friendship.'

'Fuck you, you prehistoric—'

'Jez!' Bailey rises from the couch. 'Just shut up, already.' He holds his hands out to calm everyone. 'We're just scared, okay.'

'Why are you scared?' I ask.

He reaches down to the couch cushions, picks something up. 'You're really a PI? And a cop?'

'Your mum has been worried about you,' I say.

'It'd be a first.'

'She's dealing with a lot.'

Now I'm staring at two red-faced teenagers. A string of obscenities are likely on the way. I need to try another tact. There *has* to be a reason they're hiding. Away from their parents. Away from anyone else looking for them. It can't just be a teenager's way of grieving for a lost parent.

Grieving for a lost parent.

Gary and I are strangers, and Bailey and Jeremy don't think we can relate to their situation.

But we can.

'My father died when I was your age,' I admit. The words make my limbs tremble, but I keep going. 'He was having an affair. The woman ended it, and he couldn't accept that, so he got drunk and drove and crashed his car.' For once, Jeremy doesn't add a snarky comment. I have their attention. 'I didn't deal with it well. I kind of lived the rest of my teenage years in a daze. Like I was in a dark dream, carried along by anger.'

'Does it…' Bailey starts. 'Does it get better?'

'I won't lie, it takes a long time. I had an uncle who did his best to get me through. My mother, she escaped into a dreamworld worse than mine. Hurt by my father's affair. Hiding a secret I wouldn't know until this year.'

'Do you speak to her now?' Jeremy asks. He blinks, tries to hide the welling tears.

'We've had a falling out because of the secret.'

There's no need to go into the details. Jeremy wants to say something, words forming but nothing escaping his lips. We all sit there, wait.

'Mum was having an affair,' Jeremy admits. 'With that fucker, Mister Pooles. I've been pretending I don't know who he is, but… he's over all the time, picking her up for drinks and shit. I didn't tell anyone, not even my sister.'

Jeremy's twin. I wonder if they usually share everything or if they're two unique personalities. Although, if Jeremy's sister is still at home, and he's here, there's a good chance he's not sharing much at all.

'Did your father know about the affair?' Gary asks Jeremy, the same thought swirling through my brain.

Jeremy shrugs. 'He just said he was making things right.'

Maybe stealing a pile of money seemed right, the capital needed to set up a better life? And if Julian helped establish the funds of the shell corporation, did he have a share in one of these properties? A nice new start for Maria, if wealth was all that concerned her.

Before I can ask who let the boys stay at this house, Bailey holds out the item he grabbed from the couch. It's a chunky purple controller. 'It doesn't work on our PS.'

'Is this from Mister Pooles' house?' I ask.

Bailey nods. I hold out my hand and he rounds the couch, hands the controller over. I find a panel on the back of the device. Slide it open. Sigh with relief as a tiny card drops onto my palm. A microSD. Data that might put plenty of people in prison.

'This is a huge help,' I say.

'What is it?' Bailey asks.

'Why were you in your teacher's house?' Gary asks, cutting off my answer.

I resist scowling at him. It's something I'd loved to know, but if they sense a lecture coming on, any information will dry up.

'Who do you think sent us?' I ask, before they think twice about keeping quiet.

'The police?' Jeremy says.

'No, I've asked you already why you were scared, and you avoided the answer. You thought someone sent us. Who?'

Bailey reaches into his pants pocket, pulls out a wallet.

'Don't,' Jeremy urges once more.

Bailey shakes his head. 'No more, Jez.' He draws out a card, holds it out for me to take. 'We got my dad in trouble. I think it got him killed.'

I look down at the card. At the symbol drawn on it. The King of Spades.

CHAPTER THIRTY-TWO
YOU DON'T GET A CHOICE

I show Gary the card, stare at Bailey. 'Explain.'

My phone rings. I ignore it.

'Dad liked gambling,' Bailey says, 'being with the lads. Except he was an arse to a lot of people, and they ghosted him. So, he went online, found some poker setup for locals. Tried to fit in, there.'

My phone rings again.

'You gonna get that?' Jeremy asks.

'Keep talking,' I say, making connections—Heath Hallid's story has an eerie similarity to Desmond's own gambling addiction.

'Well, we were all supposed to go on this holiday, right,' Jeremy says, taking over. 'Up to Moore River. Both our families. My dad arranged it.'

That would have been awkward, with all the parental separations. 'Go on,' I say as my phone vibrates, a message incoming.

'And, well…' Jeremy says '…dad would've given me an extra hundred dollars if my grades were up to scratch.'

'He paid you for good grades?'

Jeremy nods. 'Only my grades were basic. So, Bailey here helped.'

'I thought you had your own bank account?'

'Extra cash is better.'

'To spend on weed or something?'

'Does it matter?'

No. Not in the scheme of things. 'How did Bailey help, then?'

'He hacked into our school system. Changed a few of my grades.'

'Hacker?' Bailey scoffs. 'I'm a problem solver.'

'Yeah,' Jeremy chuckles. 'He solved the problem of my grades. I mean, I *could* have hacked in, if he showed me how.'

'Yeah right,' Bailey says. 'Your laptop's password is *boobs*. You have no idea how to access anything beyond the Wi-Fi.'

'Don't want to rush,' Gary says, 'but can we get to the card?'

'Why *are* you rushing?' Jeremy asks.

'No reason. The hacking?'

'Problem solving,' Bailey says. 'I taught myself years ago how to break the school's old reporting software. Take cash from kids to do what I did for Jez. It didn't take long to change his grades, so I snooped around on their server. I was gonna rig some weird music to play over the school's PA. But I found a Junior School subfolder labelled KOS, and it just felt off.'

'KOS?' I ask, sighing as I make the connection.

'Yeah. Someone had tried to hide it and delete most files, but there were some lines left I could put on Notepad, sort through. It was, like… stuff the school bought that had nothing to do with school. Like houses.'

'Like this one?'

'Different ones.'

'Who made the purchases?' Gary says.

'Dunno. There were no names. It was almost like a draft before someone grew a brain, put it all on their personal computer. Like, they accidentally saved it to the school's server first, or they hid it on purpose and didn't care.'

'So, it has to be a teacher,' I say, 'not a parent.'

Bailey shrugs. 'I told dad about it. He seemed to know something but wouldn't tell me. A few days later, he meets Mister Pooles, and…'

'You think the folder you found got him killed?'

Bailey shrugs again. But of course, he does. Tears are already springing forth. 'The morning my dad went to the meeting, that card showed up at our doorstep. I took it before anyone could see. There's no phone number on it or anything, just a symbol. It's KOS, though. Right?'

Bailey's right. A folder labelled KOS, a card with the King of Spades symbol on it. People have already asked if I believe in coincidences; they're popping up everywhere.

'The timing is crazy, I'll give you that,' I say. 'But nothing that happened to your father was your fault.'

'You don't know that,' Bailey whimpers.

He's right. I don't.

Before I can offer more sympathy, Gary asks, 'Did someone say you could stay here? A teacher?'

'Jez had the idea,' Bailey says. 'He'd written a few of the houses down, from the list.'

'We had a look,' Jeremy explains, 'saw these places were empty. We tried a mate's house the first night, after… Well, this is much nicer.'

I can't argue with that. 'Except you're hiding in one room.'

'Bigger than my bedroom,' Jeremy scoffs. 'What happens now? Can we stay here, just another night?'

Gary shakes his head. 'I'm afraid you need to go back to your families now. Help them.'

'What if we don't want to?'

'There are officers waiting downstairs. You don't get a choice.'

It takes a while to run through things with the awaiting officers, explain why we were in the house with two runaway teenagers. That Gary is on their side doesn't seem to matter. Officers take details, record statements. At least we avoid a trip back to a station.

When we're finally in my car, Bailey and Jeremy unable to avoid a trip to the station, I check my mobile, see who's been trying to contact me.

My wife. I give her a ring. Maybe she read Gary's mind, wants a coffee so I get a few things off my chest? Although, why would she call three times in as many minutes?

'Where are you?' Lucy asks as she answers the call.

I give her a quick summary. 'Everything okay?'

'No. Mum and dad took the kids for a play down the park. When they got back, Sarah was gone. Only, her handbag was on the bed. Mobile and everything in there.'

I put the call on speaker. 'How long were they at the park?'

'About an hour.'

'Would Sarah have walked over to meet them? Maybe she went a different way and—'

'She would have taken her mobile. Besides, it's a ten-minute walk, max. It's been another hour since my parents returned.'

Shit. 'Was she meeting with Desmond?'

'I've called him. He hasn't seen her.'

'Report it,' Gary calls out. 'Call your local police station.'

'Doesn't she have to be missing for—'

'No,' Gary and I chorus.

'Any genuine concern,' I say, 'report it straight away.'

'Done. I'm leaving work now; can you meet me back home?'

'Of course.'

I end the call, push down on the accelerator, fly towards the Freeway.

'It might not be connected,' Gary offers as we reach the on-ramp.

He could be right. Sarah could have just gone for a long walk, some time to herself. But given the rise in coincidences, this feels like all the snooping around I've done has come back to bite me.

I arrive in my street, thoughts pinging in so many directions I'm not even sure how I drove there. As I park and start exiting the car, there's a honk. Lucy pulls up beside me.

'How did you beat me?' she calls out.

I shrug. I have no idea.

Lucy steps out, grabs her handbag and a mini suitcase on wheels. 'Mum called while I was driving. Still no Sarah.' She approaches Gary, gives him a hug. 'You've been helping Henry all day?'

Habit makes me go check the mail.

'We found the missing teenagers,' Gary says, giving Lucy the quick rundown of events.

I grab out a few envelopes. A couple of flyers slip through my fingers, fall onto the paving surrounding the letterbox. I reach down, pick one up at a time. Freeze as my fingers grasp a smaller item.

'Lucy! Gary! Fuck!'

I'm holding another business card. The same as Bailey handed me, with the King of Spades symbol. Only, this one has a phone number handwritten across it.

My snooping has come back to bite me.

Gary, Lucy and I sit in my car. Away from Lucy's parents and the kids, so they don't hear what's about to happen.

I dial the number on the card.

'Name?' a modulated voice answers, its pitch deep.

'Henry Herbert,' I play along.

'It was easy to track you down. Too much interfering, there had to be a price.'

'What price?' I manage to ask.

'Find the controller and its card for us. Bring it to Perth Zoo. Eleven am tomorrow. Nocturnal house.'

'I've got it. You can have it right now. Just—'

'No… Not now. Um… Eleven am tomorrow. Nocturnal house. No police. Keep your phone on you.'

'But don't you want it now? We can make a deal tonight.'

'If you cannot follow simple instructions, you will never see your wife again.'

'But—'

The call cuts off, leaving me to process everything said, everything implied. When I can force my stare from the mobile's screen, I turn to Lucy to see tears streaming down her face.

'What have you done?' she snaps.

I know she's not angry at me, entirely, but the sting hurts the same.

'I'll fix this,' I murmur.

But I can't tell her how. Because none of this makes sense. Someone knows me enough to be worried about the information I've found, but they think Sarah is my wife. They know I've been searching for the controller, or at least know of its existence, but don't know I've met the teenagers who've handed it over.

'I just need a moment to think.'

I need to focus my thoughts, pool everything I know about the case, look at things a different way—spot the truth amongst the lies.

I can't wait until tomorrow morning. There's still plenty of today left; time to show King of Spades they tried to intimidate the wrong person. I'm not some pushover teacher or entitled parent. They can't just a leave a card in our mailbox and expect us to… be… scared…

Or intimidated.

Aunty Janice intimidated my mother and her siblings. Watched them like a hawk, forced them to bury a secret and go along with her schemes. She blackmailed locals in the area, too, had them do her bidding. Because she recorded them, had dirt on them, made them feel like they had no other choice.

Who's been intimidating a cohort of teachers, getting them to do their work, mark their tests, say how great they are?

Joseph Pooles.

I have fallen for his lies.

My first case as a PI, and I have royally fucked everything up.

CHAPTER THIRTY-FOUR
THE MILLION-DOLLAR QUESTION

We can't just turn up to the prison, though, demand answers from Joseph. For one, we need to schedule a visit, since Gary's not here on any official capacity. It may also alert Joseph that we're on to him, endangering Sarah. So, we need to look at who Joseph's connected to, press them for answers.

I park the car. 'Be back in a bit.'

Lucy doesn't respond. Gary's still on the phone. We figured whoever spoke for King of Spades has no idea I'm with Gary, at least that he's with the police. So technically *I'm* not contacting the police about the abduction, Gary is. Unlike us, they'll be able to visit Joseph soon, take some more statements without tying their whole enquiry to Sarah. Even so, we need to work fast. And hope King of Spades doesn't have a connection in law enforcement.

I get out my car, hear the distant ocean, look up at the City Beach house before me. I work my way through the gate, the jungle in the courtyard, head up an endless set of stairs.

The front door opens as I near it. 'I've just gotta grab my phone and keys,' Desmond says, retreating inside.

I enter the house. It's like stepping back in time. The interior is no longer a beer bottle-laden mess, a potential bachelor's squalor. Everything is neat, packed away. It's so clean, the floor is shining.

Desmond's trying to get Sarah and the kids to come back home, to see how hard he's working to repair things.

Now I've fucked things up for him.

'Can't believe they thought Sarah was your wife,' Desmond says as he reappears. 'We've got some racist abductor on our hands, thinks all Asians look alike.'

I fill him in on our plan as we hurry down the steps. We're going to finally see Maria Bortoni, track her down if she's still out. By then, Gary may have found the details for the Junior School principal, Talitha Hills. We'd tried looking her up using the same site I'd tracked the missing Year Four teacher on, except *T Hills* has over forty results to sort through. We don't have hours to waste. From there, we hope the police have started their own interview process, working their way through anyone at Isidore College attached to Joseph. It doesn't matter who finds Sarah first, as long as she's found alive.

'Carina couldn't find any info on King of Spades,' Desmond offers. 'They're not on AUSTRAC's radar.'

'We'll get some answers, soon,' I try to assure him.

We hop in the car, drive to Maria Bortoni's house. Trying not to think about how this is all going to end.

I tcall Jensen but get her voicemail; leave a message, implore her to get the list of P and F members from Joseph as soon as possible; don't say why I need it.

We round the corner to Maria's. There are no news vans hovering now, but someone has just pulled up to the driveway. I park on the kerb a few houses down, kill the lights. We watch as a woman exits the vehicle in Maria's driveway. It's Maria herself. Just as I've seen her on the news. She hurries into the house, the door banging behind her. This is our chance, before she disappears again.

I start to open the car door.

'Wait,' Lucy cries.

My hand hovers by the handle. 'What's wrong?'

'Everything.'

I let go of the handle. 'What do you mean?'

'I'm sorry. I was so furious, I made you rush to save Sarah. But think about it a second. Why did they take her in the first place?'

'Because I was close to exposing the truth?' I venture.

'The truth to what? Keeping Joseph in prison?'

I try to process what Lucy's saying. I'd already told myself I needed to focus my thoughts, but the rush to find anyone attached to Sarah's abduction has taken over everything.

'The card,' Lucy explains. 'You told me someone paid debt collectors to leave the King of Spades card as a calling. It's a scare tactic, a warning for a deadline to owing money.'

'She's right,' Desmond murmurs.

'A warning,' Lucy emphasises.

Something clicks in my tired brain. 'Nobody has been abducted before.'

Lucy nods.

This is completely different. 'Why now, then?'

'Exactly. Which is why everything seems wrong.'

'The fact that they want to meet up tomorrow, at a public place, seemed wrong,' Gary chips in, no longer on the phone. 'You even told them you have the microSD. Why not just meet you now?'

'Why would they even need the card?' Lucy asks. 'Have you looked at what's on it?'

'No,' I say. 'We haven't had time. We just got it and now this.'

Lucy points to the house. 'They'll have a computer in there. Kids going to a fancy private school? They'll have devices everywhere.'

'Then let's go inside.' I try to ignore my wife's visible frustration, the fact that we haven't resolved everything she's raised. 'We might get some answers there,' I try. 'It's a start.'

She opens her door. 'Okay. It's a start.'

We leave my car, hurry to Maria's front door. Knock. Wait. There's movement inside, a lot of hurried steps. If Gary wasn't with us, instinct might make me look for a quicker way inside. But I knock a couple more times, let time drag out.

It feels too long. Maria could be calling for help, could have run out the back, could be getting makeshift weapons ready to defend herself.

'I'll go round back,' Gary says, thinking the same thing.

As he steps away, a blinding light snaps on above us. We freeze. The door opens and I blink away spots to make out a silhouette at the threshold.

'Maria?' I ask, rubbing my eyes.

The security light clicks off. 'Yes.'

'My name is Henry Herbert. I've been investigating the teacher-parent murder.'

'You lot reporters? Because I've had enough of reporters.'

'You're not the only one. We're not reporters, though. We're looking into a group. P and F.'

Maria steps back, light within her entryway creating shadows around her fierce scowl. 'That group doesn't exist anymore.'

'Doesn't exist?'

Maria begins to shut the door. 'I've got to rush off with my daughter, pick my son up from the police. You might have heard about his disappearance through your investigation?'

'Please,' Lucy calls out. 'You must be able to tell us something about P and F. They've got my sister.'

Maria pauses. Her scowl almost falters. 'Are you sure?'

That is the million-dollar question; one we can't answer. I hold up the controller instead. If Maria recognises it, her stoic expression hides the truth. 'Your son stole this from the teacher's house. Joseph Pooles?'

'You can keep it,' Maria scoffs. 'We've got too many of those already.'

So, either she's brilliant at acting or Maria has no idea that anyone is looking for a controller.

'You want to talk about why he took it?' I try anyway, needing to extend our conversation. 'Maybe as payback to the man his mum's been seeing?'

She shakes her head but opens the door wider. 'That *piccola merda* has had me worried for days, he can wait another ten minutes.'

CHAPTER THIRTY-FIVE
AGES YOU HORRIBLY

As we enter Maria's house and work our way down a passageway, Gary pulls me aside, tells me he received a message from a colleague. The police tried the principal's house, but nobody was home. However, there was a King of Spades card wedged into her screen door.

'Someone's collecting every debt today,' I whisper. Which might be why they want the trade for Sarah to happen tomorrow morning.

'It looks that way,' Gary whispers.

I need to know if Maria has any idea whether her relationship with Joseph was a shared one. If she knows anything about Talitha Hills, she might know where the woman has gone.

We reach the end of the passageway, beyond a painting that's worth more than my car, and step into a large kitchen. I catch the aroma of baked bread but can't see any loaves. Maybe it's that scent some people spray? It would match the opulence of the place. Maria's house looks as old as Robyn Hallid's from the outside, but she's sunk more money into renovating hers. Everything within is grey marble and shiny white tiling, decor from the latest trend-setting magazines, paintings from established artists.

'What do you do, Missus Bortoni?' Gary asks, reading my mind.

'Looking after the kids takes most of my time,' Maria says, opening her fridge. 'I've got Hammond in Year Six, the twins in Year Nine. Sparkling water, anyone?'

We refuse the refreshment. Maria pours herself a drink, guides us into an adjoining dining room. We sit around a large oak table.

'In my spare time,' she continues, 'I help at an actors' studio. Mostly with kids. We run workshops.'

'You're an actor?' Gary says.

'Oh, I used to be. The well runs dry once you near forty.' She takes a sip of her sparkling water, stares at Gary. 'It's Miss Bortoni now, by the way. Julian's my ex-husband. Another thing that ran dry. I'll change the surname I'm legally entitled to when I feel like it. But that also means I have the right to see who I like, so if you were all hoping to start a lecture about me seeing Joseph, you can ditch that now. And Jeremy can act out about the relationship but it's not going to stop things.'

Maria tucks a strand of curly brown hair behind her ear. She's a striking woman, her appearance in line with the surrounding opulence. She's short, no more than five and a half feet, but her curly hair adds some height, her bright-green eyes drawing everyone in. She's covered in jewellery, with one small tattoo of a hummingbird on the side of her neck. As she takes another sip of her water, bangles jingle around her wrist.

'You'll keep seeing Joseph,' I ask, 'even if he's in prison?'

She keeps staring at Gary. 'Well, no. I should set a good example to my children. I'd have to find someone else, I guess. A woman needs to satisfy her needs.'

Gary clears his throat, shuffles on his chair. It's the most uncomfortable I've seen him. He's saved by a girl entering the room, a junior version of Maria.

'I thought we were going to get Jezza,' the girl says. I've seen her before, on my last visit. Jeremy's twin.

Maria snaps her gaze from Gary, takes in her daughter. 'Five minutes, Chloe.'

'But—'

'*Five* minutes.'

Chloe manages to groan and roll her eyes at the same time, then storms out of the room.

'Teenagers,' Maria says, 'you got any?'

We each shake our head.

'Well, it's a super-fun time. Ages you horribly. Worth it at some point, I'm told.'

We chuckle, but all I can think are that her choice of words seems scripted, as if she's talking to the media or acting a scene; maybe that's just how she learned to talk, after years of trying to make it on the screen. So… maybe Maria has been acting this whole time? Maybe she knows all about the controller and abduction and she's playing us, seeing what we know.

I reach out, leave the controller on the oak table. 'I need the toilet. I know you're pressed for time, but I won't be long.'

Maria points the way. I leave the table, head for the toilet, wink at Lucy as I pass. Gary, Desmond and her can ask what they need to, pry more into her relationship with Joseph. I've got something I need to try, a point Lucy raised outside.

There's bound to be a computer in this house.

I take a passageway. Down it are two closed doorways, various posters adorning them, plaques with children's names on them. There's one opposite Chloe's, but this is open. The door has a plaque with *Jeremy* written across it in a gothic font.

Jeremy could have taken his school laptop with him, to the empty Swan River house. But I'm willing to bet he didn't want any reminders of school where he was hiding. I enter his bedroom, make sure it's empty, close the door until a slight gap remains; just enough to hear someone coming. I take in his room. It's not the usual dark, brooding teenage chamber I imagined. It's as clean as the rest of the house. A couple of posters of sports stars and some busty manga figurines on a bookshelf are the only indication a teenage boy inhabits this room—although these days, it could be anyone's room, of any age.

No wonder the kid wanted a few days away, free to play video games in a junk food squalor.

There's a single bed in the room, the sheets scrunched up at the end. I imagine Maria's left it for Jeremy's return. *Welcome back, now make your bed.* Beside the frame is a small writing desk with a computer chair. Centre on the desk is a laptop. As I predicted.

I hurry to the laptop, flip open its screen. I'm asked for a password. I know this. Bailey told me, back in the Swan River house. What was it? Something real stupid, like…

I type in *boobs*.

The screen comes to life; proving why Bailey needed to change Jeremy's grades.

I take a small Ziplock bag out of my pants pocket. I removed the microSD from the controller back at home, placed it in the bag along with a spare SD adapter. I grab both items, slide the microSD into the adapter, push it into the laptop's SD slot. Wait for the folders to appear, the truth to unravel.

Except a blue window appears on the screen, prompting me to input a password.

I type *password*.

No luck. I have two attempts left.

I don't understand. If the card is password protected, will the people who want it have the right code, or do they just want to destroy it? Won't they want to check the contents before destroying it anyway, make sure the damning information is on there, confirming the card is not one big MacGuffin?

I get on my phone, look at ways to unlock a protected SD card. The internet has helped in so many situations so far, I'm hoping there's a way around the encryption.

There is; running an Administrator Command Prompt. I just need a few minutes to wrap my head around that, a few more to go through the steps on the website.

There are no minutes spare. Someone's coming, I can hear footsteps. I have seconds to hide. I eject the card, close the laptop lid, look for somewhere to duck behind. There's nowhere. I can't fit under the bed or the desk. I pull at the lone cupboard. It's full of clothes and boxes and God-knows-what.

'Yeah, the controller's right here,' Maria says, her voice just above a whisper. 'No, I want to meet tonight.'

She's right outside the door. I hurry, hide behind it.

'Look, I want to end this. Enough is enough.'

The door opens. I move with its arc, keeping out of sight. Maria enters the room, walks right up to Jeremy's bed. With her back to me, I edge around the door, slide out the room. Tiptoe back down the passageway, turn to where she told me the toilet was. Step inside the water closet, close the door behind me.

Breathe.

Fuck, that was close. I'm not made for that, am I?

I close the lid of the toilet, sit down. Try to hear footsteps. I stare at the gap between the door and tiling, waiting for a shadow to appear. When it doesn't, I glance up at the wall opposite, read an inspirational quote on a wooden plank: *"I can't" isn't a reason to give up, it's a reason to try harder.*

'You're right, plank,' I whisper. Expert advice at the right time, from an inanimate object.

'Everything alright?'

I jump at the voice. Maria's right on the other side of the door.

'Yep. Great, thanks,' I squeak out. I get up, flush the toilet for show.

When I open the door, Maria's already gone. As I re-enter the passageway, Chloe appears from her doorway. A younger boy opens his door, emerges. They walk behind me as I head for the dining area, mini security guards tagging along.

'Sorry I took a bit,' I offer as I reach the oak table.

Maria's gathering a few things in a large black leather handbag. I notice the controller's missing from my spot, don't point it out. I catch Lucy's eye. She motions to the handbag, flickers a smile.

'Thanks for the chat,' Gary says. 'I hope you're able to sort out everything with your son.'

'He'll be fine,' Maria says. 'He's more responsible than his father. Speaking of which, Chloe, I want you to stay home with Hammond.'

'I thought we were all going to get Jezza,' Chloe pouts.

'It might take longer than I first thought. There are leftovers in the fridge, reheat them if it's late.'

'Fine. But I get ice-cream.'

'Fine. Two scoops only.'

'Fine.'

We follow Maria outside as she hurries to her car. 'Where did you park?'

'Just down the road,' I point.

'Well, good luck in your investigation. Though if you're looking into P and F, I'm still not sure what you hope to find.'

'I wish we got to ask you more about it,' I say.

'We got enough,' Gary murmurs.

'Good luck with Joseph,' I call out.

'Thank you.' Maria beams a smile, starts the engine.

'I heard he likes you far more than the principal.'

The smile vanishes. Maria slams the driver's-side door. Shifts her car into reverse. Screeches out of her driveway, crunches into drive and tears down the street.

'So she knows about the principal.'

Lucy thumps me on the arm. 'She told us she hears about it all the time, you idiot. She hates it.'

I point to my vehicle again. 'My bad. Race you to the car? We've got an angry mother to follow.'

CHAPTER THIRTY-SIX
THE PENNY STARTS TO DROP

Lucy's driving, which is a good thing. She's a race car driver in another life, better at getting somewhere fast. Since Maria went onto the Freeway, that's a good thing. Plus, it gives me time to sit back and think.

'I hope I get to do something this time,' Desmond calls out from the back.

I turn to reassure him. 'Just help make sure she's safe, when we find her.'

'Of course.'

I flick my gaze to Gary. 'We can drop you off somewhere, you know. You've already got in trouble for helping me out in Margaret River, let's not keep the streak going.'

'Kind of in this a little deep now, mate,' Gary says. He waves his mobile phone at me. 'Besides, I've been updating my contact. Being as accountable as I can be. Right now, though, I'm just a citizen helping a friend. If something happens before the police arrive, I was just being shown around the city, I didn't know what was about to eventuate.'

Gary eases back in his seat and chuckles.

Did I make him like this? Willing to look the other way to get things done? Or is this a result of having members of his squad betray him, one leaving an old woman for dead? Regardless, I can't change his mind. He's here with me now and we'll let him crash on my couch later. There's no getting rid of him.

I turn back to Lucy. 'All good?'

'She's veering to the left, heading for the South Perth exit.'

'Her ex lives there.'

'The zoo's there, too. Traffic's thick…' Lucy flicks the indicator to change lanes.

'I can't believe she just took that controller off the table,' Desmond calls out, 'then carried on like she thought nobody saw. We *all* saw.'

'I think Maria's got her own problems,' I say. 'From what I overheard, she wanted the controller to strike her own deal. So, she's not the one who's abducted Sarah.'

Gary leans forward. 'What do they have on her that's worth the same risks we're taking?'

'Great question. There, she's turned off. Hurry.'

'I am.' Lucy tries pulling into the exit lane, the off ramp a hundred metres ahead, but another car runs alongside her, blocking her path. 'Move, buddy!'

She accelerates. The other car matches her speed.

'Fuckwit, move!'

She brakes at the last second, swerves behind the car. Both vehicles take the off-ramp. It rounds a bend, hits a traffic light.

We go through it, reach another traffic light. This one is red; and Maria's car is not waiting.

'She made it through,' Lucy says. 'Which way though?'

Julian's apartment and Perth Zoo are straight ahead. The apartment to the left, the zoo to the right. 'Straight.'

As we wait for the light to turn green, I do some of that thinking I told myself I'd achieve while Lucy drove. If Maria is heading for Julian's apartment, the reasoning escapes me. I thought he owed money to King of Spades, ran off with it after shooting Viktor the debt collector. If Maria brings King of Spades the controller, does that cancel Julian's debt? The last nice gesture of their relationship? If Maria is heading for Perth Zoo, then perhaps they've abducted someone she knows? Maybe King of Spades tried to incentivise an entire group of people, hoping statistics meant at least one person would bring them what they needed. Maybe Julian still factors into things here? Maybe they caught him? I don't know anything about the rest of Maria's family. If I could go back in time, I'd approach this case differently, dedicate an even spread of my investigation to all people involved in the case.

We near the apartment block. 'Slow down,' I urge.

There are two cars in the visitor's lot. Maria's isn't one of them. She could have parked elsewhere, or…

'Can you cut across the lanes, turn right into the zoo?'

Lucy signals, lets a car go past, pulls over. We cross a double lane and enter the start of the zoo car park. Only, there are bollards in front of it, a gate closed beyond that. Maria didn't park here.

'Where'd she go?' Desmond says, winding down his window, leaning out and looking around.

'She hasn't gone to pick up her son,' Gary says, 'since this is nowhere near either of the stations she would've been called to.'

'Maybe Robyn Hallid's collecting them both?' I try.

'She'd only be allowed to take her own kid.'

Her own kid.

'Turn round,' I urge. 'Head back to the lights, turn left.'

'Where are we going?' Lucy asks.

'Somewhere close by. It's the only other place that ties to everything.'

This *has* to be the place they've taken Sarah. It's minutes from the zoo. Empty. Three storeys overlooking the Freeway and Swan River, another building worth millions. Owned by the same shell corporation that had procured the other teenage hideaway.

Which Jeremy didn't discover by chance.

I hold that thought as Lucy drives past the new, scaffold-covered building. We round it, come out at a stretch of parkland to our right.

'Let's grab a spot here,' I suggest.

Maria's car is parked on the kerb. We pull up alongside it. Maria isn't inside. She's hurried off, carried with the same urgency. Still, I don't understand why.

We exit the car, hear the *whoosh* of cars on the nearby Freeway. People heading to their own dilemmas. It's almost six and sunset isn't for another hour or so, but the sky is gaining a red hue. I try not to see that as an ominous sign. We make our way to the front of the three-storey building. The sheeting covering the window frames makes a constant crinkling sound, pushed in and out by an unfelt wind. There's a scrape near the entrance door, beside the scrap-filled skip bin. We move as one to the source, find Maria at the front door. She's got a timber offcut in one hand, her other fist raised to knock on the door's surface.

'Maria,' I call out.

She twirls round, the timber plank held high. Then she recognises who's calling her name, and her resolve disappears, the plank lowering. 'You need to go.'

'No,' Desmond says, 'we need to be here, too. They have my wife.'

Maria catches the hitch in his voice, sighs. 'I just want this to end.'

'So do we,' I try. 'Tell us what happened, before whoever's in there opens that door.'

'I haven't knocked yet.'

'They'll hear the voices soon.'

Maria sighs again, emphasising her discomfort for everyone. Overacting, as if it's a display she learned in an improv class. 'Fine. You were going on about P and F. How much do you think you know about them?'

'A group of parents and teachers at your kids' school made their own little club,' I say. 'Gambled. I'd say they also invested money in things, like this house.'

'I started P and F,' Maria says, 'with Julian, when we were together. It was just the regular group of parents who attended the school's Parents and Friends meetings. We didn't want to rush home afterwards, so we'd just take our little social gathering to a restaurant or pub. And that was all the group's agenda was about. Meet up, have drinks. Bitch a little about everything going on. In school. In our lives. Then some teachers heard about us and wanted to join. I was against it but the others voted them in.'

'How many members?' I ask, having already heard a similar story from Robyn Hallid.

'I left after they proposed a merger.'

'A merger?' I ask, confused. This part of the story wasn't similar. Robyn had insisted the group had stopped before someone else started it up again.

'The school's part of a group,' Maria says. 'Eight private schools. All happy to charge high fees, compete in sports against each other and live in their own little bubble. With ties to a huge alumnus in many well-to-do places.'

'So, someone created a giant P and F?'

'Someone convinced three of the schools to join. Current parents, teachers, and alumni.'

'How many people?'

'Over two hundred that I saw, when the merger was proposed. More now, I'm sure, if it happened. Each person having to commit twenty thousand dollars in a one-off payment, an additional seven thousand dollars per year.'

'When did this begin?'

'Two years ago.'

I do the quick math. Over four million dollars raised from the outset. Two hundred times seven, add some zeroes, times two… just under three million more from ongoing fees. And for what?

I look up at the house. 'What were the fees for?'

She looks up at the house, too; it's the only response she needs.

'Did everyone get a share of the investments?'

Maria shrugs.

'So, this could all be about some fallout after a member embezzled money?'

'I don't know, and I don't care. I just want to clean my slate.'

'But you said you left P and F,' Lucy says.

'I did. I told you, this isn't about them.'

The front door flies open. 'Please can you keep quiet?' The speaker sees me. '*Tu pues la marde!*'

Silas raises a hand, as if to waves us inside. Only, in his hand is a gun. Pointed at my face.

Too late, the penny starts to drop. Silas has been collecting debts for King of Spades, leaving their card at different scenes. I'd assumed it was a name that P and F used for its gambling division, a way that a few of the top parents and teachers could scare the others in their group. But what if they are two different groups?

What if King of Spades is not associated with P and F at all?

What if I have put everyone at risk by getting everything wrong?

'Drop the plank and get inside,' Silas grunts. 'All of you. Now.'

CHAPTER THIRTY-SEVEN
BATSHIT INSANE SITUATION

This should not have been how my first case played out. I should have taken something easy, some kind of tail, like sitting in my car taking photos of an arsehole cheating on his wife. Learning little skills as I went along, developing them enough to help in a murder case involving multiple people and their secrets. Instead, I've thrust myself into a nightmare and I don't know what to do.

I'm forced to brush against Silas as I enter the house. He shoulders me, sends my body thumping against the wall. I try not to cry out in pain, depriving him of the satisfaction.

'Got your pants on this time, I see,' I say, turning to look straight at him. At the gun in his hand.

'I could shoot you right now,' Silas says, 'dump you in the skip.'

'Have you done that to anyone else lately?'

Silas grunts, holds the gun to my temple. Presses it against my flesh.

'You don't need to do that,' Lucy says, strength in her voice. 'We'll cooperate.'

Silas grunts again, gives it a moment, lowers the gun. His eyes fuelled by rage but his arm shaking. I can only hope he's having his doubts in whatever role someone's tasked him with playing.

'Head upstairs,' he says, pointing to an archway to the right.

The interior of the house is all concrete, brick and rubble. Nothing finished yet—walls awaiting plaster and paint, ceilings awaiting cornices and lighting. In another hour, when the sun sets, things could get interesting. I stop to the side of the archway, let Gary go first with a nod, Lucy and Maria behind them. It's only after seeing everyone, taking in their nervous glances, that I realise we are one short.

Desmond is no longer with us.

Did he enter the house, or hide before the door even opened? If Maria's noticed him missing, she hasn't said.

What is that man up to?

The staircase is dog-legged, so it has a landing halfway up before continuing in the opposite direction. Silas remains behind me, pointing the gun at my back, overseeing everyone's ascent. Except, by the time he reaches the landing, Gary has exited through an archway onto the next floor; and he's determined to be as sneaky as Desmond.

As Lucy and Maria reach the next landing, Silas calls out, 'Keep going up the stairs.' More dog-legged steps lead to another of the three storeys.

Lucy and Maria continue upwards. As Silas and I reach the landing, he realises we're down a line leader. 'Where is—'

A blur moves through the archway. Gary appears before Silas, grabs the barrel of the gun, twists it towards Silas's body, steps back and yanks. Silas has the gun wrenched from his hands, screeching in pain. He steps back in shock, teeters over the step. Starts to fall.

Gary reaches out with his free hand, grabs a handful of Silas's shirt, pulls him upright.

They stare at each other. Gary seems to dare Silas to retaliate. Silas considers it, relents. Holds his hands up in surrender.

'Where are they?' Gary asks.

'Top floor,' Silas murmurs.

Lucy and Maria watch, frozen on the stairs.

'How many?'

'A few.'

'Any more weapons?'

He shakes his head. 'This one isn't even real.'

'I thought so.'

'I'm sorry.'

'You will be. I'm police, you idiot.'

'Fuck.'

'You didn't even take our phones off us. Guess who I'll be calling.'

'I'm sorry. Let me take you upstairs, let them explain.'

Gary thinks about this, catches my eye. We nod in unison. 'Okay. Lower your hands. You go up the stairs first.'

Silas mutters something before obliging, stepping up past Lucy and Maria. For someone who threatens people to pay their debts, who wanted to kill me back at the hotel, he's not even trying to fight back now.

'What just happened?' Lucy whispers as I take the steps, join her.

'Sergeant Gary fucking Winters happened,' I whisper back, trying not to laugh.

We continue ascending the stairs, a fresh wave of emotions rolling through me. I didn't want to focus on the gun pointed at me before, on the worst-case scenarios it could have led to. My mind's rolled through those scenarios in Margaret River; no need for a sequel. But I'm elated we're no longer in the danger I thought we were. Now it's just a matter of seeing who's waiting up on the third floor, how they're holding Sarah, and what we can do to end this whole batshit insane situation.

Things get crazier as we step through the top floor archway. Because I can hear laughter, as if everyone's having a good time. We walk across uncoated concrete, tiptoe around a pile of plastic buckets and assorted sheeting, head around to the front room. Once it's complete, there will be wall to ceiling glass looking out at the Swan River and city. Now, it's just blue sheeting blocking most of the sunlight, still crinkling with the wind. Joining in with the laughter. From the four women seated near it.

Silas coughs. The women stop, take us in.

'We have visitors,' he says. He motions to Gary, who still has the fake gun in his hand. 'I apologise. I was trying to help, but I think I made it worse.'

One woman stands, folds her arms. Glares at Silas as if he's about to receive a verbal spray that'll send him scurrying down the stairs. Then she unfolds her arms, laughs again. 'It's okay, Uncle Silas. We kind of thought this would happen.'

Uncle Silas?

Robyn Hallid points to a circle of metal folding chairs. There are three spare. Two small, portable floodlights on the outside of the circle illuminate the room. 'Who'd like a seat?'

I take in the others in the room, the floodlights throwing shadows around them. Talitha Hills, the Junior School principal at Isidore College, her glare suggesting she's the least pleased to see me. Jensen Healy, the woman who hired me to help in a case she's somehow involved in, avoiding eye contact altogether. And Sarah, seated unrestrained, her smile suggesting she'd been laughing along with the others.

I don't know where to start. The first thing that escapes my lips echoes my bafflement. 'Just what is going on here?'

'Simple,' Robyn says. 'We're cleaning up the mistakes of the men in our lives.'

CHAPTER THIRTY-EIGHT
MYSTERIOUS THIRD PERSON

Lucy runs to Sarah, wraps her in a warm hug. Sarah tries to tell her sister she's fine. Nothing happened to her, they've treated her nicely, she understands what they've been going through. Lucy's brain is only half listening, though. She lets go of Sarah, whirls round to stand tall in front of Robyn Hallid.

'What the fuck do you think you were doing, taking my sister?'

Talitha rises from her chair, her principal instinct seeing what's about to happen. 'Let us explain before things escalate, then decide if you want to call the cops.'

'Too late,' Silas says, gesturing to Gary. 'He's police.'

Gary tucks the replica pistol into his belt. 'I haven't called anyone yet.'

I don't believe that's true for a second, but it seems to ease some of the tension in the room.

'Uncle Silas thought Sarah was your wife,' Robyn says to me. 'I guess he thinks all Asian people look alike?'

'*Je suis désolé*, Robbie. You're never going to let that go, are you?'

'No, we'll be talking about it for years.'

'I'm sorry,' I cut in, 'but *Uncle* Silas?'

Maria takes one of the empty seats, sick of waiting for her turn.

'We're not related,' Robyn explains, 'but Silas's mother has been our neighbour for years. We see him all the time.'

I wonder if his mother knows he's a debt collector. Or what he gets up to at hotels.

'You hired him as King of Spades' debt collector?'

Silas shakes his head. 'Mister Hallid used to hire me.'

'Someone's going to have to explain everything,' Gary says. He points to Sarah. 'Starting with her abduction.'

Ignoring Gary's excellent point, I think about Silas's comment, put a few things together. 'Heath Hallid started King of Spades.' I look at Robyn, Jensen, Maria. 'You've all told me a version of the truth, but twisted things into your own reality.'

I run through the facts as I see them, the tangle of thoughts that've been fighting for attention. I was told about Heath Hallid being rejected from Julian's fantasy basketball group. Rejected by the people he was trying to socialise with, for reasons he couldn't understand. I don't think he just went to the pub, settled for being alone. He said *fuck it, I'll start my own group*. He named it King of Spades. 'Am I right so far?'

Robyn sighs, nods. 'He even got a tattoo of a King of Spades card on his arm. Then he roped a few parents into joining him. Pub dwellers at first, parents who'd rather have a beer near school than watch their children grow up. Mostly a group of rich dads who wanted to pretend they were gangsters. You know: meet up late, drink, smoke cigars, gamble. Straight out of a cliché American movie. Poker, sports bets, online gambling… that kind of stuff.'

'Then he expanded to teachers?' I try, glancing at Talitha; thinking about Joseph and the missing Year Four teacher, Kristen.

'Heath was loud and frustrating,' Robyn says, 'but his passion could captivate people. He homed in on the Friday crowd, teachers who came in for a pint to take the edge off a long week. He offered them a way to boost their income, do something different.'

'He'd used everything he'd learned as an accountant,' I say, 'set up a shell corporation. Started investing everyone's money.'

'He pretended they were investing on behalf of someone called The King, only he never revealed it was him. He spoke about the leader of the group as if it was a mysterious third person. You see, the gambling and all that, that was for Heath to have a group of people to hang with, whether they wanted to or not. Outside of the gambling, Heath grew King of Spades until it became too big to handle.'

'It needed debt collectors?' I ask. 'Not for gambling debts, but for investment capital people had promised to contribute?'

Robyn nods.

'You knew all this,' I say, 'and you tried to get me to look at P and F instead? But P and F no longer exists.' I point to Maria. 'She told me this. She wondered why we were looking into it, talked about leaving before a merger. But that merger never happened, did it?'

Maria holds up the controller. 'Can we just get this over with?'

'You've taken over King of Spades, haven't you?' I ask Robyn. 'That's what you meant about cleaning up the mistakes. You told me you weren't part of P and F, and that was true. But you're part of something bigger.' I look at Maria. 'Everything from outside, the merger that was proposed. It happened with King of Spades, not P and F, right?'

Maria waves the controller. 'I have the card, let's make that deal.'

'For fuck's sake, Maria,' Robyn says, 'this wasn't part of our plan.'

'Why are you trying to play each other?' I ask.

And which lie have I fallen for?

'Can we get back to the abduction?' Gary calls out. 'Because when the police arrive, that's what they'll be asking about first.'

'When they arrive?' Lucy says.

'Come on, did you think I was just listening?'

'How long?'

'Ten minutes? Twenty? Depends if my contact believed my message.'

'I take full responsibility for Sarah,' Jensen says. 'Her abduction was my idea.'

'I don't even understand why you're here,' I say, my brain not quite registering her presence.

'My father, Simon, is an Old Boy at Isidore College.'

'And?'

'He's on the college board. He was tricked into siphoning a portion of student fees to the cause. If what happened makes the news, the college will be in more trouble, and our law firm will lose the trust of its clients.'

'Then you're here to negotiate something with Robyn? Just like Maria?'

'Henry,' Robyn says, 'you're jumping to conclusions.'

'You abducted my sister-in-law, who you thought was my wife!'

'No,' Robyn says, glaring at Jensen. 'I didn't want that. Things are spiralling.'

'They were going to use my abduction to draw the police to the zoo,' Sarah explains. 'They changed their mind, though. Once we got talking about the men in our lives and the shit they've done… They offered to take me home tonight. I was going to call you all soon, let Kat and Tommy and mum and dad and everyone know I was okay. But I wanted to stay for now. I told them I'd help.'

I have lost track of the threads of our conversation. 'We were panicking, thinking you'd been abducted, and…' I take a seat, take a deep breath; try to hide my frustration. 'What do you mean, you told them you'd help?'

Robyn nods, urging Sarah to continue. 'There are a few key people, one in particular, who know about this microSD, and it was the only way they thought of to get everyone in the same spot at once.'

'They could have been here right now.'

'It had to be somewhere public,' Jensen says. 'Lots of witnesses. Less chance something could go wrong.'

'What about the city? Elizabeth Quay? Places full of people right now.'

'We panicked, too, okay,' Jensen admits. 'When you said you already had the card, we didn't know what to do. I just wanted to stick to the plan, and… Okay, it was horrible, and I'm sorry I scared you all.'

'But who's after the microSD? Joseph? He's in prison.'

'It doesn't matter,' Maria chips in, 'I have it now.'

'And only a handful of people know about this house,' Talitha says. 'It's listed under the shell corporation.'

Bailey and Jeremy knew about the house, I think.

'But who are you hiding from here?' Lucy says.

Hiding. That's the key word here; my wife has read the room with far more intuition with me. After all, Robyn told me I was jumping to conclusions.

'You haven't taken over Heath's group,' I try.

'Why would I?' she snaps.

Shit.

'Then the debt collectors?'

'Heath contracted them. Nothing to do with us.'

I've got everything wrong.

'They've been busy since his death.'

'So I've been told.'

'Until Silas realised he wasn't working for you.' I turn to Silas. 'Your partner, Viktor. He was shot as a warning. To keep him in line. You took time off, stress leave. But Viktor's still been working for someone. Leaving calling cards.'

A loud noise echoes around the room, something smacked against the concrete wall. We turn to the source, look back at the room's entrance. At the man standing beside it.

'I gotta say,' the man calls out, 'that was the most roundabout way to get to the truth, and I still think half the people here are clueless.'

The man steps into the room. The floodlights reach his face, the gun in his hand.

'To answer a previous question, they're hiding from me.'

CHAPTER THIRTY-NINE
I'M NOT DOING ANYTHING WRONG

If I live to conduct another private investigation, I will ensure I interview as many people as possible in connection to the case. Then follow up on the information they give me, using my Notes app far better than I have this week. Because I'd already questioned what someone who works in wealth management services actually does, failing to see them as the threat they are.

I should have known better.

Julian Bortoni shot one of the men who came to collect the debt he owed. I thought it was an act of self-preservation, someone scared after that knock on his door. I thought it was because of a gambling debt, but he told me he avoided gambling. It wasn't good for business. I remember that now; too late. If it wasn't for gambling, it was for something else. An investment. One he tried to back out of. Something his wealth management experience knew he shouldn't associate with. Something that required forty thousand dollars. Maybe the whole scene was an act, though. Maybe Julian had called the debt collectors on himself. Now he's here to tie up loose ends.

'Look at everyone all gathered together,' Julian says, swinging the gun to point at everyone. 'Are we doing a rehearsal for Heath's funeral? I'll get the ball rolling. He was a cunt.'

Maria rises from her seat. 'Julian, enough. I've got the card. We can give it back. You can start fresh. *I* can start fresh.'

'You don't want that,' Julian says. 'You wanna keep sticking it to the teacher while I get stuck with your part of the investment. I have bigger plans.'

'We're divorced, Julian.'

'You still kept my name.'

'It's a legality, nothing more.'

As Julian calls his ex-wife a slew of awful names, I make the connection between the money he ran off with and the explanation Maria gave me outside. If P and F ever merged, they were going to charge investors an initial twenty thousand dollars to join. Heath must have stolen the merger model when he started King of Spades, made it a requisite that people needed the same injection; it's where the money for houses like this came from. All these cards left at teachers' places weren't for debts owed in poker nights or online gambling. They were for pledges the investors made, an investment they couldn't renege on because they'd been privy to the group's existence.

Two times twenty is the forty thousand that Julian ran off with.

Julian had helped set up the shell corporation, so he knew about the upcoming purchases. Two investments, two people.

I stand, swing my gaze from Julian to Maria. 'The both of you were supposed to invest in King of Spades?'

'You don't understand,' Maria says. 'Julian said he heard about it from school. We definitely didn't know Heath was part of it. We pledged an investment, then backed out. Only, there was no backing out. Heath expected us to pay. You know what it's like to have someone try to control you that way?'

I think of Aunty Janice, the way she controlled her siblings, my mother, her town. Everybody too scared to speak up about her. 'I don't, but I can imagine how awful it would be.'

'I told Julian to cut our losses, but forty thousand is a lot of money to forget about.'

'You left the group behind, though?'

'I never joined.' Maria points to Julian. 'He didn't, either.'

'Not after I realised Heath was a part of it,' Julian scoffs. 'He couldn't even manage his fantasy basketball team. He had Jokić, for fuck's sake; best Centre in the league, he should have dominated. How's he going to be higher than me on the King of Spades hierarchy and make solid investments with my money?'

'What does this have to do with Heath Hallid's murder?' Gary asks.

'Great question,' Julian says. 'That gun in your belt, place it on the floor, kick it this way.'

Gary obliges.

'Thank you. Your question's irrelevant. I'm here for the controller. I need the information on it.'

'How did you know Maria had it?' I ask, before Gary screams in frustration.

'She phoned, told me she had it. I didn't know she was trying to strike a deal herself.'

'How did you know where she was?'

'Her phone's still under my family plan. I can see where everyone is.'

'You knew where Jeremy was all week?'

Julian nods. 'I told him about this place. I'd helped to set up the corporation that made the purchases, confirmed its existence with Joe.' Sensing blank stares, he adds, 'I met him a few times to talk about Hammond's schooling. We bonded over basketball. He joined my fantasy basketball league. We met up for drinks a few times, after he ceased to be Hammond's teacher. I didn't know he was doing my wife, but our connection was strong. I thought maybe there could be more between us. One day.' He waves the gun at us, as if daring someone to speak up. 'I like everyone, okay. Women, men. It's not a big deal. People should be more tolerant of it. I'm not doing anything wrong.'

Back at his apartment, Julian had worked himself into a rant about people being intolerant of Bailey's sexual orientation. I'd wondered if his reaction related to his own upbringing. Another instinct I should have trusted, but how does it relate to the case?

'Joseph confided in you, told you about King of Spades,' I try. 'About the info he'd saved onto a microSD, the details of their whole operation.'

Julian nods. 'Joe had a system. He'd collated info on his workmates, found ways to control them. When he'd stumbled onto a group that a pile of them were part of, he realised he'd hit the jackpot. That's why he got closer to my wife, to the principal there. They told him about the people in King of Spades and he ended up with a spreadsheet. Investors and their connections, assets, fraudulent activities. Enough info to take hundreds of people down. He saved the file on the card, kept it hidden.

He didn't have the foresight to back things up on the cloud, or print everything out, or make multiple copies. Literally one memory card, hidden away to access later, if he needed to start pointing fingers.'

'And Heath found out?' I guess. 'Confronted Joseph at the parent meeting?'

'Heath didn't care about seeing his kid's teacher to discuss their academic progress. He'd never done that in the past, why show up for that now?' Julian shakes his head. 'The meeting was a chance to have a one-on-one chat, an isolated confrontation after sending him notes to scare him off. Heath knew Joe was controlling lots of people with knowledge about his group.'

I look over at Robyn. 'Heath didn't have his own spreadsheet? Surely he knew about everyone in King of Spades?'

'If he did, the police have it now.' Robyn points to the controller. 'That's the only copy a civilian has access to.'

'So, whoever can access it controls King of Spades.' I glare at Julian. 'You couldn't hack it that the guy you kicked out of your fantasy basketball league went off and started his own group. Became the King. You wanted what he had.'

Julian shakes his head. 'Fuck you.'

'Did you get Joseph to push Heath over that railing, or did you do it himself?'

'I didn't push Heath, but I was there. It was an accident. Now give me that controller, Maria.'

'Then it was Joseph who pushed him?' I guess, even though I don't believe it. 'He was going to take over King of Spades, since he already had the information. Did you think you could be his sidekick?'

'I'm not a *sidekick.*'

'You've tried not to be one. You even contracted the same debt collectors as Heath, right? Probably pretending to be someone from King of Spades. That was your idea, wasn't it? Not Joseph's? I bet you even had Viktor drop a card at Maria's. That's why she's here, thinking she's helping with your debts.'

Maria gasps. 'The card was in my mail.'

'That's right,' Julian snaps. 'All my idea. Joe loved it, loved the way it took the focus off him.'

'Since he killed Heath?'

'I said he didn't push—' Heath stops himself.

I shake my head, exaggerating my disappointment.

'Look,' Julian says, 'I'm not getting into the grand scheme of it all. I just want the card.' He points the weapon at Maria. 'Just hand it over. I know the card's inside.'

'You could have grabbed it off us at the zoo tomorrow,' Robyn says, 'without the need for a gun.'

'With police waiting to see if I showed up?' Julian says. 'I'm not the idiot you think I am. And I guess... since the card's right here... I guess I can't let any of you get away now. I think that's what Joe would want.'

'Of course you can,' Jensen squeals; silent until she realises the direction this is taking.

'If you let us go now,' I say, a thought forming in my mind, 'you can have the controller, and you'll walk away with all the info on King of Spades. But if something happens to us here, the police will start digging deeper, and the group will get shut down, anyway.'

'Yeah,' Gary adds. 'One death is alarming. Several deaths will bring multiple departments into the hunt. They'll pry into everyone's records and uncover the truth themselves. You'll join Joseph in prison instead of being free together.'

I hear a distant rattle. Someone coming up the staircase. Does everyone else hear that? Julian doesn't appear to; he's started to pace the room, deliberating his next move.

'I can find a way to make you disappear,' he mutters, 'with no attention on me or the school. I'm sure I can.'

'How are you going to make us all disappear?' I ask, hoping to drag this out.

'I'll find a way.' Julian takes a step towards Maria, the gun still aimed at her. 'Hand me the fucking controller, Maria.'

'It's useless without a password,' I call out.

'It doesn't matter. Joe has that.'

'He hasn't told you?'

There's another rattle in the distance. Are the police here already, storming up the staircase?

'Just let him have the controller,' I urge Maria.

She relents, hands it over. Julian opens its backing, feels round for the microSD. 'What the hell? Where is it? It was supposed to be in here.'

I reach into my pocket, pull out the Ziplock bag. 'She never had it.' I throw the bag on the ground. 'And you'll never be the King.' I lift my foot, ready to stomp down.

Time seems to drift into slow motion. Julian screams so loud, several people clasp hands to ears to block the noise. He swings the gun round to point at me as Maria cries for him to stop, desperate for this to end. And Desmond appears at the threshold, sans police, sees what's happening and starts sprinting towards us.

Too late. Julian doesn't pull the trigger. Instead, he lowers his stance, starts charging. An enraged bull with nothing to lose.

Before I can stomp on the Ziplock bag, he strikes my body; connects with so much force, the wind escapes my lungs, my limbs collapsing. I smack against the concrete flooring, Julian hovering above me. He turns to face me, reaches down with his free hand, trying to push me aside, desperate to grab the bag. I reach around, feel the plastic first, grab the bag and pin it against my chest, refusing to let go.

Julian swings the gun to point at my face, and—

I think of Lucy. Family. The trip we're supposed to take. The sister I'll never find. My sick mother.

Things I've never finished. Amends I've never made. Time I'm not ready to give up, love I'm not ready to part with.

I squint, trying to force my eyes closed. Then a blur crashes into Julian. Desmond. He lifts Julian off the ground just as there's a *bang* from the gun. A concrete chip flies into me, slicing my cheek. But the bullet has missed. Desmond keeps the momentum, throws Julian backwards against the wall.

Only, it's not a wall. Julian collapses against the blue sheeting that covers the window frames. The force of his body pushes the material outwards, the wind whipping it more, and there's a loud tear. Julian has time to look at us in sheer shock before his body continues its descent. Out of the building. Three storeys down.

There's an awful stretch of silence, then a crash.

Dust in the skip bin plumes into the sky. A cloud of white against the red sunset.

CHAPTER FORTY
COULDN'T LIE ANYMORE

The sky is almost dark, illuminated by a series of flashing red and blue. The sight should comfort me, a sense of camaraderie from my time as an officer, but there's only one reason such lights switch on. Something terrible has happened, and I've been part of it once more.

We're hovering round a large silver van. It's often used as a mini booze bus, but it's got a mini command unit inside. Chairs and desktops, IT equipment. Enough to take our statements while everything's still fresh, process us as needed. It's taking a long time to get through the routine, but I don't mind. Whatever draws my attention from the skip bin they've sectioned and screened off, the mess of limbs within.

Desmond and Sarah don't seem to mind, either. They're whispering things to each other, holding hands. Using the adrenaline and Desmond's life-saving gesture to reconnect. I can't wait to see the look on the kids' faces when we get back home, their father back in their life. Luckily, nobody is mentioning that it was Desmond who caused Julian to fall from the building, the incident downplayed as an unintentional outcome of defending oneself from a would-be killer.

I touch the sticking plaster on my cheek, try not to imagine Desmond's life-saving gesture going the other way.

Thankfully, Maria Bortoni raises her voice inside the van, a nice distraction. They will be asking her about her involvement in King of Spades, something I still don't understand entirely myself. She said she pulled out before making the investment, but maybe Heath never stopped harassing her, hence the need to get the microSD and end things, the group's secrets exposed. It's just like when my Aunty Janice was controlling everyone with dirt and debts, making them work for her, getting them to install illegal servers on their property. Once someone controls you, makes you do something you'll regret, it's hard to go back, hard to speak up against them.

Maybe that's why Joseph hired me. Sure, there was the familiarity of our time together as teachers, but it wasn't until he'd read about me exposing the vicious cycle my aunt had created that I'd returned to his radar. Even though he never told me, he knew all about King of Spades; trapped in their pocket in his own way. Controlling others with the dirt he found, then threatened by its leader, urged to bury all secrets. Reacting in a way that led to murder.

A man approaches. Tall, tanned, looking like he spends more time at the beach than on the beat. He sees Gary, shakes his hand. Gary leads him over, makes the introductions. He's Senior Constable Templesmith, the contact Gary had been messaging a fair bit this week. He thanks everyone for their help, then brings Gary and me aside, gives an update.

'We've got a confession.'

As much as I didn't want to hear it, a confession means that Julian didn't lie.

'And it was an accident?' I ask.

'That's the angle everyone will take, for now. It might not have been an accident if he hadn't appeared, but...'

'He won't go to prison, then?'

'His lawyer will make sure he avoids time.'

'Run through what happened.'

'It was just like you said.'

I nod. Digging up dirt on King of Spades and P and F, whether it existed or not, highlighted the myriad of people they had control over. Like someone I've overlooked until Julian's words, his insistence that Joseph didn't push Heath, made everything click.

Someone was controlled. Silenced.

Living in luxury all week. Angry. Acting like a toxic friend because a secret was festering within them.

Bailey Hallid was half-asleep when Senior Constable Templesmith and his partner came in to interview the teens.

'When's mum coming?' was the only thing he asked. Because she should have picked him up hours before.

'I just assured him she would be there soon,' Senior Constable Templesmith explains to us. 'Then we arranged for a Justice of the Peace to come in as an independent person and asked to speak to Jeremy.'

Jeremy wasn't asleep. He was very much awake, watching something on his phone. He was reluctant to acknowledge them.

'When my partner placed a hand on his phone, asking him to put it away before they confiscated it, the boy snapped, "Hey, I'm watching an Aussie kick butt in 2K." We didn't know what it meant, and we didn't care. Since Bailey was cooperative, I asked him whose idea it was to stay at the empty houses.'

'Jeremy's,' I say, interrupting Senior Constable Templesmith's story to add the detail I'd relayed through Gary. 'His father had told him about the houses.'

'Correct,' Senior Constable Templesmith says. 'Good catch, by the way.'

He details the same thoughts I'd had when comparing the hiding places the boys could have chosen. The house we found them in was pretty much complete, days away from a handover. Furniture and furnishings in most rooms, everything far out of my budget. Yet the boys had created their little gaming cave in a smaller, upstairs room. Hidden away. What odd choice in living circumstances led them there? They could have been back home with their mothers, in the comfort of their own bedrooms. Or at a friend's house, or even at grandparents or any other relatives I'd never asked about. Or, if they really wanted to be alone, they would have known about the Willetton house, too, and stayed there. The one near basketball courts, bus stops and fast-food outlets. The one much more suited to them, instead of a lifeless mansion.

'Why hide away in a house only a handful of people knew about?' Gary asks.

'Because the police had been to the South Perth house,' Senior Constable Templesmith says, 'on a callout from Henry here, leaving it marked in their eyes. Even though it wasn't on our radar, since it's still under construction. And because his father was using the Willetton house to hide in. Two of our constables entered it, found signs of habitation.'

'But why hide for so long at all?' Gary says, still working through everything that's happened. 'I thought they were just teens blowing off steam after the awful murder.'

'Because Jeremy didn't want the police to find him,' I say. 'Because then they would have asked about the moment that Heath Hallid died, and he was worried he couldn't lie anymore.'

Senior Constable Templesmith nods, tells us about the moment he asked Jeremy the question, 'Did you help to kill Bailey's father, or did you just watch?'

The confession poured out of Jeremy after this. About how he'd broken his freestyle record at the swim meet, looked for his dad to celebrate, saw the man leaving the area. How he followed him out the swimming pool area while the last heats were running, crossing over to the Junior School in pursuit. How he saw him walk up the stairs, sprinting to follow, nearing Joseph's classroom, hearing raised voices. Walking in to see his dad already arguing with Bailey's.

Jeremy hadn't understood what they were arguing about. He could only watch as the two men started grabbing each other, pushing, swinging fists. Then, Heath had stumbled towards the classroom door and seen Jeremy. He'd started saying everything was his family's fault, looked like he was about to attack Jeremy, too. He'd reached out to grab him, but the boy shrugged his way free of the man's grip. Heath had tripped on the door sill, stumbled forward, hit the railing. He'd reached out for Jeremy again, but it was too late. He just kept going, up and over the railing. There one second, gone the next. Julian had hurried his son back to the swim meet, made them continue as if nothing had happened, later urging Jeremy to hide in the vacant house until they sorted things out.

Julian had said the death was an accident. Jeremy believed that version of events. I didn't.

'You think Heath just tripped and fell?' Gary asks, reading my mind. 'I saw the photos. That railing should have been enough to stop him.'

'We couldn't pursue any more, for now,' Senior Constable Templesmith says. 'Jeremy was on the verge of hyperventilating. We had to cut the interview there. The news horrified Bailey. He couldn't believe his friend knew what happened and kept it a secret, hiding with him for a week. We made the call, had his mother rushed from this scene to our station.'

'What will happen to Robyn Hallid?' I ask. 'We still don't know what her involvement is.'

'Robyn knew about her estranged husband's King of Spades activities, but didn't want any part in it. She'd already been working with us to take it all down. She knew Julian Bortoni was trying to get the microSD to extract all the information on the group, take it over. But she had no idea what he'd done to Heath. Or if he had anyone else working with him. He'd called her, told her he'd be taking over King of Spades as soon as he had the information. Scared her to death.'

'You didn't have any detail watching her?' Gary asks.

'We did for the most part, one group disguised as reporters. But we had a change of guard, and Robyn took the opportunity to flee.'

'She's got two younger kids,' I say.

'Watched over by their neighbour, Juniper Raymond.'

Silas's mother. I glance over at Talitha and Jensen, waiting by the end of the van. 'Sarah's abduction still feels off, even after Jensen admitted it was a mistake.'

'We know. They were supposed to arrive at the zoo tomorrow with the microSD, where we would be ready to arrest Julian and anyone else working with him. Maybe, because they didn't have the card, they changed the plan, did what they thought they needed to do to get it. We need time to look into a few things, to decide how we'll pursue this.'

Maria screeches inside the van again. I think about the call she made while I was hiding in Jeremy's bedroom. I'd thought it was to the people who'd abducted Sarah, Maria trying to strike her own deal. But she'd called Julian, tried to get him to ease off the chase for the microSD since she thought she had it. So, she didn't call Sarah's abductors, but somehow knew where they were. She'd driven straight there.

A whole lot of craziness centred on the data contained on a tiny piece of circuit board and plastic. Which everyone only knew about after Joseph told them; at various intervals, his way of letting each person know he had dirt on them.

Dirt on the people he was sleeping with. Dirt on the people he worked with. Dirt on the families of the children he taught.

I glance at the time on my phone. Seven-forty. 'What if I could get some answers tonight?'

'Henry, you've completed your role in the case, going far beyond your duty as a PI. Unless you're called to present evidence at trial, you don't get to see how we're following up on everything from tonight.'

'Look,' I try, 'Julian pretty much admitted he didn't work alone. And in our gut, we know Heath's death was no accident. I realise I'm a civilian, but I need to interview someone in prison, and the only way I can do that is if I accompany you.'

'Who do you want to interview?'

'Joseph Pooles. The teacher.'

'You want to interview him right now?'

'It's my last chance to act on a hunch.'

'You think you can get an admission of guilt?'

'I do.'

Senior Constable Templesmith looks at Gary, who nods with a grin. I can only hope this doesn't get Gary in further trouble. He's under review for going beyond duty to help me, already. Now, he's vouching for me when we could just be heading home. His friend doesn't have to agree, though. He's tapping away at his phone, clearing something. Gary and I wait until Senior Constable Templesmith looks up at us, shrugs. The best *what the hell* gesture I could hope for.

'Regulations state we can have access to a prisoner at any time,' he says, 'if it's for an official purpose. Given the development in this case, I can take you and Gary now. But if your hunch plays out, I take over.'

If we're going now, it means I need to say goodbye to my wife. After an ordeal threatening our lives, where she almost saw me shot in the face. That, and, while waiting to be interviewed, I'd told her about everything that's happening to my mother, too. So, I should be spending every second holding her. Sticking close to Sarah, Desmond, and the rest of our family, taking comfort in the fact that we've made it through yet another ordeal.

As I walk over to Lucy, her face tells me she's perceived what I'm about to say.

'I'll start packing our suitcases,' she says, trying to smile.

I lean in for a kiss. 'I have two things I need to take care of, then I'm done with it all.'

'Sure you are.'

CHAPTER FORTY-ONE
PERTH'S A TINY PLACE

We enter Hakea Prison, go through the motions of signing in, wait
for Joseph in an interview room. It takes ten minutes for him to
arrive. I want to say he looks far worse than our last encounter, his
curly brown hair falling out in places, puffy eyes and sallow skin,
more bruises across his body. Only, he looks refreshed. Well rested.
Making me want to reach over and punch him in the face. Instead,
I've got this one chance to act on a hunch. To dig into the reason
for Joseph's swing in demeanour. After that, the police will
continue running their investigation methodically, arriving at the
right conclusion.

I wait for Joseph to take the three of us in, his eyes settling on
me. 'Last time I visited,' I say, 'you were being treated for an
attempted suicide.'

Joseph rattles the handcuffs linking him to the table. 'Not
exactly living my best life.'

'Our choices often come back to haunt us.'

Joseph chuckles. 'I heard through the grapevine that arrests are being made, that someone's being charged for Heath's murder.'

'Then you'll be living your best life soon,' I say, wondering how in the world Joseph was privy to such information so fast. I glance at Senior Constable Templesmith, thinking he might want to follow up on such a revelation, but he nods at me, urging me to continue. 'Did you ever want to hire me, or did your lawyer suggest it?'

Joseph opens his mouth to answer, pauses a moment. Deciding what to say. 'She suggested it. She'd been reading about you in the papers. She brought me the clippings.'

'So, you hadn't been following what I'd been up to?'

'Get over yourself, Henry. I'm in my own shit, why would I care what you've been doing?'

Ouch. There's a truth to Joseph's words, but they still hurt.

'Why are you even here speaking to me,' Joseph continues. 'My lawyers paid you for your services, I'd say you're done.' He points to Senior Constable Templesmith. 'This guy in the uniform should be asking me the questions, since he got me dragged out of my palace.' He points to Gary. 'I don't know who you are.'

'I'm just along for the ride,' Gary says, beaming.

Senior Constable Templesmith leans forward. 'I'm allowing this man, who is still under the employ of your lawyers, to ask what he needs to first. His credentials are backed up by this man, another member of the law. Let's continue and perhaps focus on answering the questions rather than avoiding them.'

We wait, watch as Joseph nods. Point made.

I clear my throat. 'How did you get involved with Jensen, your lawyer, in the first place?'

Joseph flashes a grin. 'Each year, the college puts on a production, the Drama students fighting for their chance to get into the performing arts academy. Sometimes it's at the college, but they last had it at the Perth Concert Hall. They invited old graduates. Jensen came along with her father. We got to talking after the event, when drinks were free-flowing.'

'You were already seeing the principal and Maria Bortoni.'

'I said we got to talking, Henry. Jesus. And besides, what if I *did* start seeing Jensen? I'm not committed to any one person. Who the fuck would want to do that?'

'Did you know Jensen's father was connected to King of Spades?' I ask, ignoring his jibe about marriage.

'I did.'

'It was luck you met her, then? And luck she ended up being your lawyer?'

'Perth's a tiny place, Henry. It's all about who you know.'

'Did you know her father beforehand?'

'Just by reputation. He's some bigwig old graduate. Still on the college board, can't let his glory days go. But why would he? Isidore College makes a huge deal of its graduates, calls them Old Boys, celebrates their achievements annually.'

'They're proud of the people who walked through their halls.'

'Can't say the same about the teachers. It's thank you and fuck off.'

'You sure that's not just your experience? Have they asked you to fuck off?'

'Even if I'm proven innocent, which it looks like I will be soon, there's no way they'll have me back.'

'Even with Talitha Hills having a say?'

'Nah. You know, a couple of years ago, three teachers left, all looking forward to retirement or new positions elsewhere. They'd all worked for the college over ten years. The most senior one, they made a nice montage they played at an assembly, photos of their early classes, some kids thanking her for teaching them. The other two teachers got a handshake and a goodbye. Now, nobody talks about them. Nobody asks them back to talk about what they've done since leaving. As if leaving was an ultimate betrayal. As if retirement was something they should never have considered. You think I want to be treated like that?'

'That's got nothing to do with your case. And it's inevitable, isn't it? Retiring? Changing schools or professions?'

'I guess.'

'And how many times did you communicate with the teachers you'd mentored along the way? You said it yourself, why would you care what I've been doing?'

Joseph tries to hold out his hands, the handcuffs rattling. 'You got me. We all move on.'

'But some of us end up richer than others, right? And that pissed you off?'

'Money's not everything,' Joseph scoffs.

'Jensen's law firm paid me ten thousand dollars to investigate your case. I didn't even put in a quote for my time. Where did they get the money for that?'

'You'd have to ask them.'

'I'm asking you. Did you invest in King of Spades?'

'Nah.'

'You just had all the info on them?'

'Don't know what you're talking about, Henry.'

'The microSD you hid in a gaming controller. The one you told Jensen about. That she didn't report to the authorities.'

'She must have misheard.'

I glance at Gary, try to look appalled. 'Not a very good lawyer, finding potential evidence and trying to cover it up for you.'

'I never asked her to.'

'Because she wanted to cover up the evidence of her father's misdeeds?'

Senior Constable Templesmith taps the table. A warning: keep it tight, wrap it up. That, or we just go round and round for hours.

'Jensen was so desperate to get that microSD, she told everyone that abducting my wife would be a smart move. To get me to find the controller faster or something, I don't know.'

'My lawyer's actions do not reflect my own.'

'I know. But they showed the reach you have. My aunt had a vast reach on other people. Did you read about that? No? She blackmailed her own siblings, the townsfolk she saw every day. She made her brother and husband kill someone who got too close to a buried secret.'

'Sounds awful.'

'It is. But for her, it's everyone else's fault. Especially that she got caught. Is that how you feel? That it's everyone else's fault you were caught?'

'I'm here for a murder I didn't commit. I wasn't caught, I was falsely imprisoned.'

'Because you didn't expect Talitha to call the police on you?'

'That was her choice.'

'More people will start making the right choice. They'll testify how you blackmailed them with the information on the microSD.'

'Ridiculous.'

'People have started to come forward about my aunt. All it takes is one person to get the ball rolling. Who will it be for you? Will Talitha have more she wants to say?'

'You tell me.'

I think about Robyn Hallid's comment, that they were cleaning up the mistakes of the men in their lives. What was Talitha's mistake? Having a relationship with a co-worker? Or introducing him to the group she was part of, King of Spades. A group she'd invested in?

I ask Joseph as much.

'You have no proof Talitha invested in King of Spades,' Joseph smirks, 'or was part of it at all. So she can't say I knew about it, either.'

'But there *is* proof she knew about the group. Bailey Hallid discovered a folder in the college's network, labelled KOS. Some leftover data that listed purchases like various properties. He thought it looked like a draft before someone made a bigger file on their personal computer. The bigger file is on that microSD, isn't it.'

'I wouldn't know.'

'But you told Jensen about it.'

'She's trying to frame me.'

'Your own lawyer is trying to frame you?'

'It's happened before. To other people.'

'I don't think so.'

Joseph shrugs.

'What will the data on the microSD show, anyway?' I ask.

Joseph shrugs again.

'Do you even know? Or was it Talitha who created the spreadsheet? She managed an entire Junior School, maybe she streamlined a way to manage the group's members, just like Heath Hallid had. Then you just copied the file off her. You were always lazy with your work.'

'Stop trying to goad me, Henry, or I'll ask for a lawyer.'

'The one who's trying to frame you?'

'I'll get another one.'

'Fine.' I take a deep breath, sigh with as much exaggeration as possible, turn to Senior Constable Templesmith. 'I guess we're done. None of this makes sense.'

'Agreed,' Joseph scoffs.

I rub my chin, thinking, putting on a show. Memories already flooding back. 'Although, we also have two witnesses who'll be able to say they found the controller at Joseph's house. So, there's that, at least.' I stare at Joseph, watch him gulp. 'That might start the ball rolling. Who will turn on you to save themselves?'

Joseph shakes his head, swears under his breath.

'Was Heath going to turn on you?' I ask.

Joseph smacks a fist against the table. 'That fucker was going to stop his own fucking group!'

I glance at Gary and Senior Constable Templesmith. Both men are wide-eyed.

'Why would he do that?' I ask, right at the moment of truth, praying we get there.

'He couldn't manage his fantasy basketball team, how did he think he'd manage a group with hundreds of members? Some people had abused their membership, gone rogue. People like Jensen's father, taking money from the college board with no approval. Heath didn't want that. He was going to dissolve everything at their next meeting.'

'How do you know?'

'The notes he left me. He knew I had the files on King of Spades. He wanted me to stop using them for my gain, was giving me one more day to put an end to things.'

'And then you had the parent-teacher meeting?'

'Where he confirmed what he was doing. I told him he should reconsider.'

'He hit you because of that?'

'I wasn't polite.'

'He knew he was killing the stranglehold you had on the people in his group?'

'He should have just handed the reins over to me and Julian.'

Ah. I resist a smile. Now we've got to their relationship without Joseph even realising.

'It was all about handing the reins over to you and Julian, wasn't it?'

Joseph realises his mistake, remains silent.

Carina had called this a few days ago, at Desmond's house. I'd told her that Julian wasn't roughed up the first time I saw Silas and Viktor outside his apartment. She surmised he'd got them running errands, that he was part of the King of Spades group. But after Julian had shot Viktor on their next visit, to get out of the debt it seemed he owed, I'd ignored that thread of thinking.

'The business cards left around, that was Julian's idea,' I say, steering back to the truth.

Joseph stays silent.

'Don't worry, he already told us, before he died. I think you gave him a few people from your list. He said he'd scare them, get a quick burst of money to help you take over the group.'

Joseph shakes his head. 'Stop it, Henry.'

'He left a card at Heath's house the day of your interview. The day Heath Hallid was killed.'

'Shut up.'

'Was the card meant for Heath or his wife, since they were separated?'

'Stop.'

'Was Robyn next on your hit list?'

'There's no hit list.'

'But Julian was doing your dirty work, right? Scaring people, making it look like Robyn had taken over King of Spades. You told him who to target. You told him about the Willetton house, the Swan River house. I think he even pretended to have the debt collectors come for him.'

'This is bullshit. Stop.'

'We could call Silas and his partner, confirm who hired them.'

'I didn't ask Julian to do anything.'

'He adored you. He probably thought you'd take over King of Spades together. A dynamic power couple.'

'This is all slander.'

'He even helped you kill Heath Hallid.'

'No.'

'His son's already confessed. During the interview, Julian made his way to your class. How did he know where to go, though? And when? I think you'd arranged a time that you'd be downstairs. A five-minute window.'

'No.'

'Maybe messaged him as you went downstairs?'

'No.'

'Police will be searching your phone records, anyway. It all happened to be right after Jeremy's winning swim meet, so the boy was looking for his father. He followed him to the class. Did you know that?'

'No.'

'He said Heath tripped, but I don't think that's true. Julian hit him, just enough to make him dizzy, and the man fell. Jeremy will revise his statement when he realises what you made his father do.'

Joseph pulls at the handcuffs, trying to rise from the table.

'I didn't make him do anything. It was his idea.'

'And you just went along with it?' I wait for Joseph to dig the hole deeper. When he doesn't, I add, 'Julian fell tonight. Did you find that out?'

Joseph pulls on the handcuffs again.

'Gone too soon. But I guess you've still got Maria and Jensen and all the other people you don't want to commit to.'

He grunts with the effort. Gary signals to someone.

'Not Talitha anymore, but... more people to do the things you're too lazy to do.'

A guard is hurrying over.

'More people to die for you.'

Joseph roars for me to go to hell, tries to leap across the table. He's restrained by the handcuffs and the guard, who pushes him down against the metallic surface.

'All this cause your free meal was about to end,' I say, bending down to catch Joseph's eye.

'You were supposed to make everyone else look guilty but me!' Joseph snarls.

'You had parents wanting to get revenge on teachers. Teachers supporting you, saying they felt like doing the same thing. When everyone goes back next year, things will be wildly different. And for no reason. The police have Heath Hallid's tech, I'm sure they'll find out about King of Spades' members anyway, shut it all down.'

A guard taps my arm, directs us from the room. Outside, I place a hand on the wall, catch my breath.

Senior Constable Templesmith is shaking his head; hopefully, it's in amazement.

'I know it's not much of a confession,' I try. 'I filled in some blanks that might not be true, and you haven't recorded anything, but… maybe it's a start?'

He glances at Gary until they both crack a broad smile. He holds out a hand to shake. 'We're looking at conspiracy to murder, at the very least. No wonder Gary tried to get you to join his department.'

We shake hands. 'I can be a consultant any time.'

'We may have to take you up on that.'

Another guard arrives, leading us to the exit.

'I need to go my station,' Senior Constable Templesmith says. 'I'll have an officer drop you home from there.'

'Actually,' I say, 'there's one more person I need to visit.'

CHAPTER FORTY-TWO
SOMETIMES WE DON'T GET OUR WISH

Visiting hours at Joondalup Hospital usually end at eight. It's past ten. At some point they'll close the automatic doors, but they slide open now. I wave goodbye to Senior Constable Templesmith and Gary, make my way inside as if the times don't apply to me. Head to the lift before anyone at the reception desk can call out. Soon, I'm on my mother's floor. Most overhead lights are out on her wing, strip lighting leading me to her room.

She's sitting up, reading a book.

'Henry?' The sight of me throws her, as if she's staring at a ghost.

I sit on the lone visitor chair. 'It's been a long day.' I sink back against the thin cushioning. 'A very long, confusing day.'

There's a sound behind me; my mother's roommate, snoring in the bed hidden by a curtain.

'Have you called Roland?'

'Mum, Uncle Roland won't talk to me. He blames me for his son's death.'

Mum nods. 'Paige was here before dinner.' Moving on.

'It's nice she's been there for you.'

'It's a connection to her father, I think. He passed away three years ago.'

And now you're close to death, I think. I should invite Paige for a longer catchup. At least she won't be assessing my ability to join Gary's department.

'Why are you here so late?' my mother asks. 'I was drifting off with this book.'

She points to the cover. It's a fantasy novel. I had no idea my mother read fantasy novels. I had no idea she read at all.

'I just wanted to see you before…' I trail off, unable to finish; unable to admit to what my mother's about to go through.

'Doctor Theodore is confident they can get a lot of the tumour out,' she says, making everything real anyway.

'But the risks?'

'There are risks with everything, Henry. I worried about risks for far too long. You think I've lived my best life because of it?' She places the book on the food tray, beside the framed photo of my father. 'Today is the longest we've been together since Graham's funeral.'

'I know.'

'They won't let me have a Coke. Can you get me one from the machine downstairs?'

'If they don't want you to—'

'It would be nice to have one, before…'

I almost smile. My mother, using my words against me. 'You'll be awake all night.'

'I just want a sip or two.'

I sigh. 'Fine, I'll be back.'

I head out the room, glance back. Mum's buried in her novel again.

Buried. Fuck, I hate the way my brain thinks sometimes. Although, it pieced together a murder, so I guess it's good for something.

I make my way to the lobby. On the way down, I check for a message from Lucy. Nothing. I'd texted her on the drive here, but she's got enough going on. I should be home with her now, can't believe a part of me was persuasive enough to visit my mother. Never mind, another hour or so and I'll be back.

There's nobody at reception, but someone's at one of the two vending machines. They're giving the contraption a nudge, trying to get it to work.

I approach the other machine, plug in the code for mum's soft drink, tap my card for payment. As the machine whirs to life, I glance at the man beside me.

He's staring straight at me. 'Henry?'

I have no idea who he is. Do I answer?

'Yeah, it's Henry. I recognise you from the paper.'

Before I can reply, the man holds out an open palm and slaps my face as hard as he can.

'The hell?' I look over at reception. Still nobody.

'That's for my mother!' the man snaps.

Did a camera just record that? Where's security?

'I don't know who—'

'Leonie Haynes!' He raises his hand again. It hovers, shaking. Then he loses all steam, sighs, lowers it to his side. 'I'm sorry. It's just...'

'Steven?' I ask. I haven't met Leonie's son, but she's told me about him. He's been living in Singapore with his wife and daughter, moving there for work. Leonie's husband had travelled there to help him settle in, to help with some family problems. When police had identified the body on Aunty Janice's property, they'd taken too long to return home, to be with Leonie; her grief and loneliness fuelling a week of revenge. 'What are you doing here? Wait, is Leonie—'

'We buried Tiff today. Properly. At Pinnaroo. Mum had a TIA.'

'A what?'

'Mini stroke. Your family gave her that.'

I close my eyes, take a deep breath. Feel the sting on my cheek. I should have been at Tiffany's funeral. I didn't even know it was today. 'Can I see her?'

'I'm not denying you that right.' I open my eyes, see him smirking. '*She* doesn't want to see you again. Besides, if you try, there's an officer outside her door.'

'Fine.' I grab mum's soda from the machine. 'At least you're here with her now.'

'I have to fly back tomorrow,' Steven says, ignoring my dig.

I hope this man isn't on the same flight. 'You're not staying for her trial?'

'It's delayed. Don't worry, you probably won't even be called to testify. She's all intent on pleading guilty now. Says she's got one last score to settle. I guess the next time I visit, I get to do it at a prison.'

I try not to wince. 'I really am sorry.'

I won't tell him why his mother will admit she's guilty. She was going to hand herself in after poisoning three women at The Ridge, but a crooked cop stabbed her, delaying the process. Now she's had a lot of recovery time to think about what she'll do next. Which, I assume, is work her way into the same prison as Aunty Janice and end the woman's life with as much pain as possible.

I could stop that, but I don't know if I want to.

I point to the vending machine. 'Can I get you anything?'

'I can manage. You seeing somebody here?'

I won't tell him my own mother is here, since she's too close to everything that happened with Leonie's children. 'It's related to a case.'

'You're still helping the police?' Steven glances down at his hand, back to my cheek, his own face reddening. 'Shit.'

'It's okay. I deserve it. For what it's worth, I would love to see your mum and apologise.'

He stays silent.

'But I guess sometimes we don't get our wish.'

I enter my mother's room, the cool can of soft drink pressed against my cheek. 'You'll never guess who I—'

But mum is asleep.

I should go home, then. Be with Lucy. With my family. Let the adrenaline run out, admit how close I came to death tonight. Again.

A nurse approaches, the same one as this morning.

'You haven't been here all day, have you?' I ask.

'Oh no, I got some sleep. Are you staying tonight? I can get a day bed, a blanket and—'

'Just some pillows would be fine. I'll use the chair.'

I *should* go home, but for some weird reason, an emotional attachment that's been dormant for decades, I can't leave my mother's side.

$$Q$$

The clank of a trolley wakes me. Before it's conscious, my brain has done the calculations. It has been eight days since I walked into Lillian's empty Yanchep house.

December 20, listen to my year of birth.

'Mum,' I start, pushing the pillow away from my face, 'let's ring Lillian together. We can—'

Mum's bed is empty.

'Mum?' I get up, check the room. The other woman is still snoring behind the curtain. Their shared bathroom is empty.

I head out, make my way to the nursing station. There are different women on duty now. One of them catches my distress as I ask their colleague about my mother, hurries over. 'We tried to wake you,' she insists. 'You were sleeping like a log.'

'I had a hell of a day yesterday,' I offer.

The nurses explain to me that they've already taken my mother in, to be prepped for surgery. An early morning start. Maybe so the surgeon will still have time for a round of golf.

'You can wait around,' the nurse suggests. 'We can bring you some breakfast?'

I ask how long the process can take.

'Around five hours. Could be longer. There are pre- and post-op factors to consider. Didn't Doctor Theodore tell you this?'

No, he didn't. I'm yet to see him. 'I'll go home for a while,' I offer, 'and come back later.'

I leave the station, glance around. Pray to a God I don't keep in touch with that my mother will be okay when I get back. That she'll be able to hear me confirm my news about Lillian.

I resist telling myself that last night, I admitted we don't always get our wish.

CHAPTER FORTY-THREE
NOT GOING ALL DOCTOR SEUSS ON YOU

The bus hisses as I step off it, pulling away seconds later. I start walking, my house quite close. I hadn't asked Lucy to pick me up, needing a moment to myself. The journey from the hospital wasn't far, anyway. Yesterday was the longest day in recent memory, one crazy moment after another. I'd said it was my last day on the case; this time yesterday, there was no way I'd expected to *solve* a large part of it. By the end of today, I'll be in another country with Lucy's whole family, ready to celebrate the Christmas season. While wondering how well my mother's recovering from her surgery; a surge of unease I haven't directed her way in far too long.

It's no wonder my brain is going everywhere.

The second I walk in my front door, I'm going to see Lucy and break down. Latch on to her, not let go.

I pause a few houses down. I'm not ready for that, *yet*. I was ready to call the number Lillian left me, hear her voice with my mother. And I want nothing more than to do that with my wife, too. But am I supposed to dial the number at all?

I've had eight days to think about this.

If I'm supposed to listen to Lillian's year of birth, I need to listen to something from nineteen ninety-three, right? That's her year of birth, after all. But how many millions of songs is that? A quick Google gives an endless barrage of Top 100 lists. Critics even argue that nineteen ninety-three was one of the biggest years in history for music. A single sold in the millions within a week for the very first time. One of the biggest pop stars headlined the Super Bowl, sparking a trend continuing to this day. So, was I supposed to I pick one of those songs? They tell me nothing about Lillian's location; another dead end.

It took four days of thinking about this. Testing different song titles, seeing how they applied to the search for my sister.

But there was a reason she had song samples prerecorded over her secret phone line.

Clues buried within clues, just like Uncle Graham left for me after his death.

If I take the digits from her year of birth, apply them to the playlist I'd created from the samples, I'm left with one possible combination of titles. Song nineteen, nine, three. Given there are only twenty-eight tracks on the list, it's the only way the digits work.

Giving me this order of songs:

Pesta Muzik, Swap Meet, The Lucky One

Three wildly different songs—pop rock, grunge, some kind of synth-powered ballad. Lyrics that don't match at all, no common theme. But they have a connection, which I realised four days ago.

Waiting ever since.

I walk ahead, reach my driveway. There's an extra car parked there. Desmond's. A joyful sight—he's part of the family again. All it took was saving me from a bullet. And a determination to clean up his act, I guess.

I reach the front door. Through the screen, I can smell a variety of food on the go. Smells that take me to happy moments in my adulthood, as I got to know my wife. Steamed rice lined with something like Pandan leaves or lemongrass. Shrimp paste I imagine boiling away in a curry or sambal-like creation. The roasted aroma of peanuts to enhance chicken or tofu. And so much more, blending to send me back to the times Lucy and I visited her parents in Singapore, to the meals her extended family cooked us as they welcomed me as their own.

Meals we've missed out on in Australia, with most of Lucy's family still overseas.

We can replicate dishes, go to food courts and Malaysian restaurants, but it's not the same. It won't be the same, once Lucy's parents leave. Unless we stay in Singapore for longer than the Christmas break.

I enter my house, call out. The house is no longer void of life. There's loud chatter and giggling echoing down the passageway. Noises deflecting what happened only half a day ago.

Lucy's father greets me near the kitchen, pats me on the shoulder. 'Everything okay?'

I shrug. If I answer, the tears will follow.

'Thank you for bringing my daughter back,' Aqil says. There's a burst of laughter outside. 'For restoring some much-needed balance.' He points to the sliding door. 'Have you eaten? Win's been cooking up a storm. She thinks an entire army is coming round for an early lunch. Don't worry, it's just us.'

I let him lead me out the back. Desmond, Lucy and Sarah are on our small patch of grass, kicking a soccer ball, keeping it off a giggling Katie and Thomas. Lucy sees me as the ball rolls towards her. It bounces off her foot, deflects into the bushes.

She hurries over. Wraps me in a tight embrace.

My brain fights for what to tell her first. News about the case, my mother, Lillian. But it makes sure I utter the words I need to tell her more. A sentiment she knows but still deserves to hear.

'I love you more than anything.'

The second the phrase escapes my lips, I start to cry.

I sit on the edge of my bed's mattress, looking down at my phone. Re-reading the email received last night. Making sure it's real. Then I turn, hold it out for Lucy to see.

'Carina directed me towards an investigator overseas,' I explain. 'I used some of the money from Joseph's case to pay for it.'

Lucy starts asking why I didn't tell her, then stops herself. She gets it. If this didn't pan out, then I wouldn't have to admit it was another fruitless effort to find my half-sister.

'And this is what you got the investigator to look into?'

I nod.

'Money well spent.' Lucy frowns. 'Do we still have money left for the rest of our trip?'

'A little bit, maybe for a few Singapore Slings.'

She smiles, puts an arm around me. 'You found your sister.'

'Maybe. I'm hoping the call today will confirm it. Maybe Lillian's changed the recording, added extra details or songs?'

'You want to make the call here? I can leave if—'

'No. I want to do it out there, with everyone.'

We ease off the bed.

'I'm proud of you.'

I lean over, kiss my amazing wife. 'I'm so sorry I haven't been around this week. I'm sorry I got you and your sister involved and—'

'It's okay. We can't change what happened.'

'I'm looking forward to our time away.'

'Especially after what you just found?'

'I was already looking forward to it.' I kick the suitcase resting near our doorway. 'Do I have time to pack a few things?'

'We leave at three, flight's at six. Plenty of time.'

I shudder at the thought of being out at the airport three hours before our flight, but we have no idea how packed the place will be. Perth International Airport isn't the busiest airport. It's tiny by world standards, poor in terms of the facilities it offers awaiting passengers, but there can be times when the boarding process grinds to a halt.

'Can we at least get a coffee there,' I say, 'while we wait?'

'We can get a coffee right now.'

Win is arranging dishes on the dining table, the family already gathered around it. Ready for an enormous brunch.

'Long Mac?' Desmond calls out, approaching with coffees.

'My saviour,' I say. When did he learn to read minds?

He hands me a mug, winks. 'Don't I know it.'

Aqil's reading the day's newspaper. 'I went for an early walk,' he explains, 'got the paper. Thought you'd be interested in the front page.'

He swings the paper round for me to see. The largest headline reads: SCHOOL OF CORRUPTION. There's a boxed image of Isidore College, with an inset image of Joseph. Someone's already connected the dots, reporting on rumours that a group of teachers and parents controlled the school, filtered money and engaged in illicit activities. Isidore College will be asking for a retraction, since the report's assuming a lot more happened than I know about; unless police have uncovered new leads. Too late for them, though. Once it's on the front page, it's hard for people to be swayed to think another way. There will be more parents pulling students out. The college will make teachers redundant; will have to make more changes, adapt.

I hand the paper back to Aqil. 'Thanks for showing me this.'

'They didn't get you for a photo this time?'

I chuckle. 'Not this time.'

'How's your mother?' Win asks, bringing a large bowl of pineapple curry to the table.

'In surgery now.'

Everyone freezes, eyes on me.

'Do you…' Win starts. 'Should we wait, change our flight?'

'It's okay.' I explain to everyone that halfway during the night, my mother woke, took my hand, and started the longest conversation we'd had in years. 'I shared the information I'd like to give everyone now,' I say, looking to Lucy for support, 'and she insisted I go to Singapore as soon as possible.'

'But she needs you here while she's recovering,' Win says.

'It's okay, mum,' Lucy offers. 'Henry, make the call.'

We all sit.

'Who are you calling?' Desmond asks.

'His sister, dad,' Katie says. 'Haven't you listened all week?'

'No, sweetie,' he smiles, 'I guess I haven't.'

'Daddy never listens,' Thomas says with a stern face.

We all burst out laughing.

As everyone recovers, I take my phone out, dial the number for Lillian's empty Yanchep house. Put the call on speaker mode.

It rings. Once, twice.

I look around the table, take everyone in. Yes, my mother's still alive and I should be there for her, but…

Three times. Four.

This is my family. The one I chose. Who accepted me for who I am. Who makes me feel more special than I could ever make myself feel.

Five times. Six.

There's a click. We wait as a hollow tap rises from the speaker. Then a voice says, 'Oh, Henry, I've moved away. A new location till Christmas Day.' I've only heard her voice once, but there's no denying it's Lillian. There's another weird scratch over the line, then, 'I'm sorry, I'm not going all Doctor Seuss on you.'

'Lillian?' I call out.

'If you're hearing this, you waited until the twentieth of December.'

'Lillian, I…' I stop though. This is another recording.

'So, you've got this recording, but you *should* be listening to the year of my birth. Maybe you'll work out where I am. Your uncle said your problem-solving skills were out of this world. After today, if you call, you'll get another set of samples. They won't mean much at first, then I might change a few selections, point to my next location. Depends how you go now. I want to meet you, Henry. I just… I have work to do and… it's hard to know who to trust, so if you find me and I don't react well, don't give up, but give me time.' There's a click, the sound of a needle dropping on a record. 'Thanks for listening. Lillian, out.'

A guitar strums, a singer says their life is pretty plain, and the recording ceases.

I grab my phone, make sure the call has ended, and stare at the faces gathered around the table.

'You get any of that?' Aqil asks.

'I did,' I smile. 'I was hoping the call would confirm things but… I already know where she is.'

CHAPTER FORTY-FOUR
THE PLANETS HAVE ALIGNED

The song echoes around our house through the tinny speakers on my phone, reaches its chorus. I keep glancing at everyone gathered around the table. Win and Aqil are holding hands, Win singing along. Lucy is smiling, already knowing what I'm about to tell the rest of the family.

'I haven't heard this song in years,' Win says.

'What is it, nan?' Thomas asks.

'*Pesta Muzik*, from a group called Sweet Charity. Singapore rock royalty.'

I nod, turn down the volume. 'Once I realised the origin to the song, instead of focusing on the lyrics, the other two titles made more sense.'

I tell everyone the other two song titles: *Swap Meet, The Lucky One.*

'If everything's at Singapore,' I say, 'there's a swap meet at Lucky Plaza. A flea market, on level six. I looked it up, made sure it's still there.'

Win nods. 'Lots of jewellery. Clothes. For younger women, mostly.'

'Your sister wants you to meet her at a flea market in Singapore?' Sarah asks.

'I assume. Except I'm not going to.'

'Why not?'

'I know where she lives.'

I open the email on my phone, show Win and Aqil the message, let them pass it round.

It's communication from the Private Investigator in Singapore, which Carina referred me to. After working out the connection between the songs, I'd sent them a digital copy of the only photograph I have of Lillian. One that Leonie Haynes gave me, when she was still talking to me. Of a younger Lillian, sure, but with enough features for someone to compare if they spotted her. At the flea market. So they could follow her home.

The PI's fee had been two thousand dollars. I'd offered another thousand if they had success within the week. She'd earned the extra money by waiting at that flea market every minute of the day, spotting Lillian in the crowd, following her back to a HDF flat.

'I have an address,' I say, finishing my explanation.

'Did your sister know you'd married someone from Singapore?' Desmond asks.

'I'll have to ask her.'

'Crazy fucking coincidence. Shit, sorry kids.'

Katie and Thomas giggle as Sarah slaps her husband's arm.

'My life seems to be filled with a million coincidences,' I offer. And I've thought about how the planets have aligned for this one. Fate. Destiny. Whatever life wants to call it.

'Pitfalls of living in Perth,' Desmond says.

'Well, I think it's all amazing,' Aqil says. 'You solved two things in a week!'

'I mean, I just kind of stumbled into the truth with the murder case. I guess I used my brain for this, though.'

'My son,' Aqil grins, 'the smart PI. Maybe you can help someone in Singapore?'

'I think I'll just stick to finding Lillian.' I smile, a trickle of warmth running through my body. It doesn't happen often, but I never tire of Aqil calling me his son.

'And your friend, Gary?' Sarah asks. 'We could ask if he wants to come along. He would be a big help.'

'Gary's got a lot to sort out,' I explain.

I'd texted Gary from the hospital last night. He's going to stay in Perth a few more days, then see if he can head back to Margaret River. See if he's welcome at work, which he's desperate to return to. I promised to visit when we return. Even though I'm not going to be working for his department, I need to make time for our friendship. Regular trips down there, at least. As long as I stay away from a few memory-triggering locations.

Gary had passed on his thanks from Senior Constable Templesmith, let me know that Kristen Silver, the Year Four teacher, was no long missing. Officers found her alive and well even further south, down in Albany. She was at her parents' house, out of touch with the news. Traumatised by seeing Heath's body, scared further by the card left at her door, her ransacked house. Nobody knows who ransacked her house—she doesn't have a housemate—but she's agreed to talk about her involvement in King of Spades' investments, should the case need it. The police are still sorting the truth from the lies, accessing the information with more depth than the local reporters bothered with.

Given I'm no longer part of the case today, that's none of my concern.

'What about your mother?' Win asks again, bringing me back to earth.

'We had a talk last night. She knows what I'm about to do.'

'You sure she doesn't want us to wait? The operation... Christmas...'

Lucy reaches out, takes her mother's hand. 'Henry and I have talked about this.'

'Mum insisted we go,' I add.

My mind takes me back to halfway through the night. When my mother woke, saw me staring at her on the chair, reached out to take my hand.

'You're not going to sit there all night, are you?'

'Yes.'

'I'll be fine tomorrow.'

'If I'm not there when you wake...' I look down at my mother's hand. Is this the longest I've held it since I was a child? It's so light, now. Skin and bone. 'I hired someone to find Lillian. And they think they've found her.'

My mother squeezes my hand.

'But I'd have to travel... She's in Singapore. And if I don't go right away, she might end up somewhere else, and—'

My mother squeezes harder. 'Go to her.'

I look into her teary eyes. 'But I'd have to leave you like this, and—'

'Your uncle died trying to find her. He put everything into righting our wrong. He wanted you to keep going, and you should honour that wish.'

'But…'

'It's my wish too, now,' my mother whimpers. She takes a deep breath, lets go of my hand. Looks up at the ceiling, staring at unseen ghosts. 'Find your sister. Show her someone in this family cares about her. Make amends for our mistakes.'

I lean over Helen Herbert, kiss her on the forehead. The first time I've kissed my mother since my wedding day. 'I'll find her, mum,' I whisper, choking back tears. 'I'll have a lot of people helping me this time. You just hang in there.'

TO BE CONTINUED IN

ESCAPE THE LION'S DEN

ACKNOWLEDGEMENTS

That's Book 3 done and dusted. Book 3? Seriously! Thank you for being part of another incredible journey getting Henry Herbert into the wild. For me, this was one of the original ideas I had for Henry, to kick-start his life on the page. His first case was always going to relate to teaching because I'd spent a decade-plus in education, as a Primary School teacher myself. There was so much backstory to the characters, though, that it didn't feel like the right point to jump off a series. So, books one and two are like the necessary prequels to me, Henry's origin story, before he becomes a Private Investigator. It was the right move—Henry's life is rich because of it, full of drama and trauma and everything I needed for him to work through. The characters are alive now—I know it's a writer's cliché, but it's true—and each subsequent novel/storyline carries more weight, guided by their past actions.

As I mention at the start of my novels, each story has real-world locations, fictionalised. Whilst I explored the Margaret River region before, this one is a nod to the city that raised me,

Perth. Perth is a confusing contradiction of a place to live. It can spark signs of life, full of wonderfully creative people and an amazing abundance of good food, key holidays celebrated with the vigour of a major metropolis. At other times, it can feel like the most isolated place in the world. Because it is. Even the rest of Australia feels a world away, and it's often cheaper to travel to our overseas neighbours than our bordering ones. But the relaxed lifestyle is a great place to raise a family, and it's one I've called home for most of my life. Singapore, Japan, Melbourne, they would be the other places I'd be happy to reside, but you deal with what life gives you, and you write about what you know. I'm happy to share my slice of the world with my readers.

Isidore College does not exist, but it has a real-world counterpart. I taught there for ten years. Definitely no secret teacher-parent groups or thoughts of pushing people over railings (I mean, that I know of), though the idea for the novel's case came from another local school. They'd fired their principal for taking board money and using it to build his dream house, as if he thought he'd get away with it. Real-world Isidore College was my second home for so long and, for the most part, I loved it. I've dedicated this story to my co-workers through those years, who made it an amazing place to work. I miss you all; I miss educating our youth; I don't miss the hundred other demands of the job that may have come across on these pages. My stress levels have dropped considerably—now I get to stress Henry Herbert out. For those who've kept teaching, your dedication is beyond admirable.

My dream is to have a map of Perth and WA with the locations of Henry Herbert's adventures scattered across it. I've set many of the homes and apartments in suburbs or buildings that exist, the places/interiors themselves fictionalised. The casino and hotels are a mainstay in Perth. Returning to them for a key scene was fun. What happened there is, of course, the actions of fictionalised characters. Which is where the joy of building them up over several novels has paid off. I've had readers tell me they want to throttle Henry's Aunty Janice. They'll have to get in line. I've had readers desperate for signs of Lillian. And I'm aware Lillian took a back seat in this novel, though she never leaves Henry's thoughts. My promise to you is that she definitely appears in the next novel, and has an enormous impact on the plot; her story arc always planned as a four story reveal, perhaps with spinoffs in the future.

The next novel takes off from the ending of this one, with Henry and family in a plane, about to land in Singapore. Its central theme is family, protecting children, and the unacknowledged people who help raise them. With some class-clashing thrown in for good measure.

I am fortunate to have grown up in a (mostly) sane household. I am fortunate my family isn't Henry's. I want to thank my parents for their support of the series. I've been writing a long time, and these are the first novels of mine my father has read and promoted to his mates (maybe because it's not horror, which I dabbled in a lot in the past). That should be all the endorsement I ever need for Henry Herbert! With my grandfather no longer around to read my tales, this means a lot to me. What means the most to me is the tireless work of my silent editor, my wife. She gets the almost-finished version of each novel and rips it to shreds before any other reader will see it. Because of that, she never sees the proper version of each novel. But I couldn't have it any other way, because she provides the honest criticism I need, our relationship stronger for it (despite my groaning as she tells me to stop rambling and cut a shitty paragraph).

And I'm rambling now, in the Acknowledgements. So, until the next one, thank you for your support—readers, and pushers of my work online, in bookstores and libraries. I wouldn't be here without it. Same goes for Henry.

If you want to stay up-to-date with news about future projects, book me for an author talk/interview, or find links to order my work, you can find the relevant information on my website. There are even links to music playlists for each novel.

www.craigbezant.com